monsoonbooks

THE BLACK AND WHITE HOU

After a childhood in Asia, the Middle East and Europe, Karien van Ditzhuijzen moved to Singapore in 2012. Karien has a degree in Chemical Engineering, but gave up her career developing ice cream recipes to become a writer and has since written and edited half a dozen books and short stories, including in 2018 her debut novel *A Yellow House*, published by Monsoon Books. *The Black and White House* was inspired by her own colonial house in Adam Park, Singapore, which has an illustrious history.

Praise for *The Black and White House*

'An absorbing exploration of friendship
in a flawlessly evoked setting.'
Audrey Chin, author of *The Ash House*

Also by Karien van Ditzhuijzen

A Yellow House

Our Homes, Our Stories: voices of migrant domestic workers in Singapore (editor)

JungleGirl Mia

Tinggi tinggi pokok kelapa,
tinggi lagi pokok durian.
Cantik cantik anak Jawa,
cantik lagi anak Boyan.

Tall grows the coconut tree,
taller still the durian.
Beautiful are the children of Java,
more beautiful still those of Boyan.

1

The air above the road shimmers in the same ruthless sunshine that hammers Anna's forehead. Despite the heat, there is a spring in her step. She turns to her husband, who is paying the taxi driver at the edge of the busy main road. 'Are you coming? I'm melting here.' Ahead, a narrow side street disappears between rows of palm trees, revealing a jumble of greenery beyond.

Tom rushes to catch up. 'Sorry. I could have had the driver drop us at the doorstep, but this neighbourhood makes more of an impression on foot.'

Anna reaches out for Tom's hand and squeezes it. She loves him for giving her – them – this opportunity, this adventure in a new country. 'Let's go. There's some shade further down.'

Tom smiles as she pulls him along. 'Funny you should say that, my secretary did mention this neighbourhood was shady. But I don't think she meant the trees.'

He gives her an ominous yet playful look.

'Odd. What could she mean?' Anna looks at the dense foliage and shudders as threads of her grandmother's ghost stories drift through her mind. Anything could be lurking in those bushes.

'I think it has to do with the history of the place. Why don't you look it up? You like that kind of thing.'

Anna nods and walks on, the muggy warmth enveloping her closely. Tom is right, this place does feel special, and she soaks up the atmosphere that feels so different from the rest of the city. With every step she takes, Anna feels herself walking further into the past and away from all that concrete. As the roar of the traffic on the road behind them fades away, all that's left is the sound of cicadas, birds and rustling leaves. The peaceful atmosphere is calming but as they continue along the cracked surface of the dead-end road, Anna becomes excited again when a large white-plastered building with shiny red roof tiles emerges amid the lush scenery.

'Is this it?' Is this the new house Tom has been so mysterious about?

'Not yet, be patient.'

'But is it like this one? It is so ...'

'Gorgeous, I know.'

Anna was going to say big, too big for the two of them. A bit daunting.

As they pass another similar house, Anna gets lost in reverie. She never expected to find old houses like these surrounded by jungle, just minutes away from a Singapore filled with skyscrapers rising up in steel and glass. These white façades with stark black beams look as if they belong in a different continent, a different era. The familiarity of the place feels almost eerie.

When they approach the third house, Anna startles. A woman, draped in blue, is sitting on a concrete barrier, staring at the building. Anna jumps aside when a car whooshes past and pulls over ahead. The red-haired driver winds down the car window and leans out. Her shrill voice shatters the gentle sounds of nature as she addresses the seated woman. 'Excuse me, what are you doing here? Why do you think you can loiter here?'

The woman gets up. For a moment, it looks as if she wants to say something. Then she scuttles backwards, pulls her dark blue headscarf deeper over her forehead, and breaks into a trot past Tom and Anna, towards the main road.

Anna looks after her, then turns to Tom. 'What happened there?'

'I have no idea.'

In front of them the car has moved up the street. Anna can hear its door slam shut, before the woman, in leggings and a sports top only a little more than a bra, disappears into the next house up.

Bewildered, Anna follows Tom to the house the blue-robed woman had sat in front of. The pillared house crouches against the incline of the hill behind it. Stately, like a posh old lady, arrogant yet a little faded.

'Are you serious?'

She blinks and peers underneath the pillars, her eyes adjusting to the sudden shade.

Tom fumbles with keys in his hands. 'It's not as big as it looks,' he says, trying to reassure her as he tries the keys one by one. 'Downstairs is nothing but the front door, some storage and a stairway up. The main house only has three bedrooms.'

Still more than they need. 'What do you mean, the main house? What else is there?'

He doesn't answer but pulls her into the shadow of the portico. 'Is this where the carriage of the masters would have pulled up, to protect them from that nasty tropical sun?' Anna jokes, then cringes. Suddenly she feels very blonde.

In response, Tom smiles and swings open the unlocked door. 'Ma'am ...'

His gusto is contagious, and Anna follows him up the stairs.

At the top, they turn into a large room with a dark wooden floor, brightened by light filtered through windows all around. Anna takes a deep breath; the air in the room tastes dusty and musky, with a faint whiff of rot. Inside, the heat is even more oppressive. She follows Tom's gaze up to the high ceiling, where white blades hang down, promising relief.

He reaches for the switch but nothing happens. 'The electricity must be disconnected.'

Anna opens a window wide and leans out. This is how she always imagined the tropics to smell, but Singapore in the past week has tasted blander than a North European summer. Only the alleys of Chinatown, where the heat bakes rubbish in open dumpsters, has smelt as strongly, everywhere else air-conditioning dulls her senses. With every breath she takes of the enticing fragrance, Anna wakes up further. She can't wait to explore this new world. Anna's father rarely mentions the place of his birth, in what is now Indonesia, but Oma, his mother, always made Anna feel Asia was inside her too. Anna takes another deep breath. Tom will start his new job tomorrow, and she will be on her own.

She grimaces, feeling like a cliché. Don't people go to Bali to find themselves, not Singapore? Living in this house, this neighbourhood, will be an adventure, she realises as she looks outside. There are trees everywhere, standing here is like being in the canopy of a jungle. A frangipani tree, gnarly with a sparse smattering of large featherlike leaves, stands in front of the window. She stretches out her hand but it is too far to pluck one of its bunched white flowers that scent the air so fiercely. Living in a house with a frangipani tree has always been her dream. They will be happy here. There is no need for her to carry around her father's colonial guilt.

Anna turns to look at Tom, who stands at the top of the stairs, looking at her in anticipation. 'What do you think? The guys at the office said we should get a nice flat in a condo. But they don't know you.'

She laughs. 'They don't know you married a crazy Dutch woman who prefers things old and enchanting, you mean?'

'Exactly. I'd prefer that condo. But I dragged you across the world, had you quit your job, so I thought ... Well, you could use something to sink your teeth into.'

From Tom, who is not a natural at expressing his feelings, the words sound almost romantic, and Anna isn't sure how to respond. 'Well, your surprise worked. I am ...' She searches for the best word. 'Stunned. How on earth are they giving us this place?'

She opens windows one by one, smiles at some green-grey pigeons in the trees outside. Tom laughs. 'You'll need to close them again in a few minutes.'

'This house needs to breathe!'

As air streams inside, the muggy room transforms and Anna revels in how beautiful it is. Even without furniture it has a great ambience. The mahogany floor gleams and above the glass windows, white latticed ventilation grilles decorate the walls.

Tom looks around again, and up, 'It looks like there is no air conditioning in this room. We'll have to put some in.'

'Absolutely not,' Anna replies. 'I'm sure this house was built before air conditioning even existed.'

There is no way she'll let that tinned air ruin this house. She tries to imagine who lived here before, when the house was new. In her mind, the room comes alive decked out in rattan chairs like the ones her grandparents had in their conservatory. She looks at

Tom. 'Seriously, where's the catch? Can we really live here?'

Tom gives her a sly grin before his lips relax into a smile. 'It's simple, the guy who did my job before me lived here. He had a large family. He had to leave unexpectedly, before the lease was up, so we're doing them a favour by taking it on.'

The words make Anna nervous. Will Tom manage the challenging job better? She doesn't want to leave anytime soon. Anna brushes aside the thought and hugs him tight. 'I love it! I love you. Let's go explore.'

A glassed-in veranda leads to a large master bedroom. Anna opens the window and notices several dead bees lying in the dust on the windowsill. She blows them outside.

'I'll ask them to give it a good clean before we move in,' Tom says. 'It's been empty for months.'

A big laugh bubbles up from Anna's belly, resonating through the empty room. 'We don't have enough furniture. Our whole flat fits in this bedroom.'

'You'll have to go shopping,' Tom says. 'We will have a generous allowance for that.'

'They will pay for new furniture too? I can't believe you kept all this a secret.' She grabs his hand and pulls him to the adjoining bathroom. 'How old is this place?'

'All I know is that it was built by the Brits, early last century.' He slams his fist on the doorframe to demonstrate. 'Solid. They knew how to make houses last. And these colonial buildings do have style, don't you think?'

Suddenly Anna remembers the photo album she found in Oma's things after she died. The white plaster, the pillared façade, the same foliage backdrop. She looks around the huge bedroom again, feeling awkward. The house, the allowance, is it all too much? She nudges Tom. 'You mentioned this house has a shady past. What did you mean?'

'Hui Ying, my secretary, says that only expats want to live in these houses; locals think they are haunted. Something to do with the war.'

Anna nods as she ponders this. She definitely needs to find out more. Maybe dust off her history degree.

'Do you ...' she starts, but Tom has moved on already, and looking over his shoulder says: 'Let's check out the garden. It's as big as a park.'

They pass through French doors opening to a small outdoor patio.

'A pool!' Anna squeals in delight and all thoughts about the past evaporate.

'Yes, you, a lady of leisure, will be floating in that pool all day.'

Anna stares at Tom, annoyed. He knows she wants to find a job. She looks away to hide her frustration, to a huge banyan tree towering behind the pool. The tree has hundreds of narrow trunks, forming arches and narrow passages, between which thinner air roots drop down. Anna has never seen such a tree. It's grand like a cathedral, exuding a similar striking aura. It is slightly unnerving. In front of the banyan is an area covered with a palm leaf roof, begging to be filled with a dining table, outdoor sofas. 'Imagine sitting there in the coolness of the evening, sipping gin and tonics.'

Her sense of wonder grows as she looks at sunbirds darting around bright orange and red heliconia flowers. 'Look, a squirrel! And banana trees!'

Tom weaves his fingers through hers and pulls Anna's body

close. 'You like it?'

She throws her arms around him. 'I adore it.' Out of the corner of her eye, she detects movement. 'What is that?'

A monitor lizard as long as her arm scampers over the grass and she stifles a scream. Her curiosity wins over, but as she approaches the reptile slowly, it scuttles under the decking that surrounds the pool. Anna dips her hand in the lukewarm water. The pool is full of leaves, and tinged green on the edges. She looks up at Tom. 'You've got your job cut out for you.'

'No way, we'll get a guy for that. Labour is cheap here. We should get one of those live-in Filipinas too for the house.'

'It is only the two of us. Do we need someone living with us?'

'Everyone at work says to hire a helper straight away, because we will end up doing it anyway,' he says. 'It's what expats here do. Locals too, apparently. It's up to you. But if you want to get a fulltime job as well, we probably won't have time to do all the work around here. It's a big house.' He points to a separate building in the garden, connected to the main house by a covered walkway. 'And we don't need to share the house with her. There are servants' quarters.'

Anna tries to ignore the jarring word as she leaves the tranquillity of the garden and follows Tom into the outbuildings that are a whole other house in itself. The first room has a massive chimney with a gaping hole underneath.

'Is this the kitchen? Are we supposed to cook on an open fire?'

'Maybe it used to be, but I think there is a more modern kitchen in the main house. We'll have to get a new cooker and fridge though. That is your first job, get all that organised.'

He laughs, but Anna does not. Why is everything a joke to

the British?

They walk through the rest of the outbuildings in silence. There are four smaller rooms and two bathrooms, connected by an open corridor. 'We'll need to hire more than one helper or she'll get lonely here.'

Anna bites her lip. Tempo doeloe, Oma called it, the good old days, long gone. Living in a big old house in the jungle – with a bunch of servants. 'It's so weird, all that space, all for the two of us.'

'That might change soon enough,' Tom winks, guiding Anna back into the main house. 'Which reminds me ...'

A bare, white-tiled kitchen leads to a spacious dining room, and beyond another glazed veranda are two smaller rooms. 'So, what do you think,' Tom asks, a glimmer in his eye. 'Which one for the study and which for a nursery?'

Anna peers into the rooms. One has no external windows and feels gloomy. She steps into the other, where sunlight streaks through the slatted grille, and visualises a crib in the corner, a rocking chair by the window. But then she resolutely shakes her head. Annoyed with her husband for bringing it up, she looks at him with tightened lips. Tom knows she doesn't want to get chained down with a baby just yet. They agreed to wait.

Tom heads back to the living room through yet another veranda, but when Anna turns to follow, a chilling rush of air creeps up her legs, freezing her in place. The hairs on her arms stand up; her fingers stiffen painfully. There seems to be a sound in the distance she can't quite make out.

'Are you coming?' Tom shouts.

Anna snaps back. 'Yes!' She wipes the sweat from her neck as she shivers. What happened there? It isn't cold here at all; it must be the intense heat that muddles her senses, making her imagine strange things.

In the living room, the ceiling fan has miraculously turned on. Lukewarm air swishes into Anna's face and she wiggles her fingers until the strange stiffness is gone. She hugs Tom tight, pushing away the remnants of whatever that was.

After they disentangle, Anna leans out for a last breath of air before closing the windows. And there she is again, hovering on the road: the woman with the blue headscarf. Anna senses Tom next to her. 'Can you believe what happened earlier? That woman was so rude!'

'She was,' Tom agrees. 'But please, promise me you won't get involved and alienate the neighbours before we even move in.'

Anna tries to formulate an answer, but when she turns to him, Tom has already left the room. Looking back out the window, she sees the woman notice her and flinch. Anna has to suppress an urge to run down and apologise to her. But for what? She didn't do anything. She stays put and stares at the figure in her long skirt disappearing in the distance.

2

Salimah stands defiantly in front of number four. Even as an adult the big house intimidates her. Curiosity has won out over her apprehension, but it takes effort to stand here. Today, she won't let any red-haired ang moh in Lycra tell her she has no right to be here.

The old house looms majestically amid the tropical trees, as if stuck in a time warp. Why is she here today, the neighbourhood of her childhood, after nearly forty years? Last month, she came on a whim, straight after the news of her redundancy. Now her notice period is over, and she is officially unemployed. Does she think she can find who she was, whoever she is – here?

She startles. There's a small bench and a potted plant by the front door – someone must have moved in. Salimah's determination shrinks a little. Then she reminds herself: this is a public road.

She walks to the side to look at the garden. It's too messy for Salimah's taste, not the landscaped grounds it used to be. Must be foreign labour taking care of it. This garden had been her father's pride and joy, and Salimah can still feel the envy she used to experience looking at it when she picked Bapa up from work. Which tree had the treehouse been in? There is a banyan at the back of the garden, could it be that same one? It is so big. Alamak, she is getting old.

Salimah notices a fence of green wire closing off the garden.

That wasn't there when she was young, surely? Why is her memory so blur? She can't see the path that led to where her kampong used to be, the greenery blocking the way to the old village is dense, uninviting. No, she won't ruin her shoes to chase a sentimental fantasy, she is no longer that girl in ragged shorts, who would climb up trees and down stormdrains to catch tadpoles. That time is long gone. Still, thoughts of the girl she used to be make her smile. How different her childhood was from that of Nazra, her own daughter.

She sits down on the concrete barrier at the edge of the drain, the empty afternoon stretching out in front of her like a desert. The thought of searching for a new job is draining, but without a job, who is she? A makcik in a tudung, a middle-aged aunty in a headscarf, whose teenager rolls her eyes at her.

She swats away a mosquito and stares at the big house. On closer inspection it looks tired, in need of a coat of paint and a scrub. A small tree peeks out from a roof gutter. Her mother always kept their small house immaculate, like Salimah herself keeps her flat tidy. No foreign help for her, thank you very much.

A couple of mynah birds peck curiously in front of her toes. One of them looks up, head cocked, and stares at Salimah with its yellow-rimmed eye, the little black quiff above its bright beak making it look like a naughty kid.

The bird flies up and lands in the frangipani tree in front of the house. Salimah shudders. No Malay would plant a graveyard tree in front of a house. But ang mohs love them everywhere – those white people have no sense. Salimah picks up a flower and sticks her nose into the yellow heart in the twist of white petals. The cloying, overly sweet perfume so close to her nose is heady and bewitching.

Suddenly, she almost vomits as the smell of rotting meat hits her. She tries to shake the stench out of her nose but it only gets stronger as she hears a wail, then a shrill voice shrieking. Something white and yellow flashes behind her. There is a whisper, in what sounds like the voice of her late mother and then ... She turns to look. Nothing. The smell is gone. But her senang good mood is gone too, and she tosses the flower into the concrete drain behind her.

She needs to leave, Salimah tells herself, she has no business being here. But her legs are glued to the concrete and she is too dizzy to stand up – a soft sound still sings inside her head. It all comes back slowly and painfully. The taunts at school. The whispers and fingers pointing behind her back. She did not understand why the adults spoke in hushed voices about that treehouse. Why her mother cried and her father sat there looking morose. No one told her anything and then they moved away.

Salimah sits in silence for a minute, her head still buzzing. Suddenly she realises the sound isn't in her head. It's real, even if it is just a soft, gentle hum: the Pan Island Expressway. The PIE. The motorway that ate up her kampong. The hum gets louder, more hostile, but she tries to push it down. She has enough problems in the present. No job. A daughter who defies her.

She covers her ears and looks up at the house, the illustrious one the government chose to preserve, and the noise subsides. It's just a house. It's quite peaceful here in fact, and she's a sentimental old woman. A sweaty woman. In the freezing cold office her layers were a blessing, but in this heat the tudung is uncomfortable and she wonders if would have kept her job had she not started wearing a tudung a few years back?

She flinches. A Caucasian lady in a red knee-length skirt and a sleeveless top is walking straight towards her, carrying a black plastic bag. Salimah stares at the woman, at her wavy golden hair. *No, don't be stupid, not all Caucasians look the same.* Transfixed, Salimah watches the woman pass by obliviously. She jerks the green bin open and clumsily drags the bag over the edge until it tears. Garbage spills onto the street. The woman drops to her haunches. Covering her eyes, she rocks back and forth slowly. She drops down further until she sits on the edge of the hot asphalt.

Salimah wants to ask whether she is okay, but instead bends down and starts picking up rubbish. A yoghurt container. Some plastic wrappers. Banana peel. As she ponders the remainder, the woman finally gets up.

'Oh my god. Why are you ...? Sorry! That is mine.' She grabs an unsavoury handful from the ground.

They finish tidying up in silence. Only when they are done, the woman looks at Salimah, her blue eyes so bashful Salimah can't help but smile at how they were huddled over the garbage together. Suddenly they both laugh out loud. The woman sticks out her tomato-sauce smeared hand, then pulls it back to wipe on her white top. She stares at her still smudged hand. 'God, I am such an idiot, I mean, look at me, I'm a mess.'

Salimah shrugs.

'I'm Anna. Thank you so much for your help. I'm sorry about all this, please come in to wash your hands.'

Salimah's been waiting so long to go inside that house, and now she hesitates. But Anna is already through the door, so she has no choice but to enter and climb the stairs, glancing left and right. When her father told her that a house like that wasn't for people like them, she'd imagined the inside in her child's mind. The real thing is bigger yet smaller. Hollow.

Anna leads her to the kitchen, and after she has rinsed her hands in the metal sink, passes the soap bottle to Salimah. Did her father ever use this sink to scrub his black nails? No, there must have been an outside tap for him. She looks at the white-tiled floor, covered in orange stains and ants all over. Bringing her attention back to the sink, which is full of unwashed dishes, she says, 'This soap smells lovely.'

'It's frangipani,' Anna smiles. 'My favourite. There is a big tree in front of the house.'

Salimah nods, lips pursed.

'Would you like a drink? Coffee, tea, something cold? I owe you that at least.'

'Water, thanks.'

Salimah follows Anna into the living room and sits down on a narrow sofa. The room has a weird smell, rotten. Salimah looks around. In the middle of the room stand unopened moving boxes, empty takeaway food containers perched on top. Anna notes Salimah's gaze and jumps up from her chair to open the windows one by one. 'Sorry, it's such a dump. Let's get some air inside.'

Anna talks so fast Salimah struggles to follow her. 'I'm not organised yet. We don't have enough furniture, this house is much bigger than our last one.'

She points at the sofa Salimah sits on. 'This small loveseat drowns in such a large room. It's almost a ballroom. I need to find more suitable things but have no idea where to go.'

Salimah doesn't know how to advise this expat tai tai on where to buy furniture. But Anna is already changing the subject. 'I don't really know anyone yet around here. Do you live in the area?'

Instinctively, Salimah wants to say yes, but shakes her head.

'No,' she mumbles. 'I live in Bishan.'

'Bishan, that sounds nice,' Anna laughs a little too loud. 'Is it far? I want to get to know Singapore, but simply buying bread and milk takes up half my day. My husband keeps nagging me to buy furniture.'

She has said that already, it must be important to her. Is she expecting an answer?

Anna waves her hands around. 'It took me hours to find a shower curtain in the right size. With all those stupid errands, I barely have time left for important things. Like finding a job.' She sighs before she continues. 'I sent out resumés. Not a single invitation for an interview came back.' She clasps her hands in front of her mouth. 'Sorry,' she says. 'I always talk too much.' She holds a tin of biscuits out to Salimah, who scrutinises Anna and wonders: does a woman like this, living in such a house, even need to work?

'Where do you get your groceries?' Anna asks.

Salimah hesitates. She usually goes to the wet market, but expats prefer supermarkets, don't they? 'NTUC supermarket has a good selection, but for fresh produce I go marketing at Chung Ling.' The bustling open-air market can be hot and smelly, but it beats the supermarkets in both quality and price.

'I did marketing for a multinational for ten years,' Anna mutters, 'but that is worth nothing here. They all want Mandarin speakers, and don't give a toss about any of the five languages I speak.'

Salimah knows exactly how that feels. When Anna leaves a gap in the conversation, she lets slip: 'Yes, I'm also finding it difficult to find a job.'

Anna looks up in surprise. She seems very pale, even for a

European. Her silence is stunning after the earlier cascade of words. Before Salimah can think of something to say, Anna asks: 'Do you have any children?'

Salimah lights up. Her daughter is her pride and joy. 'Yes, I have a daughter. Nazra is 16, she is studying at junior college. How about you?'

There are no toys or signs of children in the room. Anna has stopped talking, but Salimah isn't sure she heard the question.

It takes Anna a while to find her words. 'Ehm, yeah, no children.' Another silence ensues. 'Maybe one day. But I'm so useless I can't even manage to hire a helper.'

Salimah forces a smile. 'Hiring a maid is difficult?'

'Yes, I mean, you can't go to a shopping centre and pick one to take home, can you? As if you are buying a new vacuum cleaner? Because that's how these agencies act.' Anna pauses, then adds, 'I'd prefer a part-time cleaner.'

Salimah looks at the dusty floor, the smudges on the windows. She notices Anna following her gaze and a blush form on her pale cheeks. Salimah's hands start to itch as more, sweeter memories from before pop up. 'My mother was a cleaner. I used to help when she went on jobs, and we'd clean together. She would say that cleaning was our language of love.' The image of her mother in yellow latex gloves surfaces and Salimah feels a sharp pang of loss.

Anna bounces up, suddenly full of energy.

'Oh, could you work here? I so badly need help. Do you have time?'

The words sink into Salimah's stomach like a lump of stone. All those years of studying, her degree, her perfect English diction, her management skills – it all swirls down the drain as this woman assumes she is nothing but a cleaner. Why is there no air-conditioning in this room? Salimah takes a big gulp of the cold water in front of her, then another. Ice cubes tinkle together, and she accidentally swallows a piece whole. She coughs.

Anna looks at her pleadingly with her eyes in that too-bright blue. The job offer is so ridiculous she can't stop herself from laughing out loud but manages to stifle it in another cough. She swallows the remaining hiccups. 'Can I use the bathroom please?'

Salimah washes her face and looks at herself in the mirror. Her father worked in this very house as a gardener, worked hard to send his daughter to a good school so she could have a better future. She should throw the offer back in Anna's face and tell her that she might be a middle-aged woman in a tudung, but until recently she was the regional sales manager for an international business, selling paper products all over Asia. At the very least she should feel offended and politely decline. But she does not want to do that.

Rubbing her fingers along the crummy ridges between the white tiles around the sink she feels the house drawing her in. Her mother was a cleaner and so were her aunts. Why should she be too good for the job?

Salimah watches herself return to the living room and tell Anna she'll take the job.

On the way back in the bus she repeats to herself that it's part-time and temporary. That she loves cleaning and needs the money.

And though all of that is true, she has no idea how to explain it to her daughter.

3

Salimah. Salimah. Anna repeats the name a few times as she stares at the orange juice on the kitchen floor, and the pretty pattern the ants make marching around it. The stains no longer fill her with despair. Tomorrow, Salimah will come to fix this mess. Tomorrow, she won't be alone and the thought gives her courage. Which she needs, especially if … no, she can't even think about that. In any case, she direly needs the home help.

Tom's new job is swallowing him whole and she doesn't want to bother him. It's embarrassing enough she's a trained professional yet incapable of running a two-person household. She wants to support Tom – this job is the reason they are here. He can't be expected to iron his own shirts when he comes home from work exhausted and she has been here all day. Kneeling down, she swings a dishcloth over the juice. What must Salimah have thought seeing the squalor they live in? She needs to make the place look halfway presentable before tomorrow. Anna gets up from her haunches reluctantly. The smell coming from the dishes in the sink makes her stomach lurch, so she decides on laundry first.

With her knee she tips the overflowing basket onto the bedroom floor and starts separating colours and whites. She picks up a corner of a bedsheet and smells it, then gags. Tom insists on sleeping in air conditioning, but even so, he sweats buckets each night. She pulls off the sheets and gathers as much laundry as she can manage. A sock falls back to the floor, but she can't be bothered to pick it up. She grinds her teeth. The downside of such a sprawling house is that the washing machine is miles away, out of sight behind the outbuildings. In the *servants'* area where, Tom had joked, it belongs.

After she has stuffed as much into the machine as it can hold, Anna falls down on a beanbag by the pool, and wipes the sweat from her brow. How can anyone do anything in this heat?

She lies back, savouring the illusion of a breeze coming off the pool. Her thoughts drift back to their first weekend in the new house, the evening they sat on these very beanbags, under the banyan, gazing at the stars and holding hands. A bush with tiny white flowers immersed them in a heady scent as the glow of the moon wove patterns through the branches of the tree and onto the surface of the pool. Soon, they'd gotten carried away by the romance of the place, under that majestic tree. Anna smiles, thinking back, glad for the greenery that sheltered them from sight. Then, feeling the queasiness in her stomach, she wants to slap herself.

The next day, they'd taken a boat trip on the Singapore River and indulged in the guilty pleasure of playing at tourists. Anna was in awe of the towering skyscrapers in the business district where Tom worked, while the row of restaurants facing the river looked old and shabby yet quaint in contrast. They took a lift to the observation deck on the 57th floor of Marina Bay Sands, where the views of the island were, as promised in the guidebook, unrivalled. Staring out over the sea, Anna nudged Tom. 'Look at those islands.'

Tom nodded as he looked up from the guidebook. 'That's

Indonesia.'

'I can't believe how close it is!'

Anna had felt on top of the world. Oma's country, right there in front of her. And she herself would be reliving her grandmother's experience in an amazing house. She simply felt so, so happy.

Anna sighs as she stares at the small patio next to the kitchen. This morning, Tom mentioned that it would be a perfect spot to eat breakfast. He smiled when he said it but all Anna could think about was where on earth she would find the right table to put there. The amazing house is holding her hostage. It's too big. Her plans to visit museums, take the MRT downtown, discover hawker centres, hike the nature reserve – all drowned in the paralysing heat and her fruitless household struggles. How can groceries and errands, all those things she used to squeeze in after a full workday, take up so much time? At night she feels drained, but also as if she hasn't accomplished anything at all.

With Tom rarely home, there is nobody to cheer her up. If only she had her own job. A job in a cool office that would make her a proper part of this city. Then she would feel like a normal human being again, not like a lunatic in an empty house.

A loud cry jolts her from her thoughts and her throat constricts. Empty? If only! The place isn't empty at all. Creatures lurk everywhere. Anna hasn't forgotten that moment in the hallway when she was first here. She still gets goosebumps thinking about it. She pricks up her ears, but all she can hear is a rustle in the palm-leaf fronds of the roof above her. When she gets up to look, a startled squirrel jumps from the roof into the trees behind it. On the grass, noisy orange-beaked blackbirds fight over a worm. Anna jumps when the loud cry repeats itself. What makes that sound? She isn't sure what is worse, the fact that there could be snakes under every bush, or the lingering feeling that what she cannot see is the most dangerous of all. A modern flat in a condo seems wonderfully comfortable right now.

Anna stares at the bright blue of the pool, glistening in the sun. The water looks clear, it is the one part of this house that feels normal. A swim would freshen her up, but getting up and squeezing her sticky body into swimwear is more than she can muster. Instead, she looks at the red roof tiles that seem to move and oscillate in the heat. She imagines rising above them, soaring into the sky, to get back the feeling she had at the observation deck, looking at the islands across the sea.

As she contemplates further, Anna's mood darkens, remembering the shopping centre she visited this morning. It had been recommended by Tom's secretary as the best place to find a helper. She found the building easily enough, but inside she felt miles out of her comfort zone. Modern Asia is not at all like she expected. What *had* she expected?

There wasn't a non-Asian person to be seen. *You wanted to see the real Asia.* She passed by several maid agencies, and in every one of them, a row of helpers smiled at her with begging eyes whenever she peered inside, and Anna found it more and more intolerable. She made herself go inside and managed to interview one woman but then felt so dizzy she ran out and grimaced at the woman at the desk, apologising and saying she needed more time.

In multicultural London she barely noticed people's skin colour. But at those agencies, Anna's white skin felt fluorescent.

Ouch. A pin prick stings her leg. She swats the bug away, thinking of how she came home, desperate for an iced coffee, but was greeted by a million ants on the not-so-shiny white tiles of the kitchen. The ants crawled up her legs, everywhere, into her underwear. She pulls up her skirt. Her legs still itch though they look as white and unblemished as ever.

She ought to go back into that kitchen and finish cleaning up before Tom comes home but nausea comes back with a flash when she remembers opening the bin, and the foul blast that hit her nose coming from it. She made it to the toilet just in time. Now, she only makes it as far as the banyan tree. She rinses her mouth from the bottle of lukewarm water next to her on the floor, then pulls off her top and skirt. In her underwear she jumps into the pool and lets the water cool her. As her stomach and head calm down, Anna pictures Salimah, her round and friendly face, the dark eyes framed by a mint green scarf, – a face that she feels she has seen before though she isn't sure where. Salimah wore a long dress in a colourful print, traditional and modern at the same time. She must be a little older than Anna, though the headscarf could be misleading.

Salimah was very friendly, a tad shy, perhaps. Then again, Anna thinks, feeling like she wants to kick herself, that was probably her own fault. Why does she always rant so much around people she doesn't know? People she wants to make an impression on.

The queasiness in Anna's stomach increases and the question she asked Salimah again resonates in her brain: *Do you have children?*

As she said it, the words hung back in Anna's throat. She doesn't remember a word of what Salimah answered. She makes a few broad strokes through the cool water and tries to make sense of the whirlpool in her mind that is picking up speed. She can't ignore her body any longer. The strange feeling in her stomach envelops her from within. She dives down until her face is submerged in the pool and she slowly composes herself. When she offered Salimah the job, the woman hadn't reacted as Anna had expected her to. Uncertain of everything now, Anna shakes off all thoughts, and pulls herself out of the pool. Forget the kitchen. She needs to go and find a pharmacy.

4

When Salimah alights from the lift, Mrs Ng is standing in the corridor, blocking the way to Salimah's flat. Salimah waits for Mrs Ng to let her past, but she doesn't move. She doesn't know Mrs Ng that well, mostly remembers her shouting at her own grandchildren, *be quiet, don't make noise*! Now that her daughter has her own place, the corridors are quiet. The last time Salimah spoke to her neighbour was when she complained about Nazra being loud on her phone. Salimah puts on a brave face. 'Good afternoon, Mrs Ng. How are you?'

'I am fine, Salimah, fine. But how is your father? I worry about him. The corridor used to look bright and green, but now …'

Salimah stares at the plants Mrs Ng points to. They are brown and wilted. 'Alamak, I never saw. How long have they been like that?'

Mrs Ng looks scornful. 'I'd say a few months at least. What is wrong?'

The plants are Salimah's father's pride and joy. Ever since he retired, he tended to his green babies diligently, teaching Nazra about gardening and making friends whilst passing cuttings to all the neighbours. 'Put in your car, scares away cockroaches' he'd tell Mrs Ng over a sheave of pandan, or 'this one good against mosquitos' when pressing twists of citronella on the Singh kids three doors down.

'I haven't seen him some time,' Mrs Ng says.

'I know, I'm so sorry,' says Salimah. 'He is …' She stops. She doesn't know; not how he is, or when or why this happened. 'I'll clear it up.' She can't have the neighbours thinking they are unkempt kampong people.

'Sure, but I mean, your father …'

'I'll talk to him, leave it up to me!' she says chirpily.

Salimah scuttles off, flustered. When she opens the front door the place is silent. She is surprised, at this time of the day her father is usually in front of the tv. He spends too much of his time slumped on the sofa. He is over seventy, but still, it pains her to see him like this. When he first retired from his job, he was out all day, taking his granddaughter along when she wasn't in school. He would stay at the kopitiam, sipping kopi, chatting to the uncles. Politics, the weather, family matters, so many opinions in a coffee cup. But one day he took the wrong bus home and ended up far away in Punggol.

As she looks into the small, dark room, she notices there are two old men sitting on the sofa in serious silence. 'Pak Long! Assalamualaikum, how nice to see you.'

Pak Long is Father's eldest brother, well into his eighties but sharp as a nail. He worked for a rich Chinese family in Bukit Timah, as a driver, until a few years back when his cloudy eyes finally forced retirement. Ever since he's seemed restless and agitated. 'Did Bapa give you a drink yet?'

Father gets up and gets all of them a glass of refrigerated water, suddenly his old helpful self. He looks at Salimah. 'How was your day? Where did you go?'

'Actually,' she starts, then hesitates as she looks at her uncle. Since he moved to Pasir Ris, out east, they don't see him much.

Visiting the big house has left Salimah's brain wedged in the past, and suddenly she remembers Pak Long in his old pondok – a Boyanese communal house, which was across the canal from their kampong and the big house nearby. The pondok was a strange place – a happy place full of families but Salimah never liked going there. Why? Because she was ashamed to be half Boyanese?

Salimah feels a headache coming on. She puts down her drink and buries her face in her hands but it's too late, the smell of frangipani and the voices are back. They whisper clearly this time. 'The Boyanese can't be trusted, they do black magic.' Her classmate's taunts too are back, echoing dull but clear. What does it mean? Her father never spoke Boyanese at home – her mother didn't understand it – and her uncle is the most devout Muslim Salimah knows.

Pak Long holds up his empty glass to Salimah and she gets up to put it on the table for him. Pak Long never had a wife.

'Were you at work?' he asks. 'Another promotion?'

Salimah sighs at the tone of his voice. Pak Long never ceases to make Salimah feel that she is thinking too much of her own advancement.

'Did Bapa not tell you? I lost my job.'

At least he has the decency not to gloat. He looks at Salimah with a question in his eyes. What else can she say? That she can't find a new job? The irony of the situation makes her grimace; she gets rejected for jobs because she is Malay, but for him, she is never Malay enough. Salimah forces a friendly smile. He is her uncle, after all. Pak Long has done a lot for her, especially after her husband died. She can't believe that was fourteen years ago, he was in her life so briefly he sometimes feels like a dream. Now it is just her, supporting a teenage girl and an elderly man. Or at least, she tries to.

'But good news, I have found a temporary job to tide us over. Bapa, do you remember when you worked at the big house at Adam Park?' Salimah says.

A flicker of something crosses Father's eyes. 'Yes,' he says slowly.

'I am going to work there, with a Belanda expat lady.'

Father's eyes become darker, and he squints. 'Do what?'

'Well, cooking.'

Anna asked her if she could teach her some Malay specialties as well as clean. 'And maybe some ehm, organising.'

Father frowns. 'Organising? What do you mean? Are you to be an amah?'

'It's temporary. She wants to learn how to make Malay food, get help with cleaning, and we need the money.' Defiantly, she adds. 'I like cleaning.'

Salimah expects her father to disapprove, but instead, he smiles. 'You are so much like your mother.'

His words warm Salimah. Their language of love. Cleaning with her mother was a togetherness she hasn't felt for a long time. Father's face shows longing too but then his frown is back and his voice rises. 'But why go study so long to be the same? And in one of those houses?'

Salimah feels defensive. 'Not one of those houses, it is the same one. Number four.' Broody, Father's eyes turn inwards. Pak Long, normally the first to voice an opinion, hasn't said anything yet. He stares at Father and fingers the remains of a beard that grows on his chin. 'Eh, Adik, cleaning is a good job lah.'

Salimah feels relieved. 'Yes, it is only part-time, so I can keep looking for a real job in the meantime.'

'This kind of work is best for a woman,' Pak Long adds.

Salimah swallows that comment down like a lump in rice porridge. 'To be honest, I am curious what it is like, to work in a house like that. These houses, are, I don't know ...'

She does know but doesn't say it out loud. It's as if the whole city grew and developed around them, while they sat there in their little time warp. Breathing history. Her history too.

Should she ask Pak Long about things that happened back then? About the treehouse? She feels the story involves him too, and his brain functions much better than her father's these days. But she isn't sure whether she trusts Pak Long, and looks at the two old men, pondering. Father seems to have retreated back into himself, and Pak Long fondles his chin hairs again.

Nobody else says anything, so Salimah does: 'The lady is friendly and the pay generous.'

Father's eyes cloud over further. It seems as if he can't find his way through his own head as he tries to speak but his speech slurs: 'That house, that tree, no good. Hantu will come and get me. That woman. Cannot go.'

Salimah looks at him. What woman, he never met Anna? *And is the house haunted?* She smells the frangipani again, her head starts throbbing, the persistent hum interspersed with distant screaming is back. She sees a white flash behind her eyes as Father's words become more and more mumbled, in a Malay Salimah finds hard to follow, peppered with Boyanese words. After a last, whispered awas, be careful, Father falls back in his seat like a deflated balloon.

At that exact moment, the front door bangs shut behind them. Nazra. The teenager, in her bright school uniform, slams her backpack on the floor and pulls the earpods from her ears, shoving some stray hairs back into her wavy black ponytail. Salimah feels herself catapulted forward into the twenty-first century and breathes easier. Pak Long is gently patting his brother's hand. Nazra's eyes dart from her grandfather to her great-uncle, then sends a piercing look at Salimah. The tension is back, in another dimension. Nazra hates Pak Long.

Salimah looks at her pleadingly, hoping the girl will behave. 'Atuk isn't feeling well. Why don't we let your grandfather and uncle be? Come help prepare dinner.'

Nazra's eyes soften as she walks over to the sofa and sits on the armrest next to her grandfather, and rubs him on his back. Nazra shoots a look at Salimah and Pak Long. 'What did you do to make Atuk upset?'

Salimah isn't sure what to say, but knows she needs to speak before Pak Long does.

'We were talking about the past, about a house he used to work in. I will go and work there part-time.'

She doesn't mention the word cleaner. The girl has a bad enough opinion of her mother already. Father stares at Nazra and shakes his head vigorously. 'Hantu. That woman. Cannot go.'

Although Nazra's spoken Malay is hesitant – Salimah speaks English with her – she understands it perfectly. Nazra turns to Salimah, 'What does he mean, who lives in that house?'

Pak Long heaves himself up from his seat. 'Your father thinks there are hantu in those houses.' He continues before Salimah can stop him. 'You want to know what happened there in the war?'

The war? The war ended decades before they lived there and Salimah isn't sure whether to feel relieved or disappointed. Nazra's cheeks develop an excited blush. 'Ghosts from the war? Tell me more.'

'Pak Long, let's stop talking about it. I try to raise her as a modern Singaporean.'

Pak Long says nothing, but Nazra is hooked. 'Please, Pak Long!'

Salimah sighs. She should be glad that the girl is interested in something other than her handphone. The last time Nazra had a conversation with Pak Long it ended in a heated fight about tudungs. Salimah sees no need for Nazra to wear one, few girls do at her new school. She had been so proud of the girl, getting into such a prominent junior college but now Salimah worries. At her old neighbourhood school Nazra was happy. Now she is always moody, never brings home friends anymore. Maybe it is better this way, the girl needs no distractions; she can focus on her studies. But she could do without her temper. And her disobedience.

'Nazra, I asked you to help me.'

She looks at Pak Long for support, but he just stares at the girl.

'Nazra!'

When her daughter still doesn't reply, Salimah gives up. Let her talk to her great-uncle. 'Never mind, I am going to make dinner.'

When Nazra finally joins Salimah in the kitchen, probably sent by Pak Long, she asks, 'Maybe Atuk was right, and there are hantu. Uncle told me about what happened there in the war, there was a battle. They say there are ghosts of Japanese soldiers still.'

Salimah considers this. Surely, even if there were Japanese hantu, they shouldn't concern them. They cannot be what upset Bapa. He mentioned a woman. She shakes her head. No, it is all nonsense. Salimah drops a spoon and looks her daughter in the eye. 'The war was a long long time ago. It's just a story.'

'It's not a story, it's history.'

Salimah shakes her head. 'Same difference.'

Nazra rolls her eyes. 'They fought there, the British against the Japanese, for days. And then they locked the prisoners up. Imagine, locking up those British prisoners of war in their own houses!'

When Salimah does not respond, Nazra continues. 'Seriously, Mak! Many people died there. Who knows if their spirits ever left ...'

'Cheh, it's superstition. We need to pray and stay strong. Allah will protect us.'

When Nazra looks back tauntingly, Salimah continues: 'Satan will flee from a house where the Qur'an is read.'

'Then that is your problem right there lor. Those ang mohs don't read Qur'an.'

Salimah pushes some plates into Nazra's hands. 'Put these on the table.'

She looks her sixteen-year-old daughter up and down. 'You need to exercise more. You are getting fat.'

5

The beauty of the house is more visible now that it's clean. Anna feels like a colonial memsahib – and hates how much she loves it. Salimah hums while she cleans.

Having slept straight through for the first time in a while, Anna wakes up feeling rested. She often wakes up in the middle of the night to the sound of barking, sometimes whining, dogs. The neighbour's dog is a yapper, this sounds bigger. Tom never hears it, he sleeps like a log, and when she woke him up once to hear it, he said she was crazy.

She should get up and get dressed, but Anna is hesitant to leave the coolness of the bedroom. And now at least she has an excuse to sleep in, she thinks, as she snuggles her face into the cool underside of the pillow. She blames the house for this pregnancy. On the beanbag, infused by gin and tonic and the magic of the sweltering garden, she was transported to another dimension where practicalities like condoms did not occur to her – and she came off birth control years ago as the hormones muddled her body.

Tom was excited from the moment they saw the second line appear dimly on the white of the pregnancy test. She didn't know what to say. *I'm not sure I am ready?*

The thing is, she knows she isn't. This is not how she planned their first year here. A bump will make job interviews tricky. And travelling to Indonesia, off the beaten track like she wants to, will be tough with a baby on her hip. Tom is more than ready, but with his new job, who will be doing the bulk of the childcare? What about *her* career? Anna has been waiting for the right moment to bring up her concerns, but the longer she waits, the more they pale until she isn't sure what she wants anymore.

On the other hand, Tom's enthusiasm for the baby has put the spark back into their relationship. He has made a genuine effort to be home more. Anna still feels tired and queasy and in the evenings he cooks, does the dishes and lets her put her feet up, although more recently he suggested they leave those dishes out for Salimah to do in the morning.

Anna rubs her stomach which is still as flat as ever. In addition to the nausea, she feels odd, not herself, thrown off course by this unexpected development. On the other hand, having this little creature growing inside her makes her feel less alone in this huge house. It clearly needs more people inside it. And having a baby that, like her father, will be born in Asia, will make things come full circle. It's just the timing that is wrong. As she considers that, Anna chastises herself for even thinking it. Some people take years to conceive, or can't at all. How can she complain she got pregnant too soon? She's the right age, has the right husband. A house that's more than big enough. She should be happy. She has it all.

What she needs is to get out, have some fun. Pondering ideas of things to do today, she slowly dozes off again.

Anna's phone beeps on her nightstand. She blinks, picks it up and stares at it, expecting it to be Tom, the only one messaging her lately, but then her heart leaps. *'Hi Anna, how RU? Settling in? Let me know if you need help, I know how it can be for a newbie. Happy to meet for coffee xx Vicky'*

Yesterday she finally managed to get out of the house. She went to a yoga class in the Botanic Gardens and met some other expat wives – despite her resistance to being one she grins at the word. She had enjoyed meeting these women who were American, French and Japanese as well as British, and after class they'd gone for coffee at the café. No one in the class was from Singapore, not even the teacher, who was Australian. It seems expats mostly socialise with other expats. Anna is desperate to get outside that bubble, another reason she is happy to have Salimah around, but for now, she is glad for any interaction.

She tries to remember which one was Vicky. Of course, the one about Anna's age, with those cute floral leggings. The one that kept checking the time, and mentioning her young baby that she left with her helper for the first time. *'Thanks! Coffee would be great, need all the help I can get ;) I'm free this afternoon.'*

'I'm away to Phuket for the long weekend, let's hook up after x'

Anna leans back on her pillow, disappointed Vicky ignored her suggestion. Is the offer even genuine or is she being polite? Even after years in the UK Anna still can't always tell. But she allows herself some enthusiasm, and wasn't Vicky from New Zealand anyway? Maybe she can ask her here to see the house? She thinks back to yesterday. When Anna mentioned where she lived, Vicky had exclaimed, 'You live in a "black and white"?'

'In a what?' Anna asked, as a platinum blonde American looked at her with a sideways glance that could only signal envy.

'One of those black and white houses, you know, the colonial ones?'

'Yes,' Anna admitted. 'I didn't know they were called that,

but yeah, it is old and it is painted black and white.'

The American snorted but Vicky had smiled. It seems these houses are a phenomenon; coveted by expats. Anna had felt a little smug, and then too self-conscious to ask more so the conversation went back to where everyone was going for the long weekend.

Anna and Tom will stay here, they've only just arrived. Perhaps they can go the National Museum? At least it would be cool inside, she thinks, dreading having to leave the bedroom soon. Maybe Tom is right, and they should get air conditioning in the living room. How did her grandparents live like this? Would they have been better at coping with the heat because they were born here?

When she hears sounds of rummaging from the living room Anna sits up with a jolt. She clicks the message away and looks at the clock. Is it that late? Salimah is there already and must think Anna lazy to lie in bed this long. She quickly throws a sundress over her head and rinses her face, then walks into the living room with a chirpy 'good morning'. As if she's been up for hours.

Salimah, busy with a broom and dustpan, smiles. 'Good morning.'

She doesn't look directly at Anna, who blushes anyway. Why the charade? 'Sorry, I overslept. I didn't set my alarm, with no job to go to I just didn't see the point.'

'Why not enjoy your rest?'

Anna feels embarrassed. Not having work is one thing, but then still having someone else clean your house, another. Yesterday afternoon, when she came home, all she wanted to do was binge on Netflix, but she felt she could not do that with Salimah around. She grabs her laptop before she sits down and opens the computer. 'I need to get on with this job search.'

Salimah nods as Anna stares at a long list of Facebook notifications. That job search is going nowhere especially since she spends more time on social media than career sites. She thought she had a strong resume: history degrees from both Leiden and Cambridge universities, almost a decade of experience at a multinational. For the first time in her life Anna is feeling too white to get a job.

When she tries to talk to Tom he doesn't understand. 'Why not relax a little first? Who knows when you will have this opportunity again, to not work and enjoy life. Maybe you can spend some time with the little one when it's born before you go back to work? We can afford it here.'

He had his hand on her belly when he said that and she felt a red hormonal wave wash over her.

'If you think I am going to be this stay-at-home expat wife whose life revolves around kids and school, and wine by the pool in between, think again.'

Tom had hugged her, and said sweetly: 'Of course, I'd expect nothing less. Let me ask around at work.'

But the following day he came home and said, 'You know what they said?'

And when Anna stared back with hopeful eyes: 'Don't we pay you enough that your wife doesn't need to work?'

What hurt the most was Tom laughing.

At the same time, Anna is not sure she would cope without her afternoon naps. The heat combined with the nausea has a lethal effect. She swallows down a gulf of bile and looks at Salimah who is wiping a cloth across the tv. 'Nothing, not a single invitation for an interview. To be honest, I'm losing my motivation to try.'

Salimah wipes her brow with her sleeve as she ponders. 'It's tough right now. I can't find anything either.'

Anna looks at Salimah, befuddled. 'Do you need more work? I can ask around, maybe one of the neighbours, or one of my friends from yoga needs someone. I can give you a glowing recommendation, your work puts our London cleaner to shame.'

Salimah turns to hide her face and works on. Did Anna say something wrong? 'Don't be modest, you know it's true!'

Salimah looks up, sheepishly. 'It's not that. I enjoy cleaning, but the thing is, I don't normally do this as a job.'

Anna's puzzlement grows. 'What do you mean?'

'When we first met, I was looking for work. But not like this. My last job was in corporate sales.'

'But, I don't get it? Why were you here, in front of the house? And why did you not say so?'

Anna plays the scene of their meeting in her mind. What had Salimah said? What had Anna said? *OMG*. The embarrassment inside Anna grows until she feels it is going to swallow her whole. To be honest she barely remembers their conversation that first day. She was hot and nauseous. Did she force this job on Salimah? She remembers Salimah confused her, she sounded smart, her English good, but the tudung threw Anna off track. None of her Muslim friends in London wear it. Suddenly she remembers the woman in the blue headscarf in front of this house, that first day. Was that Salimah too? Embarrassment grows into full shame. She stammers. 'I'm so sorry, I didn't mean to ...' Mean what? Anna wishes she can go back to bed and turn back time. Salimah too seems to have lost her natural composed self. She has sat herself down on the chair across from Anna, something she hasn't done since that first day. 'No, I am sorry, I should have told you. But ... I could use the money ... And I ...'

Anna stares at Salimah. She is the only one who ought to say sorry, a hundred times, simply for being obnoxious and ignorant. 'Please don't apologise. I was probably bulldozing all over you. I do that.'

'It's okay.'

'No, it's not.' Still puzzled, Anna adds: 'Were you visiting the area, do you have friends here?' *But then, why did Felicity chase you away?*

Salimah stares out the window. 'When I lost my job, I felt detached, from myself, my life. I grew up in this area and came back here to, I don't know. For remembrance, I suppose.'

Salimah grew up here? 'Really, that's so fascinating.' Anna has to pinch herself to stop asking questions that Salimah might not want to answer. *Did she live in one of the houses? How, when, why? And does she know more about the history?*

Salimah turns back to Anna. 'We lived in a kampong, a small village nearby. My father worked in this house. He was the gardener.'

A gardener! In this very house? As Anna ponders a reply, her phone rings. It's Tom. 'Sorry, I need to take this.'

She walks to the bedroom to talk in private and when she comes back, Salimah is gone from the chair. Anna finds her in the kitchen staring into the fridge. 'You seem so pale lately, you need some proper food. Shall I teach you to cook soto? I'll buy you the ingredients for the Javanese chicken soup, the way my mother made it. We can cook it later this week.'

'That sounds amazing.'

6

Salimah and Nazra are riding the bus into town. It is cold inside and Salimah cradles her handbag close on her lap. She has been struggling more and more with Nazra these last few weeks. The girl has changed so much since she started junior college. And she has a temper that makes Salimah afraid to scold her. Nazra is always in her room, on her handphone, and barely speaks to anyone in the house. And she stays out late. Once, Salimah suspected alcohol on her breath. When Salimah asks her where she's been, or tells her to be home for dinner, Nazra gives her an angry glare. But sometimes, Nazra is her little girl again and asks for her favourite chicken curry or sits up with her Atuk for hours reading him the newspaper and watching his favourite shows with him. Nazra's mood swings are unpredictable. As she was in a good mood this morning, Salimah invited her to lunch at a foodcourt.

'You know where I want to go?' Nazra answered. 'Adam Road.'

Surprised, Salimah nodded yes. It is the one right next to Adam Park.

It is a great foodcourt; good nasi lemak is to be had there, they say it is the prime minister's favourite. This building is new, of course. The old hawkers were by the canal, before the PIE and the flyover were built, before the hygiene police moved the stalls across the road, built them a roof and toilets. She remembers the muddy grass, the smoke from the grilles, and the rickety wooden chairs they had in her childhood, chairs you could gather together, unlike the modern plastic stools – cast in concrete and unmovable. Six is the maximum amount of people that can eat together now. Imagining the old hawkers makes Salimah feel nostalgic. Singapore doesn't value its heritage. This is something she's been thinking about recently, especially at the big house. Has she done the same by burying thoughts of her childhood? A snippet from long ago floats up from a deep cellar in her brain. 'There was a long hard time when I kept far from me the remembrance of what I had thrown away when I was quite ignorant of its worth.' Dickens always could articulate things better. She mulls the quote over as her daughter continues scrolling her handphone in silence.

When they alight, a loud clap sounds straight above and a flash carves open the sky. A deep rumble ensues and it doesn't take long before the rain hammers down on the roof of the bus stop, the kind of tropical shower that soaks you in seconds. Salimah fumbles in her bag for her umbrella, until Nazra points to a covered walkway along the road. 'One day we will wake up and find the whole island covered in one huge climatised dome.'

Nazra is right, it is crazy, but Salimah is glad of the protection from the elements. But when they approach the foodcourt, they realise the walkway follows the road to the MRT stop on the other side. They need to wait or make a quick dash across. Hunger wins out. They run through a curtain of water and sink down onto two plastic stools. Salimah's wet fabric drips water on the concrete floor, and onto her leather sandals. 'What do you want to eat?' she asks Nazra.

'Mee rebus, of course.'

Salimah smiles. They always make a point of trying mee rebus, noodles in curry gravy, at various stalls in order to compare them and determine which is the best. She can't remember ever eating it here. 'Yes, me too,' she says.

'You sit here, Mak, I'll go get it.'

Whilst Nazra queues for their noodles, Salimah's wet feet bring back more memories. The old hawkers were flooded regularly – dredging through knee-high water was a common occurrence in seventies Singapore. The new Bukit Timah canal is the most gigantic longkang she's ever seen, an ugly concrete ditch that would hold an ocean. When empty it looks ridiculously oversized, yet it will fill close to overflowing if this weather endures, keeping everyone's feet dry.

The noodles arrive and, stirring them, Salimah slowly warms up. 'Nazra, we need to talk. I don't know you anymore, what is going on with you?'

The girl shrugs. 'Can we not talk about something else? Like the sogginess of this noodle.' She holds up a strand that breaks, creating a small splash in the sauce. 'See?'

Salimah laughs. 'But the gravy is excellent.' She slurps loud to prove her point. 'Anyway, don't change the subject. Why do you stay out late? And why have your grades dropped?'

Nazra rolls her eyes. 'Why not? Where did all that studying get you, still cleaning a house.'

Salimah, offended, sinks her spoon back in the noodles.

One job interview is all she's had lately and the 'thank you, we'll be in touch' says it all. She can't clean for Anna forever. Salimah sighs, she has become an old woman. Her mother wasn't much older when she died, and Salimah misses her every day. What would her mother say to a disrespectful daughter? Her mother had dreamed of Salimah becoming a teacher. She herself had been indignant at the idea of becoming the cliché of a kampong child done well – a makcik in a flowery dress teaching children. Salimah wanted something more. Now her mother is gone and Salimah asks herself: has she ever really liked her job? She remembers her last day at the office, when she saw that girl walk in, and Salimah lost her usual composure. Cast from the standard 'office girl' mould, full of confidence in a mini skirt and high heels. The opposite of Salimah in her swaths of fabric. It was as if not just her job but her very self had been made redundant. She wasn't a team player, her boss had told her, she didn't connect well with modern consumers. Her impressive monthly sales figures meant nothing. Or had her boss been right and had her heart never been in it?

'Mak?'

Salimah looks up. 'Sorry. What were you saying?'

'Nothing,' Nazra says. 'Actually, I do wonder. Why do you work there? Aren't you too good to be a maid?'

The question briefly takes her breath away. When she gets it back, Salimah finds herself happy that her daughter finds her worthy. 'There is nothing wrong with a job like that, remember your Nenek was a cleaner too. But to me, it's only temporary, until I find a better job. I think the house has things to teach me. And Anna treats me well, more than a cleaner, we talk about all sorts of things. She's very friendly.'

Nazra smirks. 'I'm sure she is. She sounds like one of those white expats wanting to be friends with the maid, just to show how good she is.'

Shocked, Salimah protests. 'She's not like that.'

When they leave the foodcourt the sun is back in full force, steam coils up from the road. Salimah stretches her wet limbs. 'Do you want to go home?'

She expects Nazra wants to rush off and meet friends as she always does, but to her surprise she nods. 'I'd like to see that house where you work. It's close by, right?'

'Why do you want to see it?'

'Well, you grew up around there, and it's my heritage too. I've never been.'

Happy to engage with her wayward teenager, Salimah points to the zebra crossing and they cross the road towards Adam Park. Salimah relaxes further as the rainwater dries from her clothes. 'Do you want to see inside the house too? I'm not sure Anna is home but I'm sure she'd love to meet you.'

Nazra shrugs. 'Why not?'

'This whole area was very different before.' How to explain to someone who never knew the old Singapore? There were no condos hiding behind the bushes, no PIE motorway rushing behind the hill. 'It was much less overgrown, and there was a path that led to the kampong. Our house was wooden but solid. My mother had a vegetable plot, with a chicken and ducks. We swapped items with neighbours, it was a tight-knit community.'

That their small village was dwarfed by the twenty imposing houses next to it was inconsequential; they had their pride, their livelihoods. 'Do you want to try and find the location of the kampong?' These shoes are ruined anyway.

Nazra shakes her head. 'Nah. Let's just see the big house.'

Offended, Salimah stands still in front of the house. 'It's not my heritage you are interested in, right? It's those ghosts.'

Nazra laughs. 'Yah. It's so cool, I've never seen a haunted

house before. My friends were really into it when I told them. They say there could be many ghosts in such an old place with so much history. Japanese, who knows what else.'

Salimah shakes her head, annoyed, but glad her daughter is taking an interest in something. Anything. 'Who are these friends? From school?'

Nazra makes a gagging sound. 'That boring bunch? No. Some people I met when I was out.'

'Out where?'

'Just somewhere, it's my life, not yours.'

'I am your mother, I am interested in you, and want to know you are okay. And that includes who you hang out with.'

'I'm fine. Do I ask you about your friends? Why you haven't had Aziza or Nurul over for ages?'

That stings. Salimah has been avoiding her friends lately. 'Okay, let's go.' She walks up to the door and rings the bell. No one answers. When Salimah looks up she sees the windows are closed.

Nazra pointedly looks around and behind them, then turns to Salimah 'Do you smell that?'

A sweet smell curls up Salimah's nose and her stomach restricts. 'That's the frangipani. Why is it so strong?'

Nazra bends to pick up a flower from the path. Salimah wants to stop her but before she can, Nazra smells it and smiles. 'It's smells so strong. You know what it signals?'

Salimah nods hesitantly as a new nausea wells up.

'A pontianak could be near,' Nazra says, looking around, and at the greenery behind the house.

Salimah follows her gaze to the banyan that looms over the back of the garden and her stomach contracts. 'You say that as if it's a good thing,' she cries out. 'First you talk about Japanese soldiers, now it's a lady ghost or pontianak. What's next, an orang minyak? Or a toyol?

Nazra grins, 'That would be cool. Do you think Anna would let me come over at night some time?'

'You gila,' Salimah mutters as she walks away. 'Let's go home.'

A lumpy feeling settles in her belly. Salimah has worked hard to get away from such dark things. Worked hard to get a good job, a good flat, a good life for her daughter. She can't let backwards superstitions ruin everything again. The girl needs to focus on school.

When they get home, Pak Long is still there. Nazra sees him and rushes to her room, slamming the door shut behind her. Pak Long comes over a lot lately. It takes him more than an hour to reach here by bus so he stays all day. Father likes the company, but the older he is, the more Pak Long gets on Salimah's nerves – she is starting to understand why he was never married.

'What's for lunch?' Pak Long grins. 'Nasi goreng?' he asks hopefully.

Is he here for the food? To be cared for? His movements have become a lot stiffer, and he often complains of hip pain. Salimah slams a packet of bread, some margarine and a jar of kaya on the table. 'We already ate,' she says. Then, in a friendlier tone, adds, 'Kopi?'

The correct thing to do would be to invite Pak Long to come and live here. He can share Father's bedroom. At the pondok, they had gotong royong, community spirit, people helping each other. This is what they do, as Malays. They don't hire outsiders to look after the elderly. They care for them, with love. But something is holding her back.

Pak Long stirs the coffee Salimah has made him. 'Salimah, I need to talk to you. About your daughter. She has no father or brother and her grandfather is more and more blur.'

Salimah doesn't need to be reminded.

After a pause, he adds: 'But Nazra has me.'

She also has me, her mother.

'Her behaviour is, how to say, disrespectful. Does she go to the mosque?'

Salimah is not sure. To her, religion is a private matter, she prefers to pray at home. In her direct connection with God she feels the most comfortable. Nazra will find her own way too. She shakes her head. Her conversation this morning went nowhere and she does need help, but Pak Long is not the right person. Who is? Salimah needs to protect her daughter, girls are judged harsher than boys and a good name is easily lost.

'Pak Long, as her mother, I think that–' In the short break it takes Salimah to catch her breath, Pak Long has cut in. 'Salimah,' he says, 'I have spoken to your father and we decided it is best I move in. I have given notice on my rental flat.'

Salimah chokes on her too hot coffee. This is her place, that she owns! Shouldn't I have a say in this, Salimah says, but then realises she did not say that out loud. Pak Long is family. Her eldest uncle. What will it look like if she refuses him?

She nods curtly and goes to check on Nazra. The girl lies curled up in her bed, the sheets crumpled around her. When Salimah gently pokes her in the side she grunts. 'Get up, why did you go lie down in the middle of the day? We just got home. Go study or what.'

Nazra, dishevelled, rises halfway, then lies back down.

'Tidy yourself and pay your respects to Pak Long. You were very rude passing him just now.'

Nazra bolts up like a jack-in-the-box. 'Why is he here again?'

Salimah sits down on the side of the bed and swallows. There is no way to break this gently.

'He's coming to live here. He is old and we are his only family.'

She pats Nazra's side gently, not sure what else to say. 'You really do need to exercise more, Naz, look at that tummy.'

Nazra jumps up from the bed and starts shoving clothes and toiletries in her bag. 'I am not staying if he is.'

'Nazra, please don't overreact, let's talk about this, together. You got along quite well with him the other day, remember. He means well.'

But Nazra is already out of the door and Salimah's heart sinks.

7

When Marivic opens the door, a blast of cold air hits Anna in the face. So *that* is why Felicity keeps her windows closed at all times; she should have brought a cardigan. Loud twittering echoes down the stairs. Anna hasn't been inside this house, or any others in the street, and glances around curiously as she walks up the stairs.

When Anna finally met her next-door neighbour she couldn't help but see her as she had that first day, snubbing Salimah – in her activewear, which she wears most days. Felicity was lovely to Anna, all hugs and invitations. Today she is hosting a coffee morning for all the wives on the street.

Marivic, Felicity's helper, quietly slips away when they reach the top of the stairs. Anna is sorry to see the back of her, she is the only person here she actually knows. Marivic walks Felicity's little white dog past their house several times a day and is always happy to chat.

The house is identical to theirs, only this one looks like it comes straight out of a magazine. Felicity is American, the furniture Asian: a gorgeous antique Chinese sideboard with painted flowers, a large bronze Buddha, some temple stools. Anna admires a print on the wall by the stairs while Felicity bustles over, and before Anna has time to wonder whether to stick out her hand or kiss her on the cheeks, Felicity has pulled her in a stiff hug. When she lets go, Anna hands her the pack of speculaas she brought over. Felicity eyes them suspiciously. 'Lovely. What are those?'

'Oh, they are a type of biscuit from the Netherlands. I found this special shop, where you can buy all things Dutch. Imagine, on the other side of the world! They didn't have these in London.'

Felicity looks at Anna, head cocked. 'Yes, that is Singapore. We have everything.'

'Yes, but at a cost, the price is ridiculous.'

Felicity smiles. 'You'll learn to stop caring about crazy food prices. Otherwise you'll never eat cheese again.'

Anna laughs. 'And that is unthinkable for a Dutch woman.'

'So are you Dutch? I thought you were British?'

'No, my husband is British. I have lived in London for years though.'

'Wow, your accent is amazing. How do you do that? I can't speak anything but English. I tried Mandarin classes for a while, but oh my god I'm useless.'

'Well, it is easier if you are from a tiny European country with a language that nobody else speaks.'

'True, true. All you Scandinavians speak amazing English,' Felicity says, and before Anna can correct her, she pulls Anna further into the room.

'Ladies, come and meet Anna from number four.'

Anna shakes a lot of hands. Everybody is friendly and welcoming. On a side table are some Pinterest-worthy cakes that make Anna's speculaas look as inadequate as her furniture. She finds herself seated between Sonja, a German lady in her fifties, and an Australian called Isabel. They soon talk about shopping. Supermarkets still daunt Anna, and apart from Orchard Road, Singapore's upmarket version of Oxford Street, she has no idea where to go for clothes. In one shop (was it Prada?) the shop assistant hadn't even looked Anna in the eye. Did she know Anna was not going to buy anything, that she had come in to escape the heat? The girl quickly scurried over when a group of heavily veiled women came in acting as if they were in a supermarket, piling purchase upon purchase. Anna escaped into Zara, only to find it full of the new winter collection. When she asked a staff member, he said: 'Yes, ma'am, of course, it's winter now.'

'It's over thirty degrees outside!'

The guy merely shrugged. 'There are a few items in the back, in the sales rack,' he added casually. She shares the story with Sonja, who laughs.

'The winter collections are for the Chinese tourists. Don't go to Orchard, go to places that cater for expats. They stock, ehm, European sizes there too.'

Anna laughs. Her waist hasn't even expanded yet but she barely fits a size XL here – in London she was a medium. They talk about Sonja's children, one is still living at home, a second is studying abroad, and then Sonja asks: 'And what does your husband do?'

Anna's jaw freezes. *Is she really 'the-wife-of' now?* She mumbles quickly, 'he's with a bank', and before Sonja can ask more, Anna blurts: 'And you, what do you do?'

Sonja continues, undaunted. 'The kids were a handful when they were younger. Driving them around Singapore, on playdates, sports, CCAs. It was a fulltime job, even with the helper.'

Even with the helper? Should she ask what a CCA is?

'Now they are older I need to find my own things to do. Of course, there are coffee mornings, lunches. I do my own groceries. I also volunteer a bit.'

Anna envisages bake sales at school. Or fundraising galas. Feigning interest, she asks. 'Really, that sounds nice, what kind of volunteering?'

Sonja puts her teacup on the table and picks up her cake fork. 'At a women's shelter. They have victims of domestic abuse mainly, some young girls too, pregnant teenage runaways ousted by conservative families. Some abused helpers.' She stares at her cake. 'I'm trained as a counsellor, so I offer my services there twice a week. I don't want to work fulltime. But this way I can give back.'

Feeling caught out for judging Sonja, Anna swallows. 'Really? That's so admirable.'

She explains how she would like to work but hasn't had much success applying.

'You really need to network here. What did you study?'

Anna laughs. 'Actually, I studied history, particularly the Victorian era.'

Sonja smiles too. 'There won't be much need for that here.'

'Or anywhere,' Anna admits. 'I worked in marketing before.'

'So, you like history then? Weren't these houses built by the Victorians?'

Anna considers this for a moment. 'I think they were built in the 1920s. Victoria was dead by then.'

Isabel turns around to face them. 'Sorry, but I happened to overhear you. I have a book on the history of the area, you are welcome to borrow it. Fascinating stuff.'

'I'd love that, thanks. I've been meaning to find out more about the history of this area. Is it true locals don't want to live here? What's the story?'

'Oh, they think there are ghosts here,' Isabel says. 'There were several days of fighting during the Battle of Singapore in 1942. Many died and the houses got badly damaged in the crossfire. And then, after the Allies lost … I'm sure you have heard of the Burma railway?'

Anna nods. Her great-uncle, Oma's brother, died there. She feels a prickly feeling building inside as Isabel continues. 'Those prisoners of war, they stayed here, in our houses. Aussie and Brit soldiers, before they were sent off to Burma. Two hundred to a house, can you believe it?'

Anna can't, and feels hot despite the cold. Could Oma's brother have stayed here? He was in the Dutch army though, captured in Indonesia, not Malaya. 'How does that even work, two hundred people? I mean, it's a big house, but still.'

Isabel says: 'Apparently many of them stayed underneath the house, in the space between the pillars.'

'Outside?' Anna gasps. 'Well, I suppose it was sheltered.'

Isabel nods. 'I'm sure they were much more uncomfortable later, in Burma.'

'So was it only military prisoners that stayed here? What about women and children?' Women like Oma.

'They were at Sime Road camp. It's very close, just across the motorway from here. You can read all about it in that book.'

Anna tries to make sense of what she is hearing whilst Isabel continues. 'I did a tour in the area, with a guide who knows all about the history. I can introduce you to her? They have added my house to the tour itinerary.'

She lives in a tourist destination! One that housed prisoners, like her family, during the war. She has heard stories of course, about Japanese guards, beatings, hunger. When she was younger, Anna tried to pry more out of Oma. Oma told her all about plantation life, the wild animals, nature encroaching on the house, the food and local magic. But that era ended with the war, and what happened after is cloaked in silence. And now Oma is dead.

Anna's throat constricts when she looks around the tastefully decorated room. At the women, all looking like her, sitting here chatting and eating cake as if nothing has changed. Soon she will be one of them, with a helper living in the servants' quarters, she ferrying children to sports and those CCAs – whatever they are – and meeting like-minded people for tea and wine, whilst tourists pass by to gape at them. Is that what she wants? Hesitantly she puts her hand on her stomach. She wants this baby, she does. But her new life in Singapore confuses her so much.

Too many thoughts stumble around her mind and her nausea starts up again with a vengeance. She stops listening as her mind wanders to a couple of unopened boxes sitting in her downstairs storeroom. They contain items she packed up when they cleared out Oma's house after she died, not long before they moved to Singapore. And suddenly she is scared to even think of what is in those boxes.

What Anna needs is some fresh new furniture. Modern Asian, like Felicity has. She takes a big bite of cake, swallows it down, and changes the subject.

'So where can I buy lovely furniture like this? I have a lot of our relocation budget still left and no idea where to spend it.'

Anna leaves the coffee morning with several furniture shop recommendations. At home, she wanders around the house, compiling a list in her mind with pieces they need. It is a long list, and their budget is generous but finite. She will never be able to fill her house like Felicity has. Anna stops at the spare rooms. The first one is really quite dark. It has no windows but verandas on two sides and two doors, one leading into each of them. She passes through the bathroom to the second empty room, the larger one which has the window. This would have made a good study, but she supposes it will have to be the nursery. Anna walks through to the veranda on the other side and stops. Suddenly she is cold. Chilly worms creep up her legs and settle in her stomach. The goosebumps on her arms are back, just like that first morning. The sound is louder this time, like distant shouting and the echo of footsteps in the roof.

Anna rushes back to her own bedroom and lies down on the edge of the bed. What is wrong with her? Are her hormones getting the better of her? She closes her eyes and her heartbeat settles. But something remains wedged in her brain. And she realises she can't hide. She needs to open those boxes.

The storeroom has only a small, barred window and smells stuffy. She pushes aside Tom's golf bag, rummages between the boxes. She opens one labelled 'books', and smiles. The colourful covers are like old friends that she is glad to see again, in this foreign new life. Then she closes the box and sets it aside. A bookcase needs to be high on her priority list.

She finds them at the back of the room. Two boxes in a darker cardboard than those of the London movers. Carefully, she opens the first one, and starts in surprise. Two pairs of big black eyes stare straight at her. Her thumping heart settles down as she observes the golden details, long white fangs and red twirls of wood. These carved masks hung on the wall in Oma's hallway, appraising everyone who entered with their piecing stare. When she was little they intimidated her so much that she had to rush past them with her eyes closed. What was she thinking, taking those?

Quickly, she closes the box and opens the second one. It contains some smaller wood carvings, colourful batik cloth, and a book with a faded green cover. She pulls out the book, it is one she knows well. They spent hours poring over it, and Anna knows a story for every image. It is the album of Oma's childhood in Sumatra. Gently she opens the fragile pages and there they are: the familiar images that seem more real now she is in Asia herself. Oma's house, so similar to this one. Groups of blonde people in white blouses and batik skirts. She stops at a man and a woman in front of a lake. *Trip to Lake Toba.* A strong sense of desire to go there, to stand in that same place, wells up inside her. Sumatra isn't far from here at all. Anna turns the pages until she stops at a photo of a baby on the lap of her babu, her nanny. That baby became the creased old lady with the grey hairs in the tiny bun at the back of her head. A woman that lived more than half of her life in the Netherlands but left her heart in Asia, forever sitting on the lap of the tropics.

Oma never went back to Indonesia. When Anna was little, Oma would sit in her armchair covered by a plaid – always cold even in the Dutch summer, and they would bring out the atlas and plan an imaginary trip, a Grand Tour. Fly to Yogyakarta to see Borobudur. Hike the Bromo volcano, then a boat to Bali. When Anna pointed at Medan, Oma would shake her head. Not Sumatra, too many ghosts there. The mystery only made young Anna want to see Medan more. She would stare at Oma's painting of two volcanoes with a vague fear that only increased her longing. The painting! It must be in here somewhere. Digging deeper, she finds the painting underneath the batik. She closes the box and takes up the painting and the photo album.

She sets the painting on the sideboard and as she stares at it, she misses her grandmother intensely. If only she could have visited her here, seen Anna's life and met her grandchild. Oma described Singapore as crowded and smelly, completely different from the gleaming metropolis it has become. Oma longed for a country that no longer exists. Indië, the Dutch East Indies, the place of tempo doeloe and plantations and baboes became Indonesia and Oma would feel homeless all her life.

A tear slides down Anna's cheek. She neglected her grandmother all those years she lived in London. She could have taken her on that trip. She needs to make it right, if not for Oma herself, then at least for her memory. Anna will make the trip Oma never got to undertake.

Oma's Grand Tour was real, it had been planned for when she came of age, to visit family members and friends all over the archipelago. But the Japanese arrived, and she went to an internment camp instead. Anna looks out the window at the birds in the trees and tries to make sense of it all. There are so many gaps. She used to fill them in with her imagination, or with things she read elsewhere. What she learned at university was shameful: Indonesian independence was paid in blood. *Indisch people don't like to talk, Anna*, papa would sigh. *Let it be.* But she can't.

She opens her laptop and starts an email to her father to ask the questions that she hasn't asked before. It is time to rip open the silence. Where was that plantation exactly? And why did he never want to come back?

8

Salimah drags the heavy bags with the soto ingredients up the wooden stairs, feeling hot and dishevelled. She had to go to a special butcher to get Anna free-range chicken. When Salimah suggested kampong chicken, Anna had rolled her eyes. 'They are not actually reared in a kampong, you know; it's just a different breed. They are raised in small cages just like other chicken here.'

Anna has only been here a short time, but already knows everything better. Could it be true what she says? Salimah thinks back to her own kampong: how a whole muddle of kids roamed free there, together with the chickens. Everywhere was a playground.

She walks into the living room where Anna is busy putting books on the shelves of a bookcase that could use a lick of paint. Anna looks as sweaty as Salimah feels. Why doesn't she get air conditioning?

Anna looks up. 'Hi, there. Did you get everything okay? I want to finish unpacking the books, could you help me bring up some more boxes?'

Salimah puts down her shopping and picks up an old, well-thumbed copy of *Jane Eyre*. 'I love this one. I did a dissertation on it in university.'

Anna takes the book from Salimah's hands. 'Yes, one of my favourites too.'

She opens it at random, her eyes dart over the pages before she reads out loud: 'I am not talking to you now through the medium of custom, conventionalities, nor even of mortal flesh;–it is my spirit that addresses your spirit; just as if both had passed through the grave, and we stood at God's feet, equal,–as we are!'

The words makes Salimah feel sentimental. 'Her prose is so beautiful. When I was a student, I used to read all the time, especially classics like Bronte and Austen. Now, I don't have the peace of mind.' Not to mention she can barely get her daughter to read anything that is not on a screen.

Anna nods. 'Same here. You're welcome to borrow some books.'

'Thank you. But before we unpack them, we should start the soto, it takes quite long to cook.'

Anna wipes her dusty hands on her shirt. 'Sure.'

In the kitchen, Salimah unpacks the groceries and lines up the spices. 'Why don't you start by washing the chicken? I'll pick some salam leaf, there's a tree in the garden. And I think I saw kaffir lime too.'

The salam tree is behind the pool, hidden by the towering banyan. Salimah feels a slight trepidation as she passes beneath the banyan's arches. She brushes aside young air roots that dangle down like tiny lianas. When one hits her in the face, she stifles a scream. It feels wet and stringy. Salimah braces herself before pushing forward, feeling enveloped by the tree, and the buzzing sound that emanates from it. *Be sensible*, she tells herself. That noise is just cicadas. The salam tree sits almost inside the banyan. Some of these banyans are stranglers, Salimah knows, and she wonders whether the salam will last. For now it seems healthy enough, and with effort she stretches and manages to pull one of its branches down enough to be able to pick a few leaves. Quickly, she stumbles backwards, out of the tree and back onto the lawn. Catching her breath, she looks around the garden. Anna's gardeners have tidied up, but it is still wilder than it ever was. It feels peaceful enough out here, now she is away from the banyan. In the bright sunlight, no spirits dare hover on the verandas that wrap around the house, at least, none that she can see.

Thankfully the kaffir lime bush is out in the open, behind the house, and as Salimah picks the leaves, she bruises them and inhales deeply. The citrusy tang of the daun perut smells clean, and uplifting. The only feeling it invokes is a slight melancholy, the scent reminding her of Nazra, who loves soto flavoured with it. She has heard nothing from the girl since she ran out, only a short text that she is staying with a friend and that Salimah should not worry. How can she not? The girl is so young. But when she rings her, Nazra never answers.

When she comes back in the kitchen, Anna is staring at the chicken in the sink. She has submerged it in hot water.

'How do you wash a chicken? Why not throw it straight into the pot?'

'Think about those sellers, the farmers, their dirty hands.'

'We're boiling it, right? That would kill all the germs. I'm not sure I should touch raw chicken.'

Salimah nudges Anna to the side with her elbow and puts her hand around the slick, chilly carcass, and rubs it up and down. 'Like this. Like you wash a baby. Why don't you chop the lengkuas. Peel it and cut it in thin slices.'

When Anna looks confused, Salimah points at some roots lying on the worktop. 'Lengkuas, you might know it as galangal?

It's the greyish one that looks like ginger, we also call it blue ginger. And chop some turmeric too, we call that one kunjit, it's the yellow one.'

'Koenjit, we say that too in the Netherlands,' Anna replies, as she sets to work. Salimah rinses the chicken under the warm tap. It is still frozen inside, she can't cut it, and decides to plunge it into the pot whole. There are no head or feet on this imported bird, which means less flavour for the broth. She covers the chicken with water and sets the pot on the stove. Anna holds the slices in her cupped hand close to her face. 'This fresh galangal is fabulous. In Europe, we have to make do with powder.'

Salimah shakes her head. 'Not the same.'

She adds the kaffir lime and salam leaves, some celery, spring onion and lemongrass stalks, as well as a generous dash of salt to the pot and turns the gas up high. 'Let's make the rempah and sambal, the spice mixes, now.'

Salimah starts to chop chilli and Anna observes her closely. She can't stay quiet for long. 'You know Isabel, from number 9? She gave me this book about the history of these houses. The Japanese fought the allies here, and afterwards, they turned these houses into a prisoner camp. Did you know that?'

Salimah stops chopping, the tip of her knife on the board, and looks at Anna. 'I thought you wanted to learn cooking?'

Anna looks flustered, and Salimah continues, 'for this chilli, no need to chop very fine, as we will grind it to a paste.'

Anna brings out a notebook and starts to scribble down notes. 'How much do you use?'

'I don't really count or weigh. I just smell, taste and see. Just like my mother taught me. Agak agak, estimate, approximate. For the rempah paste, we need a handful of candlenuts, some garlic and fresh turmeric.'

Salimah tosses them in the blender, thinking how her mother would cringe. She ground everything on a mortar stone, but Salimah's back is grateful for this modern invention. She adds powdered white pepper and nutmeg.

The groaning of the blender obscures Anna's voice, going on about that book, and asking whether Salimah's family already lived near here during the war. With Anna, Salimah sometime feels that *she* is the one on a chopping board. She asks so much about the past and acts as if it is not a big deal that Salimah's father used to work here as a gardener, that Salimah herself is paid staff. Salimah grunts with the sound of the grinder. She pretends she can't hear Anna talk and scrapes the paste into a wok with scalding hot oil.

Inhaling the singeing spices, she looks out the windows which are covered with a metal mesh and shudders, thinking about how she had felt inside the banyan. What is it that needs to be kept outside exactly? Her father's warnings to stay away echo in her mind. But surely she needs to show whatever is here that she is strong and can't be scared off, not this time. She has a job to do here. The simple household tasks, the cooking, even – maybe especially – the cleaning, feel like a break. Working here connects her to her late mother. She takes a deep breath as she stirs the aromatic paste.

The paste sizzles and she hands the spatula to Anna. 'Just fry it until it smells good.'

Anna is finally quiet. 'Oh my, this smells delicious. It reminds me of my grandmother's cooking.'

Salimah instructs Anna to peel garlic, shallots, and blanch them with the red chillies – big ones for colour and little ones for heat. Those will be ground to make sambal. 'And, with chilli, never take out the seeds. Just use less if you don't want spicy.'

When all the spice mixes are in bowls and the chicken is simmering away, Salimah scrubs the frangipani soap over the yellow turmeric stains on her hands, but they don't come off. 'Later, we prepare the toppings. Now, let's do your books.'

Salimah eyes the books strewn over the dining table, and picks up a large one, old and frayed around the edges. Not a regular book. Anna walks over and takes it off Salimah's hands. 'That's my grandmother's photo album. Do you want to see it?'

She shoves the other books aside with her elbow and carefully opens the old pages. Anna points at a house not unlike this one, in black and white, surrounded by palm trees. 'This is where my grandmother grew up.'

Puzzled, Salimah asks, 'Where is it?'

'In Sumatra. My father's family came from Indonesia, they had a plantation there.'

She flips the page gently. Men in white shorts and funny hats and little girls with large white bows in hair of indefinite grey. An old lady in baju kebaya holding a white baby.

Anna points at the baby. 'That's Oma. My grandmother.'

The lady in baju kebaya reminds Salimah of her own Javanese grandmother, who would dress just like that, her hair in a similar bun. She smiles gently, knowing Anna does not need to be prompted to say more.

'My family lived there for generations, but after independence, they were forced to leave. Only my grandmother was left by then, her parents and brother died in the camps. My father was the last one to be born in Indonesia, after the war.'

Anna leafs through the book, more photos of white people in

white outfits. 'My grandmother never really acclimatised in the Netherlands, she was always cold and hated the food.'

What can Salimah answer? 'Why did she not go back?'

'I'm not sure. I guess she didn't feel welcome anymore. They left in, well, a bad way I suppose. It's complicated. That was the 1950s.'

'My mother's family moved here from Java around that time too.'

Anna looks surprised. 'I thought you were Malay?'

'Yes, I am. Many of the Singapore Malays originally came from Indonesia.'

'Really, wow, I didn't know. Whereabouts? Why and how did they come here?'

Salimah doesn't want to admit she doesn't know that much. She has no albums of black and white photos, the wedding photo of her parents the oldest she owns. But the recipe she uses for the soto, whose fragrant smells waft into the dining room, is Javanese. It was her grandmother's. 'My father is Boyanese, and like I said, my mother's family came from central Java, near Solo.'

Salimah feels embarrassed she can't answer Anna's questions, but slowly her discomfort subsides and her curiosity grows. You need to chop spices and sear them before their full taste develops. 'The Boyanese are a minority amongst the Singapore Malays.'

'Where are they from, Boyan? Never heard of it.'

'Actually, a place called Bawean. It's a small island in the Java sea. The Boyanese were seafarers and a number of them ended up here, in the port of Singapore. Not sure when my family came, centuries ago already. Boyanese are highly spiritual people. Many practise traditional medicine.'

As she says it, another sentence rings in her mind. *They do black magic.* Quickly, she changes the subject. 'I didn't know my mother's family that well. They could not forgive my mother for marrying a Boyanese.' Salimah trails her finger around the photo of an Indonesian kampong. 'We didn't speak about it really.'

'Like my family,' says Anna. 'My grandmother only talked about the food, the heat, the people. Never about how they were made to leave Indonesia. Your ancestry is so interesting. I assumed the Malays were all born here or came from Malaysia.'

Salimah laughs. 'In Singapore, we call everyone Malay who speaks Malay and is Muslim. My father used to speak Boyanese as well as Malay, my maternal grandparents spoke Javanese. We all speak Malay now.'

'Amazing,' says Anna. 'Singapore really is a hodgepodge isn't it? I heard all the Chinese here speak different dialects too.'

Salimah nods.

'It makes me feel so useless that I don't speak any of those languages. My Dutch, German and French are useless here. Can you teach me Malay?'

'Why would you want to learn Malay? Everyone wants to learn Mandarin.'

If Salimah knew Mandarin, she could apply for all those jobs asking for Mandarin speakers. She suppresses a laugh. As if speaking Mandarin makes you Chinese.

'Malay seems, I don't know, more fun. You would make a great teacher.'

Salimah ponders the compliment; it touches her unexpectedly. She enjoys showing Anna how to cook. Teaching seems a useful kind of job, more fulfilling than sales. Anna looks at her keenly. Hesitantly, Salimah says. 'I could teach English, perhaps. I have a degree in English.'

Salimah could not even make herself send in an application for the last few suitable job openings. It felt all wrong, and between this cleaning job and Pak Long pitching in for household expenses, there was no rush.

Anna has started rattling again and Salimah shelves the thought.

'It is so frustrating, I don't even get invited to interviews, my experience in Europe means nothing here.'

Salimah sighs. Plenty of people struggle, people that don't have rich husbands. She clears her throat. 'Welcome to being a minority.'

Anna looks chastened until Salimah smiles, then bares her teeth in an apologetic grin.

'You are right. I suppose I have no right to complain. With my privileged white ass in my huge villa.'

They both laugh now, and when the laughter gently fizzles to a stop, Anna looks at Salimah conspiratorially. 'Shall I tell you a secret?

'Sure.'

'The reason I want to find a job quickly. I'm pregnant.'

Salimah's smile grows even bigger. 'That is great news. Congratulations!'

But suddenly she sees the shape of Nazra, and her thoughts drift away to her daughter lying in bed. Her dishevelled face. Her languid movements. Then, she remembers how she put her hand on Nazra's hip, and felt that hard belly. That can't be fat. Alamak, how can she not have noticed it before? In front of a bewildered Anna, Salimah puts her head in her hands and bursts into tears.

9

Anna is startled. Why would Salimah react like this to the news of her pregnancy? Is she worried Anna will now fire her in order to get fulltime help? Hesitantly, she gets up and brings Salimah a glass of iced water. 'What is wrong? Is it something I said?'

Salimah shakes her head through her tears. 'No, I'm happy for you, really. It's Nazra. My daughter. I think …' She looks up and sniffs. 'I think she might be pregnant too.'

Shocked, Anna holds a hand over her stomach, still flat but alive nonetheless. 'But how old is she? How is that possible?'

'She is sixteen. She is … I don't know. I didn't even know she had a boyfriend. But it explains everything. Her moods. Her stomach that got so big.'

'What will you do? Should she have an abortion?'

Salimah shoots her such a fiery look, Anna wishes she had put a sock in it. 'I'm so sorry, I should not have said that. What I mean is, what …'

Anna stops talking. She doesn't know what she means.

Salimah continues more gently, 'No, Allah will provide for us. We need to, well, I suppose she should get married. If I am right, based on her stomach size, she is probably quite far along. I can't believe I didn't see this earlier.'

She slinks down into the chair and covers her face with her hands. 'My baby girl! Has she even been to a doctor? She never tells me anything. And now she's run off.'

'What do you mean she's run off? She ran away?'

Salimah tells Anna about her uncle, traditional, conservative and religious, and how Nazra fights with him. 'When he announced he would move in, Nazra ran away. She messaged me to say she was staying with a friend, but since then I haven't heard from her. I called the school; she does still go there, alhamdulillah.'

Anna's own pregnancy hormones soar and she feels a knot of worry building up inside her. She already feels turned inside out by her own unexpected pregnancy, and she is an adult, with a husband. How desperate must the girl feel? She stands up. 'We need to go find her. What time does school end?'

Salimah looks at the clock on the wall. 'In a few hours. We can finish the soup first.'

Anna takes a deep breath. 'I'll drive you. We can bring her here, so you can talk to her, away from your uncle.'

'Thank you, but I'll take a bus.' Salimah walks to the kitchen and starts washing bean sprouts in silence. Anna wants to follow her, tell her the car would be much quicker, but something in Salimah's rigid face stops her.

When Salimah has left, Anna looks at the now full bookcase with satisfaction. It is a gorgeous Thai-style bookcase in royal turquoise with a distressed look. It matches the colonial feel of the house. The place is slowly filling up. She is still contemplating a Chinese wedding cabinet for the nursery and a dining table made from an old Indian door. But the table is extremely expensive. For now they use their oak one from the UK, which is too small for the dining room. She still hasn't seen a sofa she likes either. Maybe she can ask advice about that on Facebook.

Vicky from yoga recommended the Expat Wife group to her – and it's as addictive as it is a lifesaver. She can ask everything there: where to buy tasty yet not too overpriced cheese, a hairdresser that can do European hair, an electrician to install an extra fan in the living room. In a few weeks time she'll ask for a maternity shop. It is also a place to meet people. Chatting about cheese, she met Bea, a Dutch woman whom she hit it off with as they continued their conversation in private messages.

Tired from unpacking and cooking, Anna lies down on the bed, and puts her hand on her stomach. Something moves, but she isn't sure whether it's the baby or just gas. Last night she went out for dinner, overpriced Italian, but the burrata was more than worth the extravagant cost, and any bloating it may have caused. Possibly it was even worth the strenuous conversation she had to engage in over dinner.

Anna knows food is the best way to settle her stomach and she can't wait to eat the Indonesian soto ayam they just made. Tom will be so impressed. Before Salimah left to find Nazra, they set out all the toppings in the fridge, in little bowls. Blanched beansprouts, fried dry shallots, boiled eggs, lime wedges, bee hoon noodles, chopped celery leaf and spring onion. Dark, sweet oozy kecap manis soy sauce. And the sambal Anna made, fiery as hell. Together they picked the remaining meat off the carcass, and Salimah fried the chicken meat in hot oil until it was golden and crisp. This too sits in a bowl, ready to be added to the fragrant soup. Salimah explained Anna how to add the spice paste to the stock, then boil it a few more minutes, and just before serving add quartered tomatoes and chopped local celery leaf.

Anna turns on her side and briefly closes her eyes. With the furnishing coming along, and she out and about meeting people, her life here should be flourishing. So why does everything still feel so remote? At dinner the previous evening, in a group of Dutch women, Anna had felt as much out of place as she had in that shopping centre full of maid agencies.

Anna hadn't expected to make a Dutch friend here, on the other side of the world, but she really likes Bea. Still, when she invited Anna for a girls' night out with other Dutch women, Anna had hesitated. She finds the Netherlands small and the people narrow-minded. But Tom had encouraged her to go, so she went.

The evening started innocuously enough. Everyone else knew each other already. Singapore boasts one of the only Dutch schools outside of the Netherlands, and all their kids attended it. When they heard of Anna's pregnancy they insisted she had to send the child there. Anna smiled wryly and joked her British husband might have something to say about that. The conversation moved on to the subject all expats here talk about: travel. Child friendly beach resorts in Malaysia. Not-too-touristy spots close to Phuket. Wine trips in Margaret River. And, of course, Bali.

'I still love Bali, even though it is exploding now,' Bea said.

Another woman pitched in straight away. 'Canggu used to be so laid-back, now it is full of bearded hipsters and their vegan lattes. It is getting too built up. And the traffic in Bali!'

Anna asked: 'What place off the beaten track would you recommend?'

They all chimed in at once. 'Lombok and Flores still have some nice places.'

'Or Raja Ampat, that is amazing, and Papua is unspoilt. I really can't do Bali anymore.'

One woman, a sturdy redhead said, 'Well, I still prefer Bali.

I'm going next weekend actually.'

There was a brief silence.

'From what I've read and seen in photos,' Anna said hesitantly, 'I must say it does look amazing. Don't you think some places are worth the hype?'

She had expected the woman to agree and smile back, but she just rolled her eyes.

Anna tried again. 'I mean the mysticism of the place, the temples, the art.'

One of the other women – Anna has already forgotten her name – nodded, 'Yes, that is true. Bali is such a special place.'

Anna felt encouraged and unfortunately kept going. 'Yes, it sure is. It looks so peaceful in photos. It is hard to imagine the terrible history.'

The women seemed bewildered. 'What do you mean? The bombing?'

'Or that volcano erupting a while back? They had to close the airport.'

'Oh, to be stuck in paradise ...'

Anna blushed, and does again when she thinks back to last night, wishing she could have shut her big mouth. 'No, I meant our shocking history there. Sorry. An occupational hazard, I suppose, I have a degree in history and took a class focusing on Bali, which wasn't fully colonised until, like, 1906 or so. It became a bloodbath, when ...'

As Anna had looked around the table she realised it was most definitely the wrong thing to say. This wasn't a classroom full of historians.

'Never mind,' she muttered.

The redheaded woman had smirked at Anna. 'Do you want

to ruin my holiday? I go there to have fun. Not to feel guilty.'

Anna stared back in silence. She still doesn't know if the woman was joking, but the frown on her face and the furtive sniggers of the rest made her throat squeeze shut.

Thankfully Bea had stepped in. 'You know what is interesting, I always felt welcome travelling in Indonesia. When you say where you are from, they always enthusiastically say "Ah, Belanda". The men will start talking about Dutch football, and name all the players in our national team. But I suppose it is good we are mindful of the past.'

Anna nodded, glad for the support. 'Exactly. I mean, we did screw things up there and the country is still a mess.'

The woman whose name Anna forgot, pitched in. 'But we Dutch can hardly be blamed for that still, they have been independent for so long. My husband does a lot of business in Indonesia and the incompetency, the corruption; it drives him crazy.'

Anna felt she needed to say something – after all, she started this. 'Yes, of course that is true. But the fact that we didn't allow them their own development, that we exploited them for centuries and left the country destitute, that didn't help, did it? It's not that long ago really; our grandparents were part of this. The effects linger longer than a generation. And then the civil war after we refused them independence.'

'Civil war?'

'Those police actions, my grandfather fought in them and yes, that bothers me.'

The woman slapped down her napkin. 'Well, that's your grandfather, not mine.'

Bea tactfully changed the subject. The rest of the evening

had been pleasant enough, but Anna could not shake off the awkwardness.

Anna puts her hands back on her stomach and kneads it until it deflates. Definitely gas, she thinks, disappointed. She exhales deeply. If a group of Dutch expats can't even talk about the past, how can they ever move on? She hasn't heard back from her father either.

Anna only knows the bare facts about her grandmother's life during and after the war. As the single surviving family member, and a young girl, Oma was to be put on a boat to distant relatives in the Netherlands. Oma had never been there before. Her family were 'totok', they had little or no Indonesian blood, even though they had been in the country for generations. Opa was her white knight to the rescue – Oma called him a 'baar' – out in Indië for the first time. He volunteered in the army but after independence became a planter near Medan. Why that change of heart, did he do it for Oma, because he had fallen in love? Opa died when Anna was still young, she remembers a stern man, her own father doesn't like to talk about him. Anna stretches her arms above her and gives her belly a final rub, then sinks deeper into her pillow. This baby, like it's grandfather, will be born in Asia. She hopes Tom is right, that living here, in this house, will help her understand her Asian past. Because how can she start a new family without understanding her old one?

10

Girls and boys in white blouses swirl around the school building – classes have finished for the day. Salimah is glad she came alone. Anna means well but the way she speaks is so direct she might scare Nazra off. She peers at the groups of teenagers intently. Isn't that girl one of Nazra's classmates? Salimah rushes over. 'Have you seen Nazra? Was she at school today?'

The girl barely looks up from her phone. 'Sure. I think she went to the toilet, is still inside.'

'Thanks.' Salimah adjusts her tudung and posts herself in front of the exit.

'Nazra!'

She hadn't expected her daughter to be happy to see her here, but the vexed look Nazra gives her makes her shake.

'Why are you here?'

'Sayang, I am worried about you. That you might run away and not come back.'

Nazra shrugs. 'Dunno. I might. But have no money leh.'

Salimah hugs her tight. 'Can we please talk? Let's go to the kopitiam.'

When Nazra doesn't answer, Salimah drags her by the hand and silently they walk over to the coffee shop down the road. Salimah tries a hesitant smile. 'What would you like? Milo dinosaur?' The iced malted chocolate drink with heaped powder on top is a childhood favourite. Their guilty treat whenever someone needs cheering up.

Nazra grunts. 'You are always complaining about my weight and now you give me Milo dinosaur? How can?'

Salimah sighs before she speaks. 'Because I want my little girl back.'

Maybe feeling the overly sweet taste on her tongue will make the clock turn back to before everything went wrong. Before her Nazra became moody and distant. Before Salimah lost her job and their world was turned upside down. Salimah returns with the drink and Nazra sticks a spoon in the sticky powder on top. She licks it off with her pink girlish tongue. Salimah likes to stir hers into the drink and for a while they both play with their drinks in silence.

'Nazra, you need to talk to me.'

Nazra stares into her drink. 'What do you want me to say?'

'I don't know,' says Salimah. 'You can tell me anything.'

Now Nazra looks up and stares Salimah in the eyes. 'Tell you anything? What for? So you can run to tell Pak Long and all of you can tell me I am bodoh?'

The words sting Salimah in the throat like a bee.

'You aren't stupid. I'm there for you always. I just want to help.'

Nazra says, slowly, 'I don't want your help.'

'Maybe. But I don't care what you want. It's about what you need.'

Nazra stands up and her voice gets louder and higher pitched. 'What I need? Since when have you ever looked at my needs? I'm only there to be the good daughter, so you can brag to your friends about my grades, my looks. Sial, not anymore because I'm fat now. Will get lebih fat. Bodoh kan?'

When did Nazra start to speak Singlish slang like that? She did not learn it at this elite school, that's for sure.

Nazra, as if spooked by her own voice, sits back down. Salimah puts her hands over her daughter's and swallows deep. 'Why did you not tell me? How many months?'

When Nazra doesn't answer, she asks: 'When was your last period?'

Nazra takes some time then answers quietly. 'Maybe five, six months. I dunno.'

'Have you even seen a doctor? This is not going to go away just by ignoring it, sayang.'

Supressing all the emotions that are surfacing, Salimah shifts into practical mode. 'We need to get you a doctor's appointment. We need to get you vitamins, you know, folic acid. Have you thought about anything? Where is it going to sleep? We need a crib. How will you breastfeed when at school. How will you …'

The panic creeps back into her voice. Will they kick her out of school? It makes her voice squeaky when she manages: 'Come home, sayang. We will do this together.'

When she says the word 'home', Nazra cringes and Salimah feels it too. At home is Pak Long. And with Pak Long the rest of the world. Salimah's heart sinks with the thought of the shame that is coming for them. How can she even think they could manage this together, as if the rest of the world didn't matter? A million thoughts bounce into her head. But there is no time for any of them. Not yet. She needs to get the girl home first. 'I'll talk to Pak Long. Just come home.'

Resigned and compliant, Nazra follows her mother to the bus stop. At home she dashes straight to her room. Salimah doesn't allow herself time to reflect. She calls the medical clinic and makes an appointment for the next morning. She needs to know what she is dealing with, how much time she has. Then Anna springs to mind. How different will the lives of these two babies be? Before she can ponder further, Salimah hears the door and Pak Long and Father come in with two suitcases and some boxes. They lower themselves on the sofa. 'Salimah, make us some tea, Nak.'

Pak Long has moved in all of three minutes and he is already on her nerves. But the tea might calm him, and calm is what she needs. When they are all stirring sugar into their cups she wonders whether it is not better to wait until tomorrow. After they have visited the doctor they will know more. But Salimah can't carry this alone, she needs someone to talk to, not to be the only adult there. Looking only at her father she says gently. 'Bapa? I need to tell you something.'

Father looks up with a questioning gaze. 'Me?'

He is still Nazra's grandfather and Salimah makes a silent wish. Let him stand up. Let him be the strong one today. There is no point in sugar-coating this so she blurts it out.

'It's Nazra. I think she might be pregnant.'

Her words don't seem to have a lot of effect at first. Father's eyes turn dreamy and seem to face inside, rather than at her. Then, he nods. 'That is lovely. I hope for a granddaughter. One as beautiful as her mother.'

Not the reaction Salimah had expected. She furtively glances at Pak Long, who stirs his tea with pursed lips.

'Yes,' Father continues, 'a baby in the house will brighten things up for sure. Her husband must be so excited. But don't let her climb up. It's dangerous.'

Climbing, danger? What is he talking about?

Now Pak Long puts down his spoon. 'Adoi, Adik, you gila is it? The girl has no husband.'

Father looks hurt and Salimah keeps staring at him while Pak Long says exactly what she had expected him to say. That she is a bad mother, that she hasn't kept an eye on the girl properly, that this girl is bringing shame on the family. That she is ruining not only her future but that of her mother and the whole family. Nothing Salimah doesn't know already.

'Pak, pak, I know, I know.'

Pak Long looks at her. 'You know but you need to do more than that. You need to act. We need to fix this.'

'Fix this? It is already too late. I think she is six months along already. Cannot get rid of this now. Anyway ...'

Before she can finish her sentence, Pak Long cuts in. 'What sin are you proposing? You cannot take a life for your own comfort. Allah will guide us and support the ones that honour him.' He takes a sip of tea and continues: 'There is only one solution. She needs to marry the boy.'

'What boy?' Salimah asks before she realises exactly which boy he is talking about.

'Apa ini? You slow today. Bring the girl here. I'll talk to her straight.'

Part of Salimah is relieved Pak Long is taking control. But part of her screams no. She clears her throat and says, softer than she wants to. 'Pak Long, I think it is better I deal with this. We have a doctor's appointment tomorrow. Let's take it slow, I don't want to scare her away again.'

Pak Long heaves himself out of the sofa with a sigh. 'There is no time for slow.'

Salimah is trying to find more words but none come. Her

father smiles at her. 'Sayang, listen to Pak Long. He knows how to handle a problem. It's what he does. He is a good man.'

And Salimah says nothing as Pak Long pulls an angry Nazra out of her room and sits her on the sofa next to her grandfather, who puts his old, wrinkled hands over her young ones.

'Who is the father?' Pak Long spits at the girl.

Nazra sinks deeper into the sofa and looks at her mother accusingly. Salimah only half listens to Pak Long's tirade. This is not how she had planned her daughter's life. She has had visions of Nazra's future husband. He would be handsome. Well educated, at least the same or more than Nazra. Work in a professional job. Religious. Just like her husband, the love of her life, had been. She met him at university and her parents were happy with her choice. She had been happy. Until he died. She curses the disease that killed him so swiftly. He would have known what to do.

Pak Long's questions are the same ones that are echoing in her mind. Who is this boy? Who are his parents? Are they Muslim, and honourable people, will they force him to do the right thing? Salimah adds more in her mind. If not, will any boy ever go near Nazra again? Will she be forced to be alone all her life, a single mother? Salimah knows how hard it was – and she is an honourable widow.

Pak Long talks about the scorn of Allah, shame and obedience, but all Salimah can think about is a future spiralling down a sinkhole.

'If you don't tell me, you can leave this house,' Pak Long yells at a still silent Nazra.

It is too much. Salimah gets up, takes Nazra by the arm and leads her out of the room and into her bedroom. 'This is still my house,' she mutters over her shoulder, but too soft.

As Nazra sits on the bed crying, Salimah wishes her husband were still alive. Together they could face this properly, lovingly. Salimah loves her daughter more than anything but does not know what to do with the love. She hugs Nazra tight and tells the girl not to worry. Salimah will worry for her. They will make it happen. 'Please tell me the name of the boy. I will talk to his parents.'

Hugging her daughter, Salimah feels they are one again, like when she rocked her as a baby. When has she started losing her? Last year, when she was studying for her O-Levels, Nazra would sit at the kitchen table with her for tea and homework after school, now she goes straight into her room with the door slammed shut. She was a happy girl then, who often brought home girlfriends. Aziza's daughter Ayu, and that Chinese girl, what was her name? Such a shame they all went to different schools. Ayu is in a polytechnic now.

Salimah wishes her husband had lived just a little longer at least; they could have had another child, a son. She imagines a good son, a young version of her late husband, one that always treats her with respect. He could help and support his sister. Boys can look after themselves, a mother doesn't need to know his hidden thoughts and desires; Allah forbid, they would likely scare her. She sighs.

There is a lot she needs to say to Nazra, so much she needs to ask her but she can't find any words. Instead she repeats, 'Tell me who it is, sayang, then I can help you. If he is a good man he will let you finish your education, have a good job. He will benefit from that as much as you, as well as your kids.'

You can be a good role model, Salimah thinks. Which she herself failed to be. She suddenly remembers the doctors appointment in the morning. 'I'll tell school you are not well. We can talk more in the morning.'

Nazra still says nothing and Salimah does not want to leave her just yet. She wants to hold her tight again but something is keeping her back. Why can't she come up with anything good to say?

'I know Pak Long is difficult. But he means well. He has always helped this family. Trust me, sayang. Be nice to him. Make him tea when you get back from school, he appreciates things like that. Maybe cook for him. He likes you, sayang, he always has and always will. He sees you as his own granddaughter, that is why he acts like this. It is out of love, not hate.'

When Salimah is by the door Nazra finally speaks up. 'He has a strange way of showing love.'

11

Dear daughter, dear Anna,

Darling, I'm sorry it took me a while to get my thoughts together. The truth is that Oma dying and you moving to Singapore opened up something in me as well. I regret never talking to her, nor to you, about Indië – or should I say Indonesia? I couldn't forgive my father, your Opa, for his dirty war. But I also couldn't forgive him for sending me to school in the Netherlands when I was eight. I never had the chance to say goodbye to Indonesia, because Soekarno nationalised all Dutch assets in 1957. They didn't let me visit, for my own safety they said, and eventually my parents were forced to come home. Or forced to leave home …

Oma was Asian. Three generations of living there, you become part of the country, regardless of the colour of your skin. Indisch people, particularly those of mixed race, were treated badly after arriving in the Netherlands, as second-rate citizens. I always thought that did not apply to us, because we were white. But it did. People didn't understand her loss and judged her for being a colonial. As if those who weren't there themselves didn't share responsibility.

My mixed feelings make talking to you difficult. We

went there and exploited millions of people for centuries, how could I complain they kicked us out? How could I tell you how much I miss it?

We need to brush the dirt out from under the carpet and come to terms with everything, the good as well as the bad. That might help us to move on. I rarely go to those reunions, with all the ooms and tantes, people who still get heart attacks when they spot a Japanese but when they go on tempo doeloe holidays to Indonesia rave about the friendly locals. Did you know the Dutch made Indonesia pay for their own independence? They were made to pay back billions in debt, we even tried to get them to foot the bill for that bloody independence war. A lot of the rebuilding of the Netherlands in the 1950s was done with Indonesian money, money that my father made in Sumatra.

Let's talk in person. Mama and I would love to come visit you, maybe when the baby is born? In the meanwhile, enjoy yourself and all that amazing food you keep telling us about. We are jealous and miss you, my overseas child.

The words sit heavy inside Anna and her resolve grows. She needs to visit Sumatra. Tom could use a holiday to distract him from work, a last trip for the two of them before a child. She only has a few months left before she can't fly anymore. Staring at the paintings of the volcanoes, Anna wonders: were they painted by Oma herself? When she was little, Oma said they had been her friends in a very difficult time of her life. 'When everything else in your life is turned upside down, there are a few things you can rely on: the sun will come up every morning and the mountains will always stay the same.'

Reading her father's email again, Anna realises he forgot to answer one important question: the location of the plantation. She sighs. Will this trip down memory lane ever happen? Can she get Tom to take time off work? When she mentioned her plan to Vicky, she had looked horrified. 'You want to go to Sumatra while pregnant?'

Bea on the other hand, was full of encouragement. She raved about Lake Toba, and said it was smart to go now, before Anna had a toddler attached to her legs. Anna felt at home in the Dutch pragmatism but she still needs to convince Tom. She sets up her laptop on the dining table – still the old too small one – and starts googling. She hadn't realised how huge the island was – bigger than Germany. Jungles, bright blue lakes, volcanoes, traditional Batak houses. Agents advertising tours that take it all in. Would a rainforest hike with orangutans be too much?

She jolts out of her daydream when Salimah comes up behind her and nods at the photo on the screen. 'Beautiful.'

'It's Lake Toba. Remember the photos I showed you from my grandmother? I've wanted to visit Sumatra all my life. We live so close now.'

'Ah yes, of course.'

'I want to go soon, it is the dry season now. If we wait until the coming rainy season is over I'll be too pregnant.'

'Why Indonesia? Why not go to a comfortable resort somewhere and put your feet up? You are pregnant. Phuket, Bali, Bintan.'

'Not you too,' Anna groans. 'Bali and Bintan are Indonesia as well. Anyway, what's wrong with Indonesia? You grew up in a kampong yourself.'

The last comment seems to hit a bit of a nerve, and Anna swallows a strained grin. But thankfully, Salimah laughs again.

'Yah, maybe my ancestors left for a reason. Things are good in Singapore. Clean. Safe. I am comfortable here.'

Anna realises that she has never been inside an HDB flat, the government-built housing most Singaporeans live in. She would love to see Salimah's flat, but is hesitant to invite herself, so she asks about the kampong. 'Did it used to look very different around here? Do you know where your old village was exactly?'

Salimah walks up to the window and looks out. Anna follows and tries to see the view through Salimah's eyes. This house is strange, as if it has moods. Sometimes it feels friendly enough, sometimes it squashes her with its weight. There is something it isn't giving away. Something dark. Perhaps it is related to the war, the prisoners that stayed here?

Salimah seems lost in thought, and judging from her face, they aren't dark ones. Growing up here must have been an amazing experience. And, with a slight smile, Anna thinks *it will be a great experience living here, for her child.*

'You can't see it from here,' Salimah says, 'it was on the other side of the hill, behind us. Close to the PIE. They put that motorway on top of most of the village.'

Salimah points at the condominiums poking through the green foliage in front of them. 'None of those were there. A few houses, a lot of trees. There used to be a path from here to the kampong, circling the hill, but I'm not sure where. Only these houses are the same. Everything else is different.'

'So did you have to move because of the PIE? When was that built?'

'I think the late seventies? They tore down houses, sliced the kampong in two. I remember when they just finished building it. All that concrete! I was very small, kids took bicycles to go racing on it – before it opened, I mean.'

'So your house was between here and the PIE? Around Arcadia Road?'

Salimah lights up. 'Where all the big raintrees are? That track led to the kampong from the other side.'

'Why don't we go for a walk?' Anna says. 'Explore? See if we can find something you recognise?'

'But it is all overgrown,' Salimah sputters. 'Bushes and trees. And I'm wearing my leather sandals.'

Anna looks down at Salimah's bare feet, and feels Salimah's eyes on her own sandals. Her Dutch mother taught her taking off her shoes in public was indecent, and she still feels naked without them. She hates the greasy marks some visitors' sweaty feet make on the dark floor boards – even if Salimah meticulously mops them off – but can't bring herself to ask guests to keep their shoes on. Her house, but their country.

'I can lend you some of my trainers. Come on, please?'

They walk to the beginning of the road where the wall of green is less dense and slip through the bushes, down the hill. Behind the line of trees is a more open area that backs onto fences blocking the condos from view. At the lowest point sits a shallow stormdrain – they have to jump to get to the other side. 'Look, little fish,' Salimah points out.

Anna peers down until she too can see the tiny silver fish. 'Amazing how something can live in a slice of concrete like this.'

At first Salimah seemed hesitant to step off the road, but now she gets a little glimmer in her eye. Their shoes sink into the high swampy grass. 'There used to be a lot of streams in Singapore like this,' Salimah says. 'We caught those little fish to keep them in glass jars at home.'

'We should have brought something to catch them with!' Anna exclaims. She pictures herself in a few years, with a net and a small child.

Salimah steps forward, 'Who needs that? I'm a kampong girl!'

She squats down next to the drain, one leg at each side and bends over, hands on the water.

'Gotcha!' She holds up her cupped hands – a tiny sliver of silver inside. 'I haven't lost my touch.'

Salimah throws the fish back, but doing so, she slips. Her left foot lands in the drain and she sways backwards. Just in time Anna manages to grab her hand and pull her up. They look each other in the eye and laugh.

'Okay, I guess I'm no longer that agile kampong girl.' Salimah looks down and her face turns red. 'I'm so sorry. Your shoe!'

Anna looks at the hem of Salimah's long dress that is covered in mud – what was she thinking bringing Salimah, who is always so clean and tidy – out here. 'No, I'm sorry. This was my idea. Never mind the shoes.'

Salimah's youthful glow is gone. Anna feels a pang of guilt, and hopes the stains will come off. Salimah walks on, and as they follow a line of tiny white flowers in the grass, her step bounces again. 'Actually, I think this same drain was there already in my kampong days. Shall we see where it goes?'

It is very beautiful here, and surprisingly quiet – bar the piercing sound of cicadas.

'Don't you feel like we're on an adventure?' Anna says to

Salimah, who seems absent.

Salimah nods. 'It's like a secret world that everybody forgot about, that nobody goes to anymore.'

'But still,' Anna says, pointing at the grass below them, which comes just above their ankles, 'someone needs to mow this grass or this will all be jungle.'

The grass is neither wild nor cut, it is something in between. Unreal. Civilisation and modern condos are a stone's throw away but in between lies this green magical world that looks as if fairies could appear anytime. Anna shudders a little.

They pass by a multi-stemmed tree and Anna is tempted to climb it. But then she remembers how Salimah almost fell in the drain, and that she is pregnant. Instead, she points it out to Salimah. 'We have a banyan like that in the garden, imagine the little one climbing it!' She visualises the tree, a small child. 'We could build a treehouse between those arches.' She rubs her belly which, if she sticks it out, has the start of a bulge. Anna feels happy. This baby will bring good things. It must. When it is born her parents will come visit, and she will finally have succeeded in luring her father back to Asia.

Salimah stares at the tree with a stricken look. 'My father's ma'am asked him to make a treehouse in your banyan. Her little girl was the same age as me. You remind me of her. I loved that treehouse, but I wasn't allowed in.'

Anna feels a twitch in her throat. Suddenly she is all too aware Salimah works for her. She talks over the thought. 'So when was that?'

Salimah counts on her fingers. 'We left the kampong in 1980, when I was in the last year of primary school. Part of the kampong was still there then. We only left after ...' Salimah breaks off suddenly.

'After what?'

'I'm not really sure. After father lost his job.'

'Why did he lose his job?'

'I don't know,' Salimah says. 'Maybe he just quit? I can't remember.'

Salimah looks much older outdoors, where she wears her headscarf. Salimah doesn't say more and Anna worries whether she's pushed her too far. But then Salimah says: 'Do you think there are ghosts in your house?'

Anna feels the hairs on her arms prick up again like they do every time she passes the hallway near the spare room. She rubs her arms and pushes a lump back down her throat. It's all in her mind. 'I don't think I believe in ghosts. Do you?'

'Do you ever hear things?' Salimah says. 'Dogs? A screaming woman?'

Anna shakes her head violently, rubbing away the goosebumps. 'Nonsense. It is all imagination. I read a lot about the history of the house, only men were imprisoned there, and only men fought in the battle against the Japanese. How can there be a female screaming?'

'Anything can,' says Salimah.

Anna shudders and puts a hand over her stomach. She needs to get away from this conversation. 'Come on, let's find that path.'

Following the concrete drain, they manage to proceed a few hundred meters more through increasingly heavy undergrowth until the drain disappears under a wired fence. Beyond is the garden of a house similar to hers; climbing over would be trespassing and Anna doesn't know who lives here. The neighbouring condo has a high concrete wall.

'There were never fences here before,' says Salimah. 'All the gardens were open. I remember that house, this is the right way. But we can't pass.'

'We can try from the other side?' Anna says.

'Let's go back, I have work to do.'

Anna does not want to force Salimah, and they walk back to the grassy area in silence. When she steps onto the concrete, Salimah grips Anna's arm tight. 'Stop.'

Right below Anna's foot is a snake as thick as her thigh. Its black and bronze body stretches ahead – the full length of the road. She shrinks back.

'A python,' Anna gasps. 'And I …'

'You almost stepped on it! I told you this is dangerous.'

Salimah points at Anna's belly, around which she has unconsciously wrapped her hands. 'The snake means very bad luck,' she mutters.

Anna pushes out another 'nonsense' as she stares at the snake slithering away. Her hands shake all the way home.

12

They take off their muddy shoes on the bench in front of the door. Salimah's wet feet make her feel chilly – or is it something else?

The world around Salimah disappeared as they followed the drain, as if she was walking straight into the past. The trees, the creepers, the squidgy feeling of badly mowed grass under her feet, all remind her how she ran around this area barefoot as a child. She can't imagine it now, being outdoors with bare feet.

These last few weeks, Salimah can't stop thinking about the old days. Is it the house? Or Anna, who is always asking questions? She was apprehensive about this walk, but how to say no to Anna, who is after all her employer. And part of her was curious too. When they walked down the hill, she started to feel excited, ready to relive the old kampong days. All her years as a modern Singaporean seemed to evaporate. People kept popping up in her mind: the girls she played five stones with; the boy Aqsad, who made chapteh from feathers pilfered from chickens running around the kampong, kicking the plumed shuttlecock high like a football; the aunty next door, Ah Soon, who taught her to make sweet kueh and watched her when her mother had to work; the uncle who fixed bicycles and showed the kampong children how to solder metal; and her best friend Leila. Leila must have left the kampong shortly after them and they lost touch. There were few phones and no Facebook back then.

But when she heard herself telling Anna about the treehouse, a black-laced veil draped itself over the friendly faces from the past. White blurry shapes materialised behind delicate leaves and dark branches. Then, she heard a high-pitched cry.

On the bench, away from the trees, Salimah sees her father staring at her with teary eyes in a young face, hears the muttering voice of her long dead mother. Salimah has opened a door to a world that she had put behind her. Why did she have to come here and do that? She should be focusing on work, on her daughter who needs her.

When Anna speaks, Salimah snaps back out of her thoughts. 'Sorry, I forgot to ask,' Anna says. 'How is Nazra?'

Salimah sighs. The present is more than difficult enough. A scan has revealed Nazra is six months along. Six! What kind of a mother is she? It's a good thing Salimah hasn't found a full-time job yet, so she can spend time with Nazra. 'The doctor says the baby is doing well and Nazra seems fine too. I mean, physically. But she is rarely home. And when she is, she is either fighting with Pak Long or shut in her room.'

And Father is just sitting there, not helping by being blur. There is real screaming as well as the screaming inside Salimah's head these days. 'I don't know what to do. She threatened to run away again. What do I do? Do I kick out Pak Long? I can't do that to my own uncle, we are his only family.'

Anna pulls off her shoe and kicks it under the bench. 'Why don't you ask Nazra to come and stay here? We have lots of empty rooms.'

Salimah stares at her feet, not sure what to say. Her failure wraps around her like the coils of a snake. 'But what will Tom say? Shouldn't you discuss that with him first?'

'Nah, don't worry, I'll talk to him. He is rarely home so why would he care?'

When Salimah doesn't answer, Anna continues. 'I mean it. The other day Tom made me go to IKEA to get furniture for the maid's room, to get it ready. He wants me to hire someone full time when the baby ...'

Anna breaks off and Salimah knows why. Anna will fire her and hire a Filipina. She can't lose this job now. The money she makes here helps make ends meet and Salimah isn't ready to move on. She needs to figure things out first. 'What do you mean?' she says, a little harsher than planned.

'Don't worry, there are still many months before I am due. You'll have found a better job by then, surely?'

Salimah can't think that far ahead. First things first. Having Nazra here would give her room to breathe, to think and also, Anna would be less likely to fire her. But is she such a terrible mother she can't even raise her own daughter in her own home?

Anna looks as if nothing would make her happier than Salimah accepting the proposal. And the longer she looks at Anna, sitting there patiently, the more Salimah realises that Anna has been the only truly supportive one these last few weeks. Anna lifts one of her feet and starts rubbing it. She smiles at Salimah. Salimah smiles back.

What she needs is someone to advise her, someone she can trust. She told her best friend Aziza about Nazra's pregnancy, but can't stop imagining her whispering behind her back. Aziza messaged Salimah a photo of Nazra talking to a boy, saying she needs to confront his parents. But Salimah doesn't even know who this boy is, whether he is the one, and when she showed the image to Nazra, the girl threw Salimah's phone through the room, cracking the screen. Now every time Salimah swipes the screen, the hairline crack irritates her finger – reminding her how she is failing.

What choice does she have? Anna's suggestion allows them a chance to figure things out, away from the toxic atmosphere at home. Without Pak Long looking over her shoulder, maybe she can be a better mother.

'I'll think about it,' she says. She drops her head and looks at her feet. The white socks she borrowed from Anna are stained grey, there are grains of sand between her toes. 'I'll go to the side of the house to wash at the hose,' she says to Anna, whilst crumbling the dirty socks into an embarrassed ball.

Anna follows Salimah's gaze to her own feet. 'Don't worry, I've wiped them off. I won't mess up your clean floor.'

Salimah's mother used to say that unwashed feet not only bring germs into the house, they also invite unwanted spirits. Remembering the snake, she recoils. But she says nothing. Anna will think her superstitious.

Cleaning is the best way to for Salimah to keep her hands occupied whilst organising her mind. But as she mops the floor for the second time that day, her brain remains a muddle. Is Aziza right, should she find the boy and push marriage? She continues to mop, moving backwards down the hallway to the spare rooms, when she suddenly stops in the corridor. She feels naked without her tudung – as if she's being observed. She walks to the back door, and as she empties her bucket in the drain, eyes the banyan tree from a safe distance. There is no wind, no movement in the leaves, yet she feels a pull from the tree calling her. The feeling of yearning it causes slowly turns to fear. Is she crazy, considering letting her daughter stay here? Or is another fight with Pak Long and her running away the real danger? Salimah shrugs off the doubt and turns back inside. That stupid girl said she wanted to see a ghost. Let her come and try.

The more she thinks about it, the more it starts to make sense. Here, at the house, Salimah can cook for her, and make the girl tidy her own room. It won't be extra work for Anna. Yes, she decides, it will buy her time with her daughter.

13

When Salimah texts to say Nazra has agreed to come and stay, Anna has all but forgotten her offer. Caught out, she realises Salimah was right – she should have discussed this with Tom first. But he hasn't been home for dinner several days in a row, and by the time he does get home, Anna is already in bed. These days she doesn't last much longer than nine in the evening, especially watching Netflix on her own. Tom is not a morning person, which makes breakfast a bad time for anything deeper than discussing dinner plans – or lack thereof.

Frustrated, she decides to send him a text message. He replies within five minutes. *'Are you crazy? Should the gardeners move in too?'*

She carefully considers her reply, then decides on: *'Crazy? You know I am ;) It's a long story, but I feel they need us. Call me if you want to discuss.'*

She waits for the phone to ring with a mixture of eagerness and dread. After half an hour, she shoves the phone under the cushion of the sofa. If he's not here, and doesn't even have the decency to call her, he doesn't get a say. She walks over to the linen cabinet, pulls out some sheets and a towel and walks over to the outbuildings to check what else the room needs. Didn't they have a small stool somewhere? That would be good to sit on or for Nazra to put her things on. It should fit perfectly next to the bed.

She walks down to the storeroom to find the stool. As she enters the dark room, she has to blink a few times before she sees it in the back. But as she reaches to pick it up, she startles. One of her oma's boxes is perched on top, open, and from it a pair of dark eyes stare at her menacingly. She shoves the box off the stool and, with a thud, it lands on its side on the concrete floor. Anna sinks down on the stool, her heart beating like crazy. Who has been in here?

After a few deep breaths, Anna pulls the box upright, planning to push the mask deeper inside, when she notices a flash of bright blue behind it. Carefully, she pulls it out. It looks like a notebook. Was it her grandmother's? She doesn't remember packing it.

The notebook is filled with a spidery, old-fashioned handwriting too small to make out in the dense light of the storeroom. Forgetting the stool, Anna walks upstairs and sinks down on the sofa.

The first page shows a place and a date: Berastagi, 1943. The shrivelled handwriting and language make it hard to decipher, and as she leafs through the book she notices the words become squashed closer and closer together. Her eyes fall on a sentence set apart from the others, more clearly legible. *Those frightful Japs made us stand in the hot sun for hours today.*

Anna's heart misses a beat as she turns back to the first page, and deciphers the first line. *We heard them before we saw them, their boots slamming the wooden floor of the hall as they came closer and closer.*

A chill jitters up Anna's spine as she hears them too, the sound of boots ricocheting off the ceiling of the corridor behind her. *They took Father away and tomorrow Mama and I will need to report to the school, where we will be interned. We thought we would be safer here in the mountains but they are everywhere and now we need to decide what to pack. It's a long hike uphill, we can't take more than we can carry. How long will we be there for? Nobody knows anything.*

Beneath is a list. Clothes, underwear, medicines, tins of food. Pencils. A lot of question marks. Bring stockings? Her good dress? Oma obviously had little idea then what she was in for, and Anna is happy to see those last items crossed off and more food added.

Anna gets pulled into the story which follows Oma to a local school where all European woman and children are locked up by the Japanese. At first the children see it as a holiday; the mountain town they are staying in is a popular destination for people escaping the heat of the lowlands. They came here hoping to escape capture in town.

Desperation slowly sets in. There is no news of fathers, husbands and brothers. The diary contains gossip as well as complaints about people taking more than their fair share of the meagre food, though at times the women show real solidarity too. Anna swings her feet onto the sofa and lies down. As she looks up at the fan and the trellised windows above her, the school in Indonesia morphs into her own building in similar white plaster. The same war. Women there. Soldiers here. She closes her eyes and the pounding noise in her head grows louder. What happened to that school after the war? Were children ever taught there again, did they play, were they able to be happy? Was it restored, like this house, that is now an object of desire for wealthy expats to live in? She dozes off slowly, noises and shouts invading her fitful dreams where frightful Japs march round and round her corridors.

When Tom comes home he tosses his phone and wallet on the table and pecks Anna on the nose. 'Wakey, wakey.'

Anna sits up groggily and looks at the clock. It's not that late, Tom's home early for once. 'Sorry, I fell asleep.'

'No worries, sleeping beauty, you're pregnant, sleep all you like. Maybe we can we order pizza and watch a movie? I'm knackered too.'

Anna smiles a half grin. 'I thought I was the one supposed to suggest things like that.'

Tom laughs. 'I'm being helpful here. That way you don't need to cook.'

'I don't anyway, Salimah made curry, we only have to heat it up. Rice is in the cooker.'

Tom pulls a face. 'I am not in the mood for Asian food. Can we have pizza? Pretty please?'

He pushes out his lower lip, bends over and ends the pout in a kiss.

Anna, melting happily into a much-needed hug, relaxes. 'Sure, pizza it is. But I thought you liked Salimah's cooking?'

'I do, it's delicious. But I don't want to eat Asian food every day. You've turned completely Asian since we came here, I keep expecting to come home one day and finding you in one of those wrap-around batik skirts. Gone native.'

Anna suppresses a grin. 'A sarong? That sounds very comfortable, my clothes are getting tight.'

She points at her tiny bump and Tom pulls up her top and kisses her belly. 'How are you feeling? Less tired?'

'Yes, I'm actually getting things done. Can't you see?' She points around the house.

'Yes, it is starting to feel like a home. What's this?' He points at the diary wedged next to Anna.

'It's my grandmother's diary from when she was interned during the war, in Indonesia.'

'Oh wow.' He picks it up but it is in Dutch – he can't read it. 'I didn't know you had that. What does she say?'

'I only read a little before I fell asleep. She just moved into the camp, which was in a school building, with her mother. Things aren't too dire, but it sounds like a right chicken coop, a lot of women and children in a small space, not a lot of food. A lot of squabbling. The Japanese mostly leave them alone. Oma never wanted to talk about it; I didn't know she kept a diary. It feels as if I'm invading her privacy by reading it.'

'On the other hand, she kept this; she could have destroyed it. She must have known someone would find it. I bet she's glad it's you.'

'You might be right. No one in my family is interested in this sort of stuff anyway. But it's pretty shocking to read. And reading it here, in this house, makes me feel it all the more intensely.'

She looks around her, at the room that glows eerily in the twilight. It is quiet now, but the stomping feet echo in her mind. 'This very room we are sitting in was part of a prisoner of war camp for British soldiers. Doesn't that creep you out?'

Tom nods absentmindedly.

'I told you about the book Annabel gave me, remember?'

Tom nods. 'Yes, I remember, sorry.' Suppressing a yawn, he continues. 'Sorry, it's not that I am not interested, I am, but can we do this another time? I'm starving and have been in meetings all day long. The only thing that got me through was the thought of getting home to you, to snuggle up and relax.'

When they've ordered the pizza, Tom grabs the remote. 'What

do you want to watch?'

Anna bites her lip. She suddenly remembers why she went down to that storeroom in the first place. Hesitantly, she says. 'Ehm, about Nazra, you know, Salimah's daughter. She's coming to stay.'

Tom puts down the remote again. 'Was that serious? I was hoping you were joking.'

'Why would I joke about that?'

'I don't know, because it's crazy? Why would you invite the cleaner's pregnant teenage daughter to come stay with us? I mean, boundaries and such? Privacy.'

'You wanted to get a helper, we have all the furniture, and the girl needs to get away from her toxic uncle. The situation is unhealthy for her, and her baby.'

'Yes, but a helper isn't the same. She would work here. And she'd be an adult.'

'This girl's mother works here; Salimah promised she'll take care of her. We have all this space, almost like two houses, just for the two of us. It's embarrassing when you think about it. They are in a small flat: Salimah, the girl, the grandfather and the uncle. The whole place is probably smaller than our outbuildings.'

Tom sighs. 'But what are you bringing into the house? What kind of a girl is this? A sixteen-year-old who is pregnant, she could create all sorts of trouble. Are we to be responsible for her? Is she going to bring friends over? Her boyfriend? Have you even met her?'

When Anna doesn't know how to answer that, he continues. 'A random Malay girl, what do we know about someone like that?'

Anna sees red. 'What is that supposed to mean, that's such a racist remark.'

Tom turns pale, then red. 'Don't be ridiculous. I'd say the same thing if she was white. Or Chinese. Or blue with purple spots.'

Anna seethes inside. 'Salimah is a good woman so I'm sure her daughter is too. Anyway, what does it matter to you? Salimah will be here every day to look after her. You on the other hand are rarely home. We moved here together, and every morning you leave me here in this ... this insane house.' A house with footsteps that echo through the halls, through Anna's mind. A house that scares Anna. But intrigues her at the same time, and she feels like she's picking up speed when she hurls more at Tom. 'And when I try to make something of my life, by helping a local girl that needs me, you get angry?'

She has hit Tom in a sore spot. 'That is mean and also unfair. We discussed that this would not be a nine-to-five job. You agreed to the move yourself.'

She had. But at the time, Anna had imagined herself in a similar high-profile job, taking Asia by storm. Not at home, pregnant, without a single invitation for a job interview. She doesn't answer Tom because she doesn't know what to say.

'I am sorry,' Tom says and hugs her. 'I know it is hard for you, being pregnant, not having a job or friends. I admit, my work is harder than I thought, and I'm stressed and grumpy. If helping that girl makes you happy, do it. But promise me you'll be careful.'

Outside, a motorcycle pulls up. Tom gets up and kisses Anna on her hair. 'I love you. Even though you are a little crazy. Or, more likely, because you are.'

14

Nazra has been at the house three days now and seems like a different girl. She is cheerful, offers to help and is polite to Anna. Maybe Salimah finally did something right by bringing her here.

Salimah is cooking rendang in Anna's kitchen and, over her shoulder, peeks into the dining room, at the slight blonde woman opposite her bulky black-haired daughter. They sip iced tea whilst chatting about pregnancy matters, casually, as if they are old friends. Nazra has such beautiful eyes now she looks up at the world with them again. The scent of roasting spices wafts from the kitchen to the dining room. 'That smells delicious!' Anna yells to Salimah.

Anna's nausea is obviously over. As Salimah washes the meat she eavesdrops on the conversation in the adjacent room. Why can't she talk to the girl like this? They talk about swollen ankles. Back ache. She hears Anna say that she felt the baby move last week, but her stomach has been quiet since and it worries her. Nazra responds by saying she is jealous, hers keeps kicking her right in the bladder.

Then Nazra drops her voice. Salimah puts down the knife and strains her ears. 'They say these houses are haunted. Have you ever seen any ghosts?'

Anna laughs out loud. 'I don't believe in ghosts. Marivic, my neighbour's helper does; she says there's a British prisoner in their back yard, he screams when there's a full moon.'

'Really?'

'Well, Felicity, that's the neighbour, says it's all nonsense. It probably is.'

Anna continues in a very soft voice. Quietly, Salimah walks to the kitchen door and leans against the doorpost. 'But there is a spot in the corridor that gives me the creeps whenever I pass by. And I hear weird things at night too: dogs, and sometimes whining. Tom never hears it.'

Nazra nods excitedly. 'I am sure there are supernatural presences in this house. I'm going to try and stay up tonight to find them. What time do you hear those noises? Midnight?'

Salimah is chilled to the bone. *Is the girl gila?* She steps into the dining room. 'Are you mad? You need your sleep, you have school tomorrow and a baby inside you!'

Nazra rolls her eyes in frustration, the comfortable atmosphere is gone. Anna looks at Nazra with a maternal look. 'You should listen to your mother.'

Salimah goes back into the kitchen and angrily hacks at the beef. She tosses it on top of the spice mixture, adds coconut, then slams the lid on the pan. She is Nazra's mother. And they need to talk. She takes a plate of grapes from the fridge and joins the other two at the table. She holds the grapes in front of Nazra. 'You need vitamins.'

To Salimah's surprise, the girl not only takes a handful, but says thank you too. When was the last time she said something like that? She presents the fruit to Anna, who takes only one and pops it in her mouth absentmindedly. She chews, but then her face distorts. 'Is it too cold?' Salimah asks. 'I like them chilled.'

Anna shakes her head. 'No, it's not that. I've been ... Excuse me. I need the toilet.'

She rushes out and Salimah and Nazra sit in silence for a minute, eating grapes.

Facing her daughter alone, Salimah is lost for words, and the silence becomes increasingly embarrassing. Nazra chatted so freely with Anna.

She can't help but wonder: who is this teenager? She is so different from the little girl she once was. Salimah remembers how a few days back, as they packed her belongings into a small suitcase, Nazra had said in a small voice. 'Mak? You will come see me every day, right?' She had looked so young, so fragile, that all Salimah could do was cry and hug her. But now, when she looks at Nazra, her eyes are vacant again. Salimah needs to say something, to fix this, and clears her throat. 'So, do you like it here?'

Nazra shrugs. 'Sure. It's okay. Anna is nice. The room is nice. The bathroom is weird. The door is like, outside. There is a toad in there sometimes.'

'A toad!' In her kampong, nocturnal visitors in the outdoor bathroom were common, she's seen worse than toads too. 'Can't you leave a light on?' At least now there is electricity everywhere.

'I tried that, but it attracted a lot of bugs. This place is crazy wild.'

Nazra suddenly giggles. 'The other day I was getting undressed when I heard this sound, pheet-wew, like a wolf whistle. I freaked out, put my shirt back on and went outside. No one there. I looked around and I heard it again.'

'Nazra! How can you get changed without closing the curtains?'

'Who is going to see me here? The monkeys?'

Salimah recoils. 'What if Tom was there?'

'He was at work, anyway, he never comes out back. And it wasn't the day for the gardeners, or the pool boy.'

She looks at Salimah defiantly. 'Anyway, the whistling continued. Do you know who it was?'

Salimah frowns. 'No?'

Nazra bursts out laughing. 'A bird!'

Relief sweeps over Salimah. 'What bird?'

'I don't know, it was black, quite big, and sitting there in a tree whistling at me!'

Now Salimah laughs too. 'Did it look like a mynah but bigger, with orange patches around the eyes?'

Nazra nods. 'It's a burung tiong mas,' Salimah says. 'A hill mynah. They imitate everything they hear. My neighbour in the kampong had one, he taught it naughty words.' She grins at the memory. 'Who would have taught him that?'

They laugh together and Salimah hasn't felt so happy in a long time. She is elated to be talking with her daughter again, even if it is only about simple things. She needs to ask Nazra about the boy, about marriage, about the future. But first, things need to be right between the two of them again. She wants the conversation to go on forever, but before she can say more, Anna comes back into the room, white as a sheet, and the laughter dies.

'What is wrong?' Salimah asks.

Anna slumps down in a chair and folds double, cradling her stomach. 'Pain,' she mumbles. 'So much pain.'

15

As Anna lies in bed, she feels like she is on a merry-go-round from hell. One that spins too fast, making her cling on for dear life lest it flings her off like a catapult. The not-so-merry-go-round spins and spins, and Anna rushes to the toilet once again. She retches but her stomach is empty and she sinks down on the seat, pants down, again confronted with the same red. She adjusts the pad and rubs some heating cream on her empty belly against the cramps.

'Don't worry,' Tom had said when they left the hospital. 'The doctor says it happens a lot at this stage.' The look in his eyes said something different.

Anna hadn't answered. She had refused to look at it. *Her*. It had been a girl. Tom had looked and later when she regretted not doing so herself, he described what sounded to Anna like a little alien, big eyes in a tiny head. The whole thing – it's easier when Anna thinks of it as a thing – was the size of his thumb. And dead. Still. Gone. All Anna is left with is guilt for not wanting it. Now it's gone, now *she* is gone, Anna knows there is nothing she wants more than to have her back.

'Rest,' Tom had said when he left this morning for work. He has taken a few days off work but has an important meeting today. 'I'm glad that Nazra and Salimah are here. That means you won't be alone.'

Anna would prefer to be alone. Nazra is at school, but Salimah keeps coming in with tea and food Anna does not want.

'Why don't you read something?' Salimah asks, signalling to the pile of books next to the bed as she straightens the sheets around Anna. There is nothing there she wants to read right now. She would prefer some chicklit or a romance but doesn't want to get out of bed so she grabs the first thing on the pile. It's her grandmother's camp diary. So far, Anna has only read random entries here and there, fragments. Right now, with a spinning head, she can't manage this. *Come on, chin up,* Anna tells herself. *Stop feeling sorry for yourself. Your grandmother had it much worse.* It doesn't help. She opens the notebook on a page that has a little bit more white and is easier on the eye. It is a recipe for a chocolate cake. *Food rations keep dwindling, but it is amazing what some people can do with so little. A boy in our room celebrated this birthday today, and his mother had saved up all the sugar for weeks and baked him a cake. We all got a mouthful, but the look on the boy's face tasted even better. This woman can do magic, I'd love to eat her food when she has real butter and whiter flour. She gave me a recipe for her chocolate cake and the thought that one day I will bake it helps me through nights when my stomach growls.*

The thought of chocolate makes Anna choke, she hasn't really eaten the last few days and she isn't hungry at all. A stitch barrels through her abdomen and Anna rearranges herself uncomfortably. She remembers another story, how after liberation her maternal grandmother was given a piece of chocolate by Allied soldiers in the Netherlands. She wolfed it down. And ten minutes later her stomach, not used to such rich food, rejected it and she spat it all up. Anna rushes to the toilet too but all that comes out is yellow bile. She drinks some tepid water straight from the tap and lies down again.

She flips through the diary, trying to find another connection in the rows and rows of letters. Her eye settles on a sentence that is underlined: remedies against period pain. Oma was a teenager in the camp, would she ever have gotten a period? Or would hunger have emaciated her body so much it stayed away? Djahe, Oma advises. Ginger, Anna knows. Raspberry leaf tea and again, chocolate. Anna retches. Maybe she should ask Salimah for ginger tea. They should have fresh ginger and the thought of it doesn't make Anna sick. She gets up but can't find Salimah anywhere. Anna boils water herself and after slicing the ginger the scent has perked her up enough to walk outside to the beanbags under the palm leaves, cradling the hot drink. Sipping slowly, her nausea subsides and is replaced by a numb feeling. She is happy to be in the fresh air, not the pounding canned cold of the aircon. She ought to open her curtains and air the room. Let the bad things be blown out. Anna left the diary inside but can't stop thinking about Oma and the camp. It is a good distraction from thinking about *her*.

A flock of birds fly up from the banyan tree above her, chattering loudly, and another jolt hits Anna. Her great-uncle. Could he have been here – in this house? All she knows is that he died building the railway. And that this, her house, where she is now living, was a prisoner of war camp for prisoners in transit to Burma. It is a long shot but it is not impossible.

If two hundred prisoners were squeezed into a single house, some of them would have slept in her very bedroom! The cold tinges rushing through Anna's body feel familiar. She has felt this before. And she knows exactly where.

Fed up with the numbness, with a desperate desire to feel something, Anna walks inside. Inside to that one spot in the corridor she usually avoids. She sinks down on her haunches in the corner and lets the icy waves roll over her, spiking her arms, pricking her neck and settling in her belly that was far too hot before. Visions fill her head – khaki and dark green uniforms, stampeding boots, mud, a lot of mud, streaks of brown that slowly turn red. The visions swivel and turn until everything is red and Anna slumps over crying.

After Salimah finds her there and slowly coaxes her back to bed, Anna drops into a deep sleep.

That evening Anna sits down to dinner with Tom and pretends to be okay; she feels better when she doesn't think at all. She eats a few mouthfuls and manages not to cry. If Tom can act normally, so can she. Maybe pretending to be fine will actually make things fine. They make small talk. About work, the heat, the tree that fell over at the entrance to their road, blocking it for hours. Anna remembers hearing the sound of chainsaws but also not registering it.

When dark falls, Anna lies in bed but she can't sleep. She already slept all afternoon. The air-conditioning hums and the window is closed but so many sounds pass through. A screech. The *chi chi chi* sound of a cicak. A car passing by, its headlights making slatted stripes on the ceiling through the air vents above the French doors. To allow for air-conditioning, all the vents have been sealed with Perspex, which increases the choked feeling of the room. A dog barks loudly in the distance. It begins a high-pitched howl, which slows to a soft whimpering. Now it is close by. It is in their garden.

Anna looks at Tom, sleeping peacefully beside her. She wonders how he can seemingly set aside their painful loss and rest so soundly. With each passing moment, her resentment towards his apparent acceptance of what happened grows stronger. It happened to them both. She curses his childhood that discouraged talking about feelings.

She waits, ten minutes on the alarm clock, fifteen. The dog's whimpering rises and falls and drives her crazy. Anna gets up from the bed and tiptoes into the living room. The street is fairly light; there is a streetlight in front of Felicity's house and it's a full moon tonight. Does that make the dog howl? Anna opens the front window, leans outside and the cloying scent of frangipani envelopes her. It is never this strong during the day and it makes Anna dizzy.

She rushes out the back door into the garden for some fresh air. The night breeze is refreshing and almost crisp. The dog is gone and the scent of flowers is weaker here. She walks over to the gazebo with the palm leaf roof and sits down. Cradling her stomach – the cramps are still there – Anna sits down and tries to empty her mind. A frog hops in front of her and onto the table. The little creatures congregate by the pool every night, croaking for dear life. Looking at the frog, and its big eyes, Anna shudders, thinking it too looks like an alien. She tries very hard not to think of *her*. But the harder she tries not to, the more *she* takes shape, like a real child this time, a rosy pink baby, with big blue eyes, who smiles but then scrunches up her tiny face and bawls. Anna covers her ears but the baby girl keeps crying loudly in her mind.

Anna rocks back and forth trying to snap out of it and does so when the frog hops off the table and onto her foot. She jumps up, inadvertently kicking the frog into the pool. It swims away with a strong breaststroke in the eerie light of the underwater lamp. Anna walks over to the pool and dips her hands in, cooling her wrists and rubbing the water over her face. The chlorine brings her to her senses. *Come on, Anna, keep it together.*

As she pulls herself up she feels fresher but then she hears it again, louder now and definitely not in her mind. There is a baby crying behind the banyan tree. Felicity doesn't have a baby. Could Anna's baby be here? On bare feet Anna slips off the decking and onto the grass. Surrounding the banyan are roots, small shrubs and piles of old leaves. Thinking of snakes, insects and whatever else lurks in those leaves, Anna stops in her tracks. Anyway, the sound seems weaker as she approaches the tree. She hurries back to the safety of the wooden decking. The crying baby seems louder here. She looks behind her. The sound is coming from the outbuildings. Is she out of her mind? Obviously, Nazra must have had her baby.

Does Salimah know? Why aren't they at the hospital? Anna rushes over to the outbuildings and stops in front of Nazra's door. It is dark and quiet. Through the partially drawn curtains she sees the sleeping shape of Nazra in bed, her rounded bulk pushing through the sheets.

Confused, Anna walks back to the pool. Now it is silent here too. She feels a wisp of frangipani wafting by, then a strong smell of rot, decay, of utter disgust and Anna imagines her rosy pink baby decomposing, and she rushes to the bushes and throws up what little she ate tonight between the arches of the banyan. As she straightens and pulls back her hair, she looks at the house. A white, thin shape the size of a woman drifts over the house and slowly the stench abates. Anna feels as if two hot hands are clawing at her insides from within. She pulls off her nightgown and submerges herself in the pool. With the cool water spreading through her hair and into her mouth, Anna's heartbeat slows and she finds peace. She doesn't notice the water turning red between her legs. She lets herself float on her back and thinks of falling asleep in this water and slowly sinking to the bottom so everything will be over.

16

The next morning, Tom finds Anna curled up like a foetus on the chair beneath the attap roof. Stark naked. She is now lying in bed, with a sleeping pill from the doctor, whilst Salimah tries to clean the stains off the chair cover. Scrubbing at the stain, Salimah feels the blood pull away from her hands. What happened last night?

She saw Nazra only briefly before she went to school this morning. The girl is growing fast, her bump now very obvious. Tomorrow they have an appointment with the school counsellor, someone at school is bound to have noticed by now. Salimah worries they will ask Nazra to leave school. A girl like that is a disgrace. And then she will have no education and no husband. Is that what the girl wants? Salimah hopes seeing the counsellor will at least force some decisions.

Salimah takes the wet chair cover to the washing lines behind the house, and is surprised to see them full of bed linen. A chill tingles her fingers as she takes down the dry sheets.

At midday she brings Anna a cup of tea and some toast with butter and Marmite. Anna likes the horrible yeasty spread and the saltiness will do her good. When Salimah enters, Anna is awake, staring at the ceiling. Salimah touches her on the shoulder, and she looks up groggily. She eats the toast with an unexpected appetite. Energised by the food, Anna starts to talk, her story incoherent. Howling dogs, a stench, white shapes. 'Did Nazra have her baby?

How is she? I heard it last night. But …'

Salimah straightens the clammy sheet over Anna's legs. 'Nazra is fine, she is at school. Relax.'

But Salimah isn't relaxed at all as she returns the empty plate to the kitchen. She chops onions, and the stinging in her eyes hurts pleasantly. Something is wrong.

When the plain chicken stock she made for Anna is simmering, Salimah hears Nazra coming home. She wipes her hands on her apron, takes it off and reluctantly walks to the outbuildings. Nazra is lying on the bed and Salimah perches down besides her. 'How are you feeling?'

Nazra shrugs. 'Fine.'

Clothes and school books are strewn across the floor. 'You could keep this room a bit tidier, sayang.'

Nazra rolls her eyes.

'We are meeting the counsellor tomorrow. Do you realise they might expel you from school? Did you think about your options?' Nazra doesn't answer. 'Have you told the father yet? Will he do the right thing, will he marry you?'

'How can it be the right thing if I don't want to marry him?' Nazra's voice rises as she speaks. 'Why is it that you never ask me what I want?' She turns sharply, and her gaze feels like daggers shooting into Salimah's soul.

'Okay. What do you want?'

Nazra lies back down. 'I don't know.'

'You can't keep ignoring this. You will have a baby soon. You need to read these.'

Salimah has carefully read all the flyers the doctor gave them, now lying discarded on the floor. Salimah picks them up and fans them out in front of Nazra. Adoption, care homes, programmes to assist young mothers. Nazra stares at them with obstinate eyes. 'And what if I would keep this baby? Would I live at home with it, and your uncle? Or will you kick him out for me?'

Salimah's resolve to be firm crumbles under the condemning looks. 'Why don't you come home tonight, just for one night, and we will talk to Pak Long. Come and sleep in your own bed, just one night.'

Nazra doesn't answer and Salimah takes this as a yes. A wave of relief washes over her as she thinks that, at least for one night, Nazra will be back home.

Salimah peers into Anna's room. She is asleep. Tom will be home soon to take care of his wife. Nazra is her priority now. She has stopped looking for new jobs some weeks now. She has stopped seeing friends – being too ashamed to face their questions – she has stopped doing anything but come here and cook and clean and try to keep an eye on a daughter who acts as if she doesn't exist, who blames her for this mess they are in.

Is Pak Long right, is it her fault that the girl has gone astray, because she spent all these years focusing on her career? Doesn't he see she did it all for the girl, to show her that a woman can be strong? Anyway, she had no choice – as a single mother, someone needed to provide. But now she's lost her job and is losing her daughter too.

At home, at the round kitchen table, dinner starts off well. Father smacks his lips as he eats his chicken curry. Pak long scrapes up every last bit of gravy with his spoon, and Nazra piles another heap of rice on her plate. Salimah loves how food brings people together, how it gives comfort. It almost feels like they are a normal family enjoying a meal together. Pak Long never likes to talk when he eats so Salimah keeps quiet too for now. A stomach full of ayam masak lemak might put him in a good mood. And anyway, she isn't even sure what to say. She can't simply tell Pak long to leave the girl alone. He would never accept it.

Bapa puts down his spoon and looks Salimah in the eye. 'Are you going to tell us what is going on?'

Salimah looks at her half-empty plate. Why is he suddenly so sharp? She swallows down her rice, and takes a swig of water to ease down the lump that is stuck in her throat. 'Tomorrow we are meeting Nazra's counsellor at school. We need to talk, as a family, about her options.'

Father screws up his eyes as he peers at Salimah. 'That is not why you bought her here. Tell us the truth.'

'Bapa!' Salimah exclaims. What is he going on about? She looks at Nazra, wondering what the girl told her grandfather but Nazra just looks relieved at the change of subject.

'It's the hantu,' Father states. The word hovers above the table and makes Salimah shudder.

Nazra adds a ladle of curry to her rice. 'I never saw the hantu, Atuk, but Anna did. She saw a long white shape flying over the house. Tell me what you know, Atuk.'

Father nods. 'It could be a ponti–' but Salimah cuts him off.

'Stop it, Bapa, don't talk like that.'

She doesn't want everything to start again. The gossip. The threats. The shame.

Father's eyes flash red. 'I warned you not to go there, it is not a good place.'

He strokes Nazra's hand. 'Awas, better you stay here.'

Pak Long chews thoughtfully on his last piece of chicken,

then pushes his plate away from him. He takes a sip of water and looks stern. 'Adik, you need to stop this. Remember before? Better not mention these things. We put our faith in Allah.'

'Ya, easy for you to say. All your fault anyway and now my granddaughter lives there. What if she wants revenge?'

What if who wants revenge? Salimah looks at Pak Long. 'You need to tell me what he is talking about. You all talk in riddles.'

Pak Long scratches his head. 'Susah all that. Better leave that treehouse in the past.'

'What treehouse?'

Salimah knows exactly what treehouse. The one she coveted. The one she was never allowed to go into. But what does that have to do with Pak Long? The python from the road is back and curls itself round the arches of the banyan, the planks of the treehouse. Father's eyes glaze over before he screams, 'It wasn't my fault! It was his friend sold me the wood.' He points at Pak Long.

Nazra has been quietly eating her third serving of curry but now looks up. 'So it is true the place is haunted? Cool. Maybe tomorrow I can find this hantu.'

Salimah want to scream too. What is wrong with this girl? But the girl's voice sounds so normal, and in the present, that it soothes Salimah and her scream never leaves her mouth.

Nazra asks: 'Did something happen in the house when you worked there as a tukang kebun?'

Father nods.

'Did someone die or what?'

Nobody answers.

Pak Long plays with the hairs on his chin and mumbles something Salimah can't hear. It sounds like a prayer. Then he continues. 'They can blame me, blame them, but what Allah means for us will happen. Things happened in that house, long time ago already, things that don't concern good Muslims. Why go and bring it all back?'

Salimah stands up. 'I'm not bringing it back. They are.' She looks at Nazra and her father. 'I brought Nazra here to talk about her. About how we can all live together without fighting. So she doesn't have to be there anymore.'

Nazra looks angry. 'Why did you suddenly want to get me out of there?'

Now Salimah does scream. 'What I want, is to talk about that real thing that grows inside you and is no ghost. It is a baby and it will be born soon. What are you going to do about that?'

Nazra gets up and screams back. 'As if you care! All you care about is your good name.'

When it looks like Pak Long wants to say something, Nazra yells even louder. 'And don't you dare say anything. You are not my father. You are not even my grandfather. You are a crazy old guy. I don't understand what I am even doing here! I'd much rather stay with that pontianak!'

Nazra turns to Salimah. 'They are only dangerous for misogynistic men like him.'

Nazra storms out of the house and as the shame bounces through Salimah's ears she isn't sure what causes it. The bad manners of her daughter, raising her voice against her elders, or the realisation that all of this can only be her fault. Real life is much scarier than any ghost story.

17

Anna sits across from Tom at the outdoor dining table and stares at her food. Roast potatoes, steak that Tom grilled on the barbecue. A side salad. Not Anna's favourite food, even if she had an appetite. Anna hates potatoes, particularly the boiled-to-death variety her maternal grandmother served, accompanied by dreary beans and meat spiced only with a smidge of pepper and salt.

But today, Anna wants to make an effort to please Tom, hoping that if he's happy she will be too. It has been two weeks. The bleeding has eased to spotting. The cramps have gone from feeling like long nailed claws gripping her insides to irregular pokes that no longer make her fold over. The worst is the fog inside her head, and the strange thoughts that keep attacking her. The world around her looks the same superficially, but it is as if she has been shipped to a parallel universe.

The fog follows her around, infiltrates all of her body and scares her. Inside the fog is the crying baby, and she can't stop looking for it but never finds her. Sometimes, at night, when she can't sleep and sits on a beanbag underneath the banyan, she hears whispers, speaking of longing, and comfort that she can cradle in her arms. She misses her unborn daughter so badly it hurts, and the only way to stop that feeling is to replace it with something worse.

Anna spends hours in the side corridor, rocking back and

forth in a whirlpool of images and noise. Black leather boots stomping. White cloth fluttering in the wind, turning grey and yellow like rags. Rusty nails that smell like blood. Desperation wells up when she realises that the one thing that could have made everything right has been taken from her.

On better days, she takes Oma's diary to that spot in the corridor where she feels the worst, the discomfort of the hard wood underneath her more soothing than the soft pillows of her bed. The distraction of someone else's pain calms her. The situation in Oma's camp is becoming worse. *Mother is sick, dysentery, like so many people right now. If only we had more food, better food. It's mostly watery cabbage. Rice with stones. Just a mouthful per person. Our own supplies are gone, and bartering with locals at the fence is harshly punished, so we need to depend on what the Japs give us. This dysentery epidemic is getting out of control; our whole room stinks from people that didn't make it to the latrines. We lost seven people already and the atmosphere in the camp is more depressing than ever. Mrs Voogd, who is a nurse, tries to help, but with no medication there is little she can do. We need clean water. She hammers on about hygiene but how, when we live like sardines in a tin?*

On the next page, Oma's mother dies. She doesn't write for a few weeks and Anna can only guess at the grief and desperation that slowly starts to feel like her own. Her daughter. Her great grandmother. Gone forever.

When Tom is home she tries to look normal, but he can see her suffering and talks about rest, about waiting a bit longer. So tonight she decides that the best way for things to go back to normal is to act as if things are normal. She prepares the food, sets the table and now sits facing her husband in the darkening twilight. It feels like she is an actress in a play, a side character. Anna has the role of the wife. Tom makes polite conversation. She asks him about work and has to listen to the answer, which doesn't interest her at all. The cicadas screech behind her, overpowering the conversation, as if they have wedged themselves in her ears. The monotonous sound of Tom's voice rustles in the background but there it is again. 'Shhh!' she says to Tom. 'Do you hear that? It drives me crazy all the time.'

Tom looks bemused. 'What? The cicadas? I just filter them out, barely hear them anymore.'

'No, not those,' Anna snaps. 'The dog. Who has a crazy dog like that, at it every night? It's not next door. Can it be a stray?'

Tom looks confused. 'What dog?'

Anna points into the night sky, behind the banyan. 'There. The barking? What are you, deaf?'

'Anna, there is no dog here. Do you want to go lie down?'

Tom is always doing this, telling her to relax, to take sleeping pills. She can't spend the rest of her life in bed being drugged, can she? She needs to feel the pain so she knows she is alive. But that night she takes the pill and sleeps a dreamless sleep. It is the first night she doesn't hear the baby cry.

When Anna wakes up in the morning the house is empty. There is a note from Tom on the table; he went to work and didn't want to wake her. *Call me when you wake up.* With xx, kisses.

Anna sighs. Tom means well but doesn't have a clue. Despite the numbing pill she took, Anna's mind feels a little clearer today. Salimah isn't coming in until later, and will bring groceries, so Anna has the morning to herself. She hasn't been out of the garden yet since it happened and she sees the glances Tom and Salimah exchange over that. Anna doesn't care. She has had some friendly messages from Vicky, from Bea, but they ceased after Anna didn't respond. Felicity came by once, all whispers and flurry and Anna had to make up a doctors' appointment to get rid of her. She feels more comfortable in the cocoon of the parallel world she is floating in. In this monster of a house, full of the hugeness of history, that shows how insignificant she is. She can't make small talk with friends who barely know her. Her old friends – some in the Netherlands, some in the UK – are too far away, they know nothing. What could she tell them? *I had a miscarriage and feel a bit weird.* They would react the same as Tom. Rationally. Prescribe rest, or worse, a shrink. They won't understand that this craziness is the real Anna.

She pours herself some iced tea and takes out her grandmother's diary again. Today she wants to read with a clear head, so not in the corridor. She sinks into a beanbag outside, where the air is fresher. Further into the book the spidery writing gets more and more condensed and reading it makes her head ache. The notebook confuses her. A month after her mother died, Oma sounds chirpy again. Is she, too, pretending all is fine? Is she too scared to show her true feelings? Anna does not recognise her Oma in the writing, the old-fashioned language sounds more Dutch than Oma's spoken words. Oma was fair haired, her Indisch heritage only showed in how she walked, how she talked. Oma used words like soedah and adoe, she called bananas pisang. It is as if she became more Asian after she moved.

The Indonesia Oma sketched for Anna as a child was a beautiful place, not this slice of hell she is reading about. She tosses the notebook behind her into the muddle of aerial roots that sprout from the banyan. She doesn't want the picture of a country she adored as a child tainted by the nightmare described in this diary. Leaning back, she ponders why this upsets her so much and then she realises: that colonial world of Oma's stories is resurrected here in Singapore. Anna experienced it during the coffee morning at Felicity's house, and whilst eating overpriced imported burrata with those Dutch ladies. She lives in that world every day in this house, which is so much bigger than anything they could afford back home, and with almost fulltime domestic help. The discomfort she felt in that shopping centre where all the helpers looked at her like she was salvation herself resurfaces painfully. How is all of this possible, more than half a century later?

When Anna told her parents about the miscarriage, she had to stop her mother from jumping on a plane. She can't face her yet. Who she needs right now is her father, but she could never hurt her mother by saying that. Papa must know more than he lets on. He sends her newspaper articles about Singapore, its history, its supersonic rush to wealth, about the current government, post-colonialism and the influence of the past. When Anna studied history in university and took classes on colonialism, she and Papa talked about the Dutch Indies – the exploitation, the suppression, everything that was wrong with it. But never in relation to themselves, to their family. 'We' were wrong in Indonesia, he said, but with a degree of separation in his voice. All of it made her feel detached from her country, her family, and herself.

Ironically, she immediately felt at home in England. Without any pressure to belong she became successful, confident – in her studies and later in her job, and she forgot about the girl that dreamed of living on a plantation in the jungle. She only saw Oma during brief visits, the occasional phone call becoming harder and harder as Oma's hearing declined. Still, when Tom heard the news about the job in Singapore, she was the first person Anna wanted to call. But there was no answer and then Papa called to tell her Oma had been admitted to the hospital. Anna didn't make it there in time to say goodbye, only to fill some boxes with a few things Oma left her and tape them up. Destination: Singapore.

But now that girl who dreamed of the tropics is back and her marriage, her career, feel fake. When she looks at her husband, smart and handsome, she sees a stranger.

She feels a pulse coming off the banyan behind her, as if it's urging her over, to pick the book back up. She sinks deeper into her beanbag, thinking instead about the stories of beauty Oma told her.

But the buzz behind her becomes stronger, it pierces her ears, so she gets up and searches between the branches until she finds the book again.

She opens it at a page covered not in writing, but with sketches of the two volcanoes. In the far corner of the page Anna can just about make out: *Today I will need to say goodbye to my two friends, my mountains. We will be moved to another camp.* There are only a few pages left in the notebook and the next page has a sketch of row upon row of trees. *The new camp is surrounded by rubber.* Oma recounts their adjusting to the hot and humid climate in the new camp, which is in the lowlands instead of in the cooler highlands. Anna knows Japan capitulated on August 15th but the story rolls on unperturbed; it is not until August 24th that Oma mentions it, underlined. *The war is over!!!* News doesn't travel fast through trees.

For a few lines Oma is optimistic. Anna stops to ponder that brief moment where Oma did not yet know that she would lose her country again, this time for good. After liberation Oma's writing sounds more hollow than ever. *We are desperate for home and news of loved ones.* The word home makes Anna recoil. *The Japanese have lost but we are still stuck with them. The only difference is they now look away when they hand us our rations, which have slightly improved, and they do not dare shout at us anymore. How I long to see soldiers in a different uniform, ones that are on our side. But here in this backwater we have to make do with what we have. The gates of the camp stay closed shut. If the war is over, why can't we leave???*

The KNIL soldiers, from the Dutch-Indies army, are dead, wounded or starving in their own camps. Oma and the other internees have only the Japanese soldiers to protect them now. On August 17th, Soekarno made his proklamasi for merdeka – independence – and a new war has started. Anna knows this, but Oma doesn't, not yet. She is still living in that other war.

Anna's cheeks turn red as she reads about the repeated attempts to transport the women and children back to Medan. Time and again the train doesn't depart. Oma gets more and more frustrated, oblivious of the seriousness of the situation outside the safe enclosure of the camp. When they finally board a train, escorted by British soldiers, it doesn't go far before screeching to a halt in the jungle night. *We sat in the dark, trying to understand what caused our stopping and then we saw them, scarier than we could have imagined: hundreds of inlanders coming up to the train, shouting. Waving burning torches, machetes, sticks. Fists raised and shouting. We sat there with our hearts in our throats, not able to believe what we saw. Were these the same people that passed us food though the fence at camp? We all cried when the train chugged back to the camp, away from freedom.*

Oma is frightened to learn that not English but Japanese

soldiers will accompany them on the next attempt at transport, a few weeks later. But Japanese soldiers are trained to follow orders, and the men posted at regular intervals on both sides of the railway allow the train to continue its way towards Medan. It is daytime now, and through the train windows, behind the upheld rifles and bayonets of the Japanese, Oma sees the Indonesians in their rice paddies and kampongs, clenched fists raised to the passing carriages. Oma made a quick sketch of such a fist. Merdeka. But freedom is four years away still for Indonesia.

We are finally in Medan and it feels like in a war zone. Where can I go, what state will the plantation be in? How can I find my father? Anna swallows down her grief for her young grandmother. She doesn't know yet that her father and brother are dead. *No letters from Broer, I haven't heard from him since Singapore.* Anna's eyes prick up. Singapore!? Was he here?

As she reads on she learns Oma received a letter at the beginning of the war from her brother, after he was transported to Singapore. Suddenly all goes icy around Anna. He could have been here, in this house!

Anna runs inside, opens her laptop on the dining table and searches lists of prisoners, articles, diaries, names, dates, places, losing herself in the abundance of data. She makes lists, jots down clues, links, not realising she is filling the empty pages at the end of her Oma's notebook. She doesn't even know her great-uncle's first name; Oma uses his nickname, Broer, which simply means brother. She finds the family name in a Dutch army battalion. It could be him. The battalion was sent to Changi prison, not here, and Anna feels almost disappointed. As she glances over her notes, her own distinct handwriting, she realises that for the last hour, doing historical research, she has felt like her normal self again.

A loud bump pulls Anna from her thoughts. There is a moaning sound, not the crying baby, not the dog, but the eeriness of it in the empty house suggests to Anna that something is out of place. Then, a bang. A tap running. Footsteps from the corridor.

Anna doesn't notice the notebook slipping from her hands and dropping to the ground. Her heart bounces as loud as the footsteps and Anna screams at the top of her voice, not noticing she has the direction all wrong. The footsteps don't come from the side corridor. They come from the kitchen and when Anna finally falls silent and looks up she sees a sheet-white Nazra cradling her stomach. 'Is my mother here?'

18

Salimah rushes into the hospital and is irritated to find Anna in the waiting room. Why is this woman here? Why not her? Her angriness abates when Anna explains how Nazra had walked in, in the middle of a contraction, with hair that she had just dunked in the kitchen sink, drips sliding down the wet coils and onto her shirt.

'She asked for you,' Anna says. 'She said, is my mother here?'

Anna explains how she tried to call Salimah, and when she could not reach her decided to drive Nazra to the hospital herself. Salimah is as much scared as relieved. She has been looking for Nazra ever since the girl barged out of the house after that last fight with Pak Long. She hadn't shown up at school and none of her friends knew where to find her – or at least, they would not tell Salimah. Nazra wasn't due for another month, and Salimah could only hope that the girl would find her when she needed her. That she went to Anna's house looking for her, for her mother, means a lot.

'How is she? Can I see her?' Salimah runs ahead, Anna follows more slowly behind.

'She is in the delivery room. When she started screaming, I did not know if she wanted me there. I wanted to give her some privacy.'

Salimah hesitates, but Anna shoves her through the door:

'Go. She needs you.'

Nazra is lying on a bed, her eyes closed, a nurse in pink and a female doctor in a white coat crouching over her quavering bulk. When she sees Salimah come in, the doctor looks up with questioning eyes. 'Are you the mother?'

Salimah hesitates. Surely that woman on the table, her baby girl, surely she is the mother here? Unsure of her role, Salimah nods. The doctor continues, urgently now, 'Come over, hold her hand. It is not going smoothly, we might need to resort to a caesarean. Labour is progressing too slowly.'

When Salimah grabs Nazra's hand and squeezes it, the girl squeezes back. 'How are you doing, sayang?'

Nazra shakes her head, too weak to speak. Salimah turns back to the doctor. 'Is she okay? What can I do?'

'She is exhausted. Labour has been going on too long. We see this often with very young girls, their pelvis is not well developed, that is why they go into labour prematurely. Also, the mental strain of doing this is huge. She says she does not want a caesarean, but she is a minor, you are her parent, what do you think?'

Why does this doctor use so many words? Salimah needs to digest them, needs time. How can she be expected to be in charge suddenly? She wipes the sweat off Nazra's face with her sleeve and looks at her with a mixture of tenderness and apprehension. What would Nazra want? If becoming a mother does not make you an adult, what does? Salimah looks behind her to the door, as if expecting her own dead mother to stand on the doorstep, but there is nothing but white corridor. Looking into Nazra's pained eyes, there is only one thing Salimah can say. 'We need to give her another chance.'

She squeezes Nazra's hand again and picks up a wet cloth

from a bowl of ice cubes next to the bed and sponges Nazra's forehead. She whispers in her daughter's ear. 'You can do this. We can, together. Mak is here now.'

A massive groan escapes from Nazra and the nurse staring down her other end sticks up her thumbs. 'Keep going.'

Sometime later, Salimah is not sure whether it was an eternity or just five minutes, there is a relieving cry. The doctor pushes a bundle in a white hospital blanket into Salimah's hands. 'It's a boy.'

While the doctor and nurse fuss over Nazra, Salimah looks at the crinkled little face. It doesn't look like Nazra at all. Does he look like his father?

The baby gets whisked away – his weight is low and he needs to be checked by a paediatrician. Nazra too is wheeled away.

'Wait there,' the nurse points at the waiting room.

Suddenly Salimah is expelled again from the little world where nothing else matters; where she and Nazra have done it together. Salimah sinks down in a green plastic chair, uncertain what to do. Should she call someone? Her father? With a shock, Salimah remembers Anna. Is she still here? She texts Anna, who pings back straight away. *Congratulations! Sorry could not stay. Feeling faint. Please do bring them back here later.*

A minute later. *Can I help, buy things? Nappies? Formula?* It takes a few minutes for Salimah to realise she means diapers and baby milk. She doesn't answer yet. When the doctor comes back to bring Salimah to the recovery room she explains they want to keep Nazra in for a few days to monitor her. 'She has a high blood pressure and we are a bit worried about her mental state. She is so young. It was a long labour and she will need a lot of support. Does she have a safe and stable home situation to go back to?

She needs peace and quiet to be able bond with the baby. Or is she giving it up? We have a good adoption program.' The doctor fiddles with a watch that is clipped on her lapel, then looks at Salimah expectantly. What Salimah hears is: *Will you look after her? Or should I give this baby away?*

Salimah hesitates, thinks of Pak Long and pushes her doubts away as her phone pings in her pocket. 'Yes,' she says confidently. 'I am there for her. Both of them.'

When she looks at the phone it's Anna again. *I have a friend from yoga that has a crib we can borrow!*

In the recovery room, Salimah sits between a sleeping Nazra and a sleeping baby. She still has no clue what Nazra wants. Keep the baby, give it up for adoption. Be a single mum, find the dad. But Anna's texts gave her confidence; at Anna's house she can keep Nazra close. In its green lushness, Nazra can recover. Salimah ignores thoughts of that other thing, that shimmering cloud of scary white. It didn't get its way, she thinks, looking at the healthy boy sleeping next to her. She texts Anna back. *Thank you, you are so helpful.*

Quietly, she prays. Allah is forgiving, she knows. Her own mother's voice comes back to her. Mak's religion made her feel safe, of Pak Long's version, she is not so sure. His Islam is one of judgement, not one of peace. Salimah is a grandmother now but she has never felt more like a little girl, in need of her mother to guide her. She thinks back to that day, not even that long ago, in a different hospital but a similar room. With her husband by her side she held baby Nazra, they were full of dreams for their little girl and Salimah was oblivious to all that could go wrong. The disease took her husband just before Nazra's third birthday.

Pancreatic cancer. The words taste sour and she swallows them quickly. It is strange, but sometimes Salimah feels her husband was in her life so briefly that it is was if he was never really there. She isn't sure how he would have responded to this illegitimate grandson. Would they have figured things out together, like a team, as her parents always had?

Salimah's mother died not long after her husband. She has so much to ask her still. What had Mak's life been like? What had Mak's dreams been? How had she felt when she held Salimah for the first time? She had given birth at home in the kampong, not in a hospital. Life was different then, was it better, or just worse as the government likes to tell them? Salimah no longer knows what to believe. Salimah's mother hated the move to the HDB flat. She missed the kampong, her vegetables, her chicken, her neighbours and friends. The kampong spirit. They all got flats in different parts of town, and there were no handphones in those days, no WhatsApp, no Facebook, many people did not even have landlines. Mak lost her friends and never got over it. On the other hand, Salimah will never forget her mother's face when she flushed the toilet for the first time. They went on a look-see and she remembers flipping the switch on the wall that turned on the light. On, off, on off. Like their feelings about the move. Excited. Apprehensive. Excited. Apprehensive.

The new school was supposed to be very good, better than her old one, and she had her good grades to thank for getting in. Speaking dialect was discouraged outside of mother tongue sessions but the Chinese ignored that. There weren't many Malay for her to talk to.

As her daughter and grandson sleep, Salimah sits and reminisces. Other shreds fly past again, the dark ones she has successfully supressed for years. The pointing fingers and giggles from former friends. Neighbouring children no longer allowed to come to her house. Her mother in tears, disappearing for a few days, staying with her Javanese parents, and coming back shouting, *why did I marry you, why did I not listen to them?* A feeling of relief at changing schools. All her life, she has been outrunning her past, trying to prove that she is better than those who sneered at her. But now she is tired.

19

Anna smiles at Nazra, who looks pale in her green hospital gown. 'How are you feeling?'

'Fine,' says Nazra, even though she doesn't look it. The baby sleeps in a transparent plastic crib in the corner of the room near the door, but Nazra mostly stares out the window. The girl was so chatty before, but now Anna doesn't know what questions to ask. She is relieved when a nurse comes in with a bottle of formula, stating 'feeding time' in a chirpy voice. Nazra looks at the bottle in her hand as if she's not sure what to do with it.

She looks at Anna. 'Do you want to feed it?'

It, not him. The baby has no name yet. Anna doesn't know whether that is a Malay custom or just Nazra. This is her first visit, she wasn't sure whether she should impose. Salimah has been at the hospital every day, massaging Nazra's belly and feeding her nourishing food. Nazra has low iron and is weak. The baby is premature and skinny but, according to the doctors, perfectly healthy. Today Salimah has another appointment, and Anna has offered to come instead.

Gently, she lifts the sleeping baby out of his crib. He weighs so little she is scared she might break him. 'He is stronger than he looks,' Nazra says from her bed, with a voice that betrays more emotion than intended.

'Are you sure you don't want to do it?'

A shrug.

Anna perches the baby on her lap, and as he purses his lips around the plastic teat of the bottle, Anna's nipples contract. With a quiver, she realises how hungry her body is for this touch. The rhythmic sounds of gentle sucking are more soothing than any pill can be. The baby is small but gorgeous, with a shock of brown curls and intelligent dark eyes, cheeky even, as he glances up at Anna whilst he drinks. The shape of the baby feels warm against her empty belly. She wonders why Nazra doesn't breastfeed him. Having a baby on your bare breast must be magical, she thinks, as an electric current jolts through her nipple yet again. When he has emptied the bottle, Anna holds him upright on her shoulder to burp him, like a pro, even though she has only seen it done in movies and books. She cradles him on her lap, unsure what to do now. If only she could sit here, with him, forever.

She makes herself get up, but when she tries to hand the baby to Nazra the girl looks away, gesturing to the crib instead. 'Let him sleep. He'll be up and screaming all too soon.'

Anna tries small talk, but her heart isn't in it, and since Nazra barely responds, she soon takes her leave, with one last look in the crib and a heavy heart.

That night, she lies awake again next to a sleeping Tom, straining her ears for the sounds of the night. It is uncommonly quiet. She walks outside, to the banyan tree. It is a full moon, and the garden is bathed in light. Even at night, the temperature in Singapore barely drops, and layers of scent drift through the svelte air. She walks over to where the beanbags are, and suddenly she is back in their poolside night of romance. Like tiny stars in the moonlight, the white flowers of the green bushes are blooming again, exuding their heady scent that makes the air pregnant of opportunity. A happiness and optimism she hasn't felt in a long time floods into Anna. She understands what the scent is telling her, it is the same one they smelled that night she conceived. Anna will soon have her baby back. She sits savouring the feeling for a while, then goes to bed and falls into a deep sleep.

Anna's good state doesn't last long. A few nights later the dog wakes her up again, and chilled by her sweat-soaked sheets in the airconditioned room, she is drawn outside. The white flowers have wilted, and around the banyan the stench is back, and with it, the desperation in Anna. Her baby is dead. The world is a rotten place. But then a slither of a floral scent wafts by, and she gets up, following it to the outbuildings, and there she hears it cry. She rushes to Nazra's room but it is empty. The scent now guides her inside the house, to the nursery, where the moonlight filters through the window and into the borrowed crib standing underneath. Anna rushes over and looks at the shape lying inside. When she bends over to pick it up, it falls apart. With a scream, Anna tosses the bundle of sheets aside, then rushes over to the corridor next to the room and sinks to the floor and cries.

There, the stomping and shouting starts again, in a staccato voice, in a language she can't make out, and she becomes so scared she runs down the stairs and out of the front door where she comes to a halt under the frangipani tree. The tree ruffles its leaves. The moon doesn't reach this side of the house, and although Anna is still terrified in the dark, the panic she felt inside subsides slowly as she catches her breath.

During the day, Anna sleeps a lot. Sometimes she wakes up, sweating, imagining tiny creatures marching through her bloodstream, all around, from toes to fingers, and when they reach her brain she sees sways of red and white with black spots and again hears those black-booted footsteps. She has put her grandmother's diary back into the box in the storeroom, underneath the masks, which can guard it. She tries reading books, a simple romance, travel books, but everything makes her more depressed. Until Boy comes home on Saturday afternoon.

Tom looks at the baby with a faint smile, and Anna can't tell what he is thinking. When she apprehensively told him the baby was coming to stay he responded remarkably calmly. *Sure, we need to help them. They can stay as long as they like. The company will do you good.*

After helping carry baby's belongings to the outbuildings, he turns to Anna. 'I'm going for a run.'

'But they just got here!'

Tom looks at Anna, bewildered. 'We offer them a room, but Salimah is here to help her settle in. What more do you expect me to do? I've opened up my house, but that's not my baby.'

Anna's body tenses up. She doesn't know how to reply so she nods, and minutes later Tom is gone. Before running out of the door, he turns to Anna. 'Give them some privacy to settle in. Go relax, read a book. I won't be long, maybe we can go out later? Do something fun?'

Anna sits down on the sofa. Reading is the last thing she wants to do now. All her brain can think of is that little body that is lying in his crib that now stands in the outbuildings. The baby isn't hers, she knows that, she's not crazy. She knows Tom still remembers the day he saw her in the corridor, and the day they found her outside, and suspects that's why he doesn't object to Nazra and the baby staying. His job is swallowing him up whole. Anything that keeps her occupied makes his life more easy. And similarly, Anna doesn't have the space in her mind to ask him about work right now. To be the supportive wife that he needs. Their lives have become two parallel universes that collide awkwardly and infrequently. And every time Tom tells her he needs to go to yet another dinner she is glad not to be invited to, Anna wonders whether to him it is an escape from his crazy wife.

Over the following week, they settle into an awkward routine. Salimah has been staying overnight too, keeping an eye on Nazra and helping with night feeds. In the afternoon she goes home for a few hours – to look after her father and uncle.

Every time Anna hears the baby cry, even from a distance, her body reacts. She finally forces herself to leave the house. She goes back to yoga, takes on extra classes. Goes shopping at all those boutiques she was recommended, trying on one outfit after another but buying nothing. Her body feels strange, all wrong. Clothes can't cover that up.

She rarely sees Nazra, who stays in her room, only coming out to go to the bathroom. Salimah is the one Anna runs into in the kitchen at all hours, sterilising and preparing bottles. The kitchen is full of baby. But Anna's room and body are empty.

Then one morning Nazra is in the kitchen. It is still early, Tom only just left for work. 'Oh, good morning. Nice to see you up and about. Do you want a coffee?'

'Yes, please.'

Anna brings two cups over to the dining table, and sits down, unsure what to say to the girl. 'How are you feeling?'

Nazra takes a big swig of coffee. 'I'm good. Very good actually. It's time to move on with life.'

'Why not allow yourself some time. Giving birth is a big deal.'

She can only imagine how a full labour must drain you. But

then again, Nazra has a baby. Anna has nothing. Nothing to do except move on. But there is only so much yoga a person can do.

'What will you do? Have you spoken to the father?'

'My father? He's dead. I never knew him.'

'No, I mean the baby's father.'

'Oh, him. Nah. He's nobody.'

Anna looks at the girl. *Mind your own business,* she hears Tom say. 'Your mother is hoping you'll marry him, but I guess you're too young. Still, it's his child too.'

Nazra shakes her head violently. 'He's not that kind of guy. I mean, he's cute and fun and all, to party with. But if I ever marry I need a man I can respect. One that respects me. Not a loser like that. I don't want a dumb guy like that screwing up my life again. Why do I get to suffer the consequences, not him? It's so unfair!'

Anna feels for the girl, slumped back in her chair, deflated of her earlier energetic and fierce look. 'You are right, it is unfair. Men never take responsibility for these things.'

She thinks of Tom, away at work, his life continuing as normal. He's not dealing with blood, cramps and nausea. With mind fog. 'Because it is in our bodies, we are the ones that have to deal with anything related to our uterus.'

Nazra grunts agreement. 'I think we need to take charge of our own lives.' She gets up from the chair. 'I'm getting changed.'

A few minutes later and the girl is back, now in her school uniform.

'What are you doing?' Anna asks, trying not to sound too inquisitive.

'I'm going to school,' Nazra says defiantly.

Anna bites her lip. 'Does your mother know?'

'She told me she wants me to go back to school.'

'But now? Didn't she mean in, I don't know, a while?'

Nazra stands unmoving, letting her eyes do most of the talking. 'I am ready.'

Feeling nervous, Anna wonders whether she should call Salimah. She has gone out to get groceries from the wet market. 'It's only been two weeks, and you had a hard labour. And what about the baby?'

Nazra turns around on her heels, half out of the room already. 'He's asleep in my room. You wanted to help, right? In fact, you want a baby, and I don't.'

20

Salimah stares at Anna rocking the baby on her lap. Anna looks more relaxed than she has in a long time. The boy too looks happy. It is Nazra who worries her. 'What did she say, exactly?'

Anna blushes and doesn't look up. 'She said she was going to school. And that I should look after him.'

Salimah feels a sharp sting of detachment, like she did when she first entered the hospital. Her voice is sharp when she answers. 'In what way? Like, babysit him when she is at school?'

Anna shrugs. 'I don't know.'

Salimah sighs as she pours the both of them another glass of iced tea. 'She is so headstrong, that girl. How to talk some sense into her? The confinement period is not even over. I don't know if the school will even take her back. They were quite rude before, those ignoramuses, ruining a girl's life even more by denying her an education.'

Anna looks up slightly. 'Maybe it is good she is back at school?'

Salimah shakes her head, muttering. 'Should I give her more time? I gave her so much already, I wanted her to grow strong first. But then she does this.'

Anna fiddles with the tiny fingers. 'I don't mind watching him. He is lovely.'

'Yes, he is,' says Salimah, looking at the sweet shape. 'But he is her son. My responsibility. You have done so much already.'

When Anna looks up it is with needy eyes that scare Salimah. 'I really don't mind.'

Salimah walks over and picks up the baby, causing him to wail. She rocks him but it only amplifies and Anna gets up. 'I'll make him a bottle.'

And as the baby screams louder and louder, Salimah feels increasingly relieved not to have to do this alone.

Nazra leaves the house early every morning and Salimah and Anna take turns caring for the baby. She and Anna talk about schedules, groceries, food, formula, diaper rash, cradle cap. They don't talk about how long this will go on. It suits them both too well.

Salimah can't worry about both her daughter and her grandson and is glad for Anna's help. She has forgotten what it is like to handle a baby. She buys his clothes and lets Anna cover the milk and diapers with the rest of the groceries. When Anna shows her a photo of a pushchair online, the price tag makes Salimah red in the face. So far she has been carrying him in a selendang, but her back is getting too old for such a sling. A pushchair would be good. 'Not that one,' she says.

'But it is the best one,' Anna retorts. 'All my friends agree. I had already done a lot of research. I'd been meaning to get this one anyway.'

She looks so sad Salimah doesn't know what to say.

'I'm getting it,' Anna decides. 'In lime green.'

When she sees Anna rubbing her stomach, how can Salimah say no?

Precisely when Salimah folds the last towel she hears a whimper from Nazra's bedroom. No! She had really hoped to sit down with a cup of tea before he woke again. Anna is out shopping, and the boy is due a feed, so she quickly piles the laundry into the basket and rushes to the kitchen to boil water. Before the bottle is ready she can hear his loud bawling all the way from the kitchen. With the hiccupping baby over her shoulder she walks to the living room and sits down on the sofa. At least when she feeds him she can briefly put her feet up. The baby drinks with greedy gulps and Salimah sinks deeper into the soft cushions. She hasn't been this tired ever. At nights, she lets Nazra sleep, the girl needs her energy for school. When she came back here that first day, Salimah's first emotion was relief: that she came home, and that the school had let her back in. But then anger took over. 'How irresponsible are you, just taking off like that, leaving your baby?' And then, to Nazra's vacant face, 'Do you expect me to raise him, just like that? Should we not have discussed such a thing first? I can't clean up all your messes. You are a mother now! That comes with responsibilities.'

The girl broke down in tears.

Salimah is too tired to think properly, to come up with a good plan to make this work. Last night was the worst so far. After his feed, the baby simply did not want to go back to sleep. She walked him round and round the garden, circling the pool. The banyan had looked quiet enough, but still, Salimah could not help but feel a slight shudder every time she passed it. Thankfully the cries of the healthy baby in her arms were loud enough to scare anything away. She looks at the baby tenderly. His eyes are closed and his lips suck slower and slower until they stop completely. Salimah arranges him in the crook of her arm and lies her neck back, closing her own eyes for a second too.

She wakes up when she hears stumbling on the stairs. It is Anna, dragging up the overpriced pushchair. Salimah shakes off her drowsiness and can't help but suppress a grin. A few weeks ago she cleaned this house and wouldn't have dreamed of even sitting down when alone in the house. Now, Anna catches her asleep on her sofa and doesn't even flinch. Excited, she starts showing her the pushchair and all its special features.

When Anna brings her some water, Salimah drinks the cool liquid greedily. 'Thanks, I needed that. I'm getting too old for this, those night feeds are wearing me down.'

Anna takes the sleeping form off Salimah's chest. 'You go rest, put your feet up for an hour or so. I'll take him for a stroll, test his new wheels. Don't worry about us.'

Before Anna leaves the house Salimah is already sound asleep.

21

Anna walks down the main road, under the flyover, past the food court and takes the bridge over the road to the Botanic Gardens. She stops in a lush bamboo grove and sits down on a bench. It is the middle of the day, a bit too hot, the bamboo only half shades them. She drapes a cloth over the hood of the pram, making sure the baby's face is protected from the rays that sneak through.

She fights the urge to pick him up, he is sleeping so sweetly. If she could, she'd hold him all day long. Cuddling him makes Anna's body relax. His smell makes all the bad things fly away. Only at night, when he sleeps far away in the outbuildings, Anna can smell, hear and see those things that make her cramp up completely. Now she is here with him, she feels normal. A mother with a newborn baby.

She sits and stares at the pram for a long time, until she hears a 'hello' just behind her and looks up. Vicky! Her yoga friend, whose messages she has not returned. She has met her at class, and they were friendly enough, but they haven't had any private contact since.

'Anna, how are you? It's lovely to see you!'

Anna smiles politely. Vicky looks at the pram with questioning eyes. Then, obtusely, lifts the cloth and peers into the pram.

'Who is this little one? He's gorgeous.'

Vicky sounds confused; she knows about Anna's miscarriage.

Anna carefully considers the answer. Boy doesn't have a real name yet, but she has no wish to explain that. She calls him Boy in her mind, and although she has never said that out loud, she needs to say something now. She takes a deep breath. 'This is Boy. Yes. He's lovely, isn't he?'

Vicky looks at Anna with questioning eyes, angling for more. Anna wavers.

'I'm just helping out. His mother can't care for him. She's only sixteen, still in school. She is ... considering her options.'

'That is amazing,' says Vicky, 'I did not know you did fostering. Well done you.'

Anna nods. 'Yes, I'm his foster mother.' The word tastes good.

They chat for a while but before too many questions can be asked Anna breaks off. 'Sorry, need to go, feeding time soon!' She kicks herself for forgetting to bring a bottle.

As they turn into their little lane, Boy starts to cry and Anna feels her breasts react, the feeling growing stronger as the sound of his cries amplifies.

A few days later Anna gets a WhatsApp message from Vicky. *'How's your gorgeous little one? I'm hosting my baby group tmr. Wanna join? Bring little guy!'*

Anna briefly wonders whether she should discuss this with Salimah. The baby spends a lot of time with her, more than with Salimah in the daytime. But they haven't talked properly at all lately. Not like they used to. Anna likes this limbo, allowing thoughts and decisions to float around, her mind set at half strength. If she opens it fully she is sure it will explode. Implosion seems more gentle. So she says nothing to Salimah, and on her daily walk to the Botanic Gardens, heads to the bus stop instead.

In the middle of the room lies a mat made of pastel rubber jigsaw pieces with letters on them. On it are four babies. Anna puts Boy in the middle. The others look like white giants next to little Boy but he has the most hair. And everyone coos over him, the newcomer, the most.

'His hair is so fabulous. How old is he?'

'About a month. But he was premature, that's why he is so small.'

'Is he back on his birth weight yet? As long as he follows the curve he'll be fine.'

Anna feels out of her depth with the questions asked. Salimah took Nazra and Boy to a check-up a few days back and all was well, they said, but Anna doesn't know any details.

She sits in silence, as the women talk of cracked nipples, leaking boobs, mastitis and thrush. They sometimes glance at Anna sheepishly, as if they are sorry for her that she can't breastfeed Boy.

Thankfully they soon switch to other subjects – baby shops, the best babychinos – and Anna joins in again. By the end of the meeting – it doesn't last long, most babies need a nap – she feels just like the others: a mummy.

That night Anna lies awake listening, straining her ears to hear the baby cry. It has always been Boy she heard, it must be. When she doesn't hear any crying, she wanders outside through the dark, to Nazra's room. She tries to peer inside, but the curtains are drawn. Apart from the hum of cicadas behind her and some rustling of leaves, it is quiet.

Taking a deep breath to compose herself, Anna walks towards the back of the house. Suddenly, the sickly smell of decay fills her nostrils again, and out of the corner of her eye, she catches sight of something. A white cloth appears to be draped from the roof of the patio door with a swathe of yellow above it, making it resemble a woman. As she approaches, the shape seems to shift and become transparent, swerving back and forth before sweeping sideways, despite there being no wind. Anna feels a clawing sensation in her insides again and senses something hot between her legs.

Anna turns towards the patio doors, to get to the bathroom, but the white shape now hovers directly above it. She tries the kitchen door, but finds it is locked from the inside. She walks back to the patio, closes her eyes, and walks straight through. She feels nothing. Inside, footsteps resonate in the distance and when Anna turns around the white disappears behind the banyan tree. Looking at her feet Anna is surprised to register she does not wear heavy black boots, but is barefooted.

Anna doesn't remember going back to bed, doesn't remember falling asleep, but wakes up in the morning to Tom sitting on the edge of the bed staring at her. Was it all a dream?

'Good morning, darling. You slept well? You looked so peaceful, I didn't want to wake you.'

Anna is disoriented but manages a smile.

'You are doing a lot better, aren't you?' Tom asks.

For a lack of a better answer, Anna nods.

'The thing is,' he starts, apprehensively, 'I have this thing. Well, a business meeting in Vietnam. It is quite important. You know, to do with the joint venture. But it would mean me being away for a few nights. Will you be okay?'

What joint venture? Have they discussed this before? Last night's white cloth sweeps through Anna's mind, the smell too real to have been a nightmare. The eerie feeling it left behind clenches in her belly.

'Sure,' she nods. 'I'm fine.'

The next day, after Tom leaves for the airport at the break of dawn, Anna lies in bed, staring at the ceiling. She feels relieved. She can drop the pretence now that she is normal, that she sleeps well at night, that she doesn't wander outside at all hours. She throws on shorts and a T-shirt and walks to the back of the house. When she peers into the storeroom next to Nazra's room, she notices a mat on the floor. The clothes strewn in a heap in the corner make it clear – Nazra has been sleeping here. Salimah must sleep with the baby, which explains the ever-darkening bags under her eyes. Anna finds her by the washing line. 'How is Nazra? She doesn't seem to be here much lately?'

Salimah shakes her head and Anna doesn't ask further. Nazra's presence in the house is starting to confuse Anna. Instead, she looks at Salimah. 'You look wrung out. Do you take care of yourself, not only of your daughter?'

When Salimah still doesn't answer, merely shrugging, Anna continues. 'Why don't I take the baby tonight? You need a rest. With Tom away, he can sleep with me.'

Salimah seems too tired to say no.

When Anna goes to Nazra's room to see if Boy is awake yet, she startles when she finds the girl in the room, staring at the sleeping baby. Why is she not at school?

'I agreed with your mother I'd watch him tonight,' Anna mumbles.

Suddenly Nazra breaks and slumps down on the bed, her face

in her hands.

'I saw her.'

'Who?' Anna says, while a chill runs down her spine. Nazra looks up with fiery red eyes. 'That woman, in white. You see her too, I know it. You can smell her.'

Anna has no idea how to reply. Seeing a ghost is one thing, admitting to it out loud, another. Nazra points out the door, to the banyan. 'I wanted to find her. I thought it would be cool, how stupid am I?'

Anna has no idea what the girl is talking about.

Nazra wipes the sweat off her upper lip. Her hands shake. 'Do you know what she wants?'

'No? Why would she want anything?'

Anna looks at Nazra's eyes, their dark pupils unnaturally dilated, as the girl blurts out. 'You know nothing about ghosts. They don't haunt a house for nothing. They need something.'

'Like what?'

'I dunno. Revenge. Closure.'

Against her better judgement, Anna wonders whether the girl could be right. 'But what has she got to do with me?'

Nazra jumps to her feet but her movements seem off, too slow. Her speech is slurred. 'Not you. Me. She wants my baby.'

My? The word stabs like a knife, but Anna composes herself quickly. 'Nazra, why are you acting like this? Are you on something?'

Nazra lets out an eerie laugh. 'I'm such a loser, how could I be a mother? You take the baby.'

Shocked, Anna says nothing. Nazra nods pointedly. 'You look like her, you know.'

The girl walks out, swaying as she almost hits the doorpost, leaving behind a confused Anna.

That night when Anna hears the crying baby, she rolls over first, burying her head in the pillow, as she has done many nights before. But the sound is too loud, too close, like it is in the room and then she realises it is. It's Boy. She gets to her feet groggily and picks him up, placing him against her shoulder and he quietens. Anna sits down for a minute, unsteady. She knows she needs to get up and go to the kitchen to prepare him a bottle. Boy, impatient, starts a soft hiccup, then a wail and is soon screaming his little lungs out and Anna's body reacts immediately. Her nipples wince and flinch as if charged with a current. Instinctively, half asleep, Anna lies down and shoves the straps of her top aside. Boy latches on straight away. It feels like a pinch and a relief at the same time when something inside Anna's breasts starts to flow. Her body has known this all along and now she does too.

Boy sucks rhythmically for a few seconds with a strange, pulling motion, then stops, and looks around in frustration. Anna pushes her nipple back into his mouth, kneading it until a drop forms on the tip. Boy smacks his lips and starts to suck again, but after three long sucks, a bolt of lightning shoots through Anna's abdomen. It is that feeling of something with sharp claws attacking her insides, but more intense than before. The pain subsides briefly, only to return with a vengeance, and Anna pushes Boy away to Tom's side of the bed. She uses pillows to prop the baby on both sides then gets up and runs to the toilet, clutching her stomach.

22

Salimah feels she is slowly getting her mind back now she has slept a few nights in a row. And when Tom stands in front of her one morning she knows why.

'Anna is doing a lot better, caring for the baby. I felt I was losing her. He … he is such a lovely boy. But we need to do this properly.'

Salimah nods. She knows this conversation has to be had and she has been dreading it. But she still hasn't managed a serious talk with Nazra.

Tom, visibly uncomfortable with Salimah's silence, talks on. 'I admit, it was a shock when I found him in our room all of a sudden.'

'I know,' Salimah says. 'I'll take him back tonight. It was only meant to be for a few nights when you were away. It's just that Anna … that Nazra …'

Nobody finishes that sentence.

It is not that Salimah didn't mean to bring the boy back to the outbuildings, or that she needs sleep so much she can't fulfil her responsibilities, but that she struggles to make any definitive decisions these days. She misses the baby on the evenings she spends in her own house, in her own bed. Before, she would massage him every night after his bath, rubbing his soft limbs, soothing her own brain. The urut bayi makes her feel close to the little boy, a closeness she needs now Nazra seems miles away, living in her own world again. Her eyes look strange. It is hard to have any meaningful conversation with her. Salimah isn't sure what is wrong with the girl. Post-partum depression? Only once Salimah has raised her voice, trying to force a conversation, but Nazra barged out and didn't come home that night. Salimah is scared to lose her again. So, nothing has been resolved and Tom is right. She needs to tell them she is grateful for their help, and that she will solve this, this … situation they are in.

Tom looks friendly and eager, albeit a tad fretful, fumbling with his handphone. 'It really is a good solution for everyone.'

Salimah's head is full of thoughts, words tumble over each other as Tom talks on. Formalise. Paperwork. Nazra. She looks up at Tom, who is still talking. 'Anna is getting very attached and I am worried what can happen to her if things change again, you know what I mean. So you agree?'

Salimah nods quickly, 'Yes, yes. I will sort it out.'

Tom looks at his phone impatiently: 'Are you sure?'

Salimah isn't sure what she should be sure about, but Tom's phone goes off and he looks at the screen, then up apologetically. 'Sorry, I need to take this.'

He talks into the phone as he walks down the stairs.

Salimah considers Toms words. What papers? Then it dawns on her. The baby doesn't even have a name! They have been hiding here in this house pretending he never really happened. The child is weeks old already and formally doesn't even exist. Self-conscious, she makes inquiries. A child needs to be registered within forty-two days of birth. That means it needs to be done very soon. She hauls the sleeping baby in her selendang, and hurries to her flat to gather the documents they were given at the hospital as well as Nazra's own birth records. What else would she need?

She is relieved to find Nazra in front of the school, looking like a normal schoolgirl in her bright uniform. 'Sayang, come, we need to go ICA. Register your son.'

The girl says nothing but follows Salimah to the bus stop.

'Nazra,' Salimah says as they sit inside the bus, 'how to register him without a name?'

Nazra looks out of the window as Salimah rocks the boy on her lap, pushing down the impulse to shake her daughter hard – after all, they are in a public bus. She says nothing and then the girl turns around and looks at her with empty eyes. 'Mak, what do you want me to say? I don't know. Why don't you ask Anna?'

Shocked, Salimah cradles the baby closer to her. 'What do you mean? He is your son. You need to name him.'

The baby starts to cry and by the time Salimah has rocked him to sleep they need to alight.

When she asks Nazra again in front of the clerk, the girl bursts into tears. Conscious of the piercing looks of the ICA officer, Salimah writes down the first name that comes to mind, that of her father: Ahmad. Nazra signs the forms where she is told to do so.

As they leave the building Salimah hesitates. She doesn't want to see Tom and Anna right now. Nor her father and Pak Long. She takes Nazra and the baby – Ahmad already in her mind but not yet out loud, not yet, to a nearby kopitiam.

Nazra stirs her ice lemon tea, and Salimah starts the speech she has practised so often in her mind, listing the options one by one, clearly, again. Nazra stares into her drink. 'Are you even listening?'

She looks up with red-rimmed eyes, eyes Salimah can't connect with. Empty eyes with pupils too dilated to be normal. Concern mixes with anger and frustration as she realises this conversation will go nowhere today. This is not her Nazra. Something is wrong. 'Nazra. Why don't we go see the doctor again? They can help, you know. Maybe you need some medication.'

Her concern only makes Nazra snap. 'Why don't you just leave me alone? I am so tired.'

Salimah wants to yell, *what are you tired for, I don't see you taking care of him at all, getting up at night or doing anything a mother does.*

Buy she composes herself, and instead says. 'Maybe you should stay home from school for a while, take some rest? Until you feel better?'

When Nazra nods, she gets up and pulls her tight. 'Come on. Let's go home. I mean, to Anna's place.'

Nazra is still her little girl and she mustn't scare her away by pushing too hard. First, Nazra needs to get better.

While Anna takes Ahmad for a walk, Salimah sweeps the decking around the pool. Every day the banyan sheds dozens of leaves, which end up in and around the pool, and every day Salimah sweeps them up. She looks down at the leaves as she shoves the growing heap forwards, on and on, until the very far end of the decking where, with a big swoop, she sweeps them off. She watches the flurry of leaves settling between the aerial roots of the banyan tree and feels a sense of desolation filling her body. As she stares at the tree, she realises with certainty that this baby will ruin her daughter's future.

But as she walks back towards the house, Salimah feels torn once again. This is her grandson. Her own flesh and blood. The boy is a gift.

She remembers all those times she came home from the office late, missing school events, serving hawker fare bought in a hurry. She also remembers being the first to leave, and colleagues getting the promotions she wanted. At the office she was that lazy Malay, going home early; at home, she was the mum coming back home too late for her family. Could she do it differently a second time round?

Her head spins as she realises that he is barely a month old and she is failing him already. Ahmad deserves a better start in life than this. Suddenly, it hits her. She will organise a cukur rambut. The ceremony will welcome him into the world properly. Feeling lighter for having made some sort of decision, Salimah heads home. Not sure how her father and Pak Long will react, she leaves Ahmad with Anna. Surprisingly – or maybe not – Pak Long immediately takes control. 'It is about time we properly meet him and introduce him to Islam. Let's do this cukur rambut. I will help. We keep it small. No marhaban, no party, not many people. I will ask Uzthad Amir to come. He is my friend, I trust him.'

Father nods in agreement. 'Yes. This will be great for my grandson. I do not even know his name.'

'Great-grandson,' Salimah smiles.

Pak Long nods. 'Salimah, tell us, what name did Nazra choose for the boy?'

Salimah takes a sip of hot tea. It is too hot and she scrunches up her face for a second, then stretches it back into a forced smile. 'His name is Ahmad.'

Her father's eyes flicker and Pak Long nods again. 'A good

Muslim name.'

Salimah doesn't invite Anna, she doesn't even tell her about the ceremony. She simply says she will take the baby home to meet her family. Anna does not seem particularly excited about the idea. Salimah changes him into the new clothes she has bought especially for the ceremony.

When she arrives home she is relieved to see Nazra is there already. As they wait for Uzthad Amir to arrive, Salimah busies herself getting everything ready. She hands Ahmad to Nazra who takes him without comment. She seems in a good mood, rocking him gently and smiling.

Salimah puts a large rug on the floor and in the middle sets out a bowl, olive oil, a jar of honey and a plate of dates. On the side table are drinks and snacks for the guests, few as they are. Pak Long and Father sit in the corner of the room near Nazra. When Uzthad Amir arrives he puts a set of scales and electric clippers next to the items Salimah has so carefully positioned. Nazra is holding a soft baby brush that Salimah took from Anna's room. She gently caresses the boy's long dark curls with it.

Salimah wonders what Pak Long has told Uzthad Amir. He must notice the absence of a father. As he talks, Nazra keeps brushing her son's hair, her mind somewhere far away – Pak Long is the only one listening attentively. Salimah stares at her father who in turn stares at Nazra. She wonders why Pak Long did not offer to do the cukur rambut himself. He has done many in the past. Why publicly display their shame to such an esteemed religious man as Uzthad Amir?

Uzthad Amir coughs and Salimah's attention snaps back as he describes the big celebrations that so many people hold these days for their babies: American-style baby showers, flashy presents and rented cribs, songs, dance and all things that that pull the attention away from what really counts in this ceremony – introducing the child to Islam. It sounds like an approval of their frugal setup and Salimah relaxes. Uzthad Amir signals Nazra to bring Ahmad, and when the girl does not respond, Salimah walks over and takes him from her and puts him on the rug in front of Uzthad Amir. Nazra keeps brushing the air and Salimah has to force herself to pull her eyes away from her daughter and look at her grandson.

Dark snaking curls drop into the bowl one by one. With slow strokes Uzthad Amir moves the clippers up and down, straight, firm lines, shearing Ahmad's head close. Salimah holds one hand under the neck of the infant so the hair falls cleanly in the bowl and not a single strand goes missing. Sweat pearls form around her neck, it is hot in the room; Pak Long has turned off the fan to stop any stray hairs from blowing away in the wind.

Unlike Nazra all those years ago, Ahmad lies still – he does not wriggle at all. Father brings out a bowl of lukewarm water and Uzthad Amir proceeds to wash Ahmad's head with it, shampoos and rinses, then massages olive oil onto the bare scalp. Salimah brings out a soft towel from behind her and rubs his scalp dry. He looks a different child. She notices a layer of cradle cap on his head; she should do something about that before she brings him back to the house. Then, with a flinch, Salimah thinks of Anna. What will she say?

Uzthad Amir now puts the bowl of hair on the scales and notes the weight minutely. Pak Long smiles proudly – it is a large amount of hair. Salimah briefly wonders who should pay the charitable donation in gold equal to the weight of the hair. She looks at Nazra again, who still holds the brush but has stopped moving, and motionlessly stares into the bowl that holds the hair of her baby son.

It is time for tahnik. Pak Long picks up the plate of dates and mashes up a small piece and mixes it with honey. He stands up and offers it to Nazra, who declines, but Father, who sits next to his granddaughter and has watched the whole ritual in sincere silence, picks up the piece. Gently he puts a tiny bit on the tip of his fingers and feeds it to his great-grandson whose name he shares. Ahmad sucks it up smacking his lips, visibly pleased with the sweet taste. Salimah can't resist the urge to snap a photo on her phone. She has so few photos of the boy, and this precious shot of these two Ahmads, three generations apart, makes her feel sentimental. She offers up a silent prayer, hoping the boy will have his great-grandfather's kindness. Tears pool in her eyes as she thinks of the people she loves and how she seems to be losing them all.

When Ahmad begins to cry, hungry for more, Salimah picks him up and hands him to Nazra before going to the kitchen to prepare his milk. She thrusts the bottle at Nazra, who is rocking her crying boy. 'Can you feed your son?'

While Ahmad drinks, Uzthad Amir and Pak Long recite a number of prayers. Salimah invites Uzthad Amir to eat from the dishes she prepared for today in Anna's kitchen. Rice, chicken curry, sweet rendang, noodles and shop-bought kueh for dessert. So much, Anna had exclaimed, and Salimah had nodded. Only the best for her grandson.

23

Anna misses Boy so much it makes her breasts hurt. When Salimah comes home and places the sleeping bundle in her arms, Anna lowers her nose to his neck. She misses his smell. But when she feels the top of his head rasp against her cheek, she screams. Salimah can only just catch the baby as Anna's arms flail weakly by her side. 'Anna,' she calls out, 'what's wrong?'

Salimah pulls Anna onto the sofa, the baby perched on her hip. 'Do you want some water? Anna!'

She puts the baby down on the soft play rug and shakes Anna back and forth. Anna looks up in shock and whispers, 'Salimah?'

'Stay there, I will get you some iced water to cool down.'

Anna stares at the baby on the floor. He is wearing an outfit Anna does not recognise, a yellow romper suit with white stripes. On his feet are tiny red socks. Her mind is thrown into turmoil with confusion. Who is this child? And more importantly, where is hers?

After Salimah leaves the room the screaming starts again. At first it is only in Anna's head. Then it seems to echo and bounce through the walls of the room, up to the ceiling. Anna looks up and sees the swirling fan chopping at the air, and the revolving blades hypnotise her so the noise inside her amplifies, echoing into that one corridor. It gets louder and louder and the banging intensifies, until it starts to seep out from Anna's mouth in a soft whimper.

It is not until the baby in yellow rolls over to its side and looks directly at her that it stops. He stares at Anna with his big dark eyes and things snap back into place. Anna picks up Boy and cuddles him close and when Salimah comes in she is rocking back and forth, holding him a little too firmly. Boy lets out a tiny squeak and Anna loosens her grip, balances him on the tip of her knees then looks Salimah straight in the face. Her face breaks into a smile. 'He just rolled over!'

Salimah sits down next to Anna and strokes Boy's cheek. 'No, really? He is still so young.'

Anna puts her hand on Boy's head and caresses it with gentle strokes. It feels rough and stubbly. Strange and unpleasant. But the weirdest thing is that the soft sandpaper feeling on her fingers makes her feel better.

What is wrong with her? Why does she overreact to everything? Is it to compensate for the numb feeling she has inside, the feeling she lives in a soap bubble – and if she is not careful small things can pierce the bubble and she will explode.

'What did you do with his hair?'

Anna half-listens to Salimah explaining how shaving the hair of babies is a tradition in Malay culture, or Islam, it's not clear to Anna. The baby's hair wasn't clean and now it's gone he is ready for a fresh start in life. It sounds like a baby shower, Malay style. Why wasn't she invited?

'I bought some leftover food back, it's in the fridge,' Salimah says, as she leaves the room.

When she is gone, Anna looks at the new Boy. He looks grown-up and rather cool. Tough. She hugs him again and sticks her nose into his neck, below where the stubble ends, and the soft downy hair still smells like him. There is something vulnerable underneath the toughness in Boy's new look. All the angst Anna felt earlier is replaced with an overwhelming melancholy that drips off the ceiling and the walls. She needs some air outside of this stifling house. That fan just moves around as if through static air. Mindful of his earlier rolling – real or imagined – Anna puts Boy on the play rug and walks to the window. It has been raining, the air is crisp and green and cool. She inhales deeply and just when she feels the freshness clearing up some of the cobwebs in her mind a tiny slither of floral sweetness hits her nostrils. The scent makes her insides cramp up again.

It has been a few weeks since her last major bleed but Anna has had spotting ever since. She knows she needs to go see her doctor but keeps putting it off. Every time she is close to picking up the phone, the bleeding stops, the urgency disappears, just like the urgency of so many things seems to have disappeared from Anna's life. Finding a job. Making friends. Exploring Singapore. Breathing in deeper, the scent becomes stronger and Anna absorbs it. Slowly the uneasiness stops. Picking up Boy again and inhaling his powdery smell settles the last of it.

When Tom comes home he is livid. 'How could they do that to the child? Without asking us?'

He looks at Anna who does not say anything back. First, Tom didn't seem to understand how she needed Boy. *But the doctor said we can still have our own, right, am I missing something?* But when he started spending time with Boy, changing his nappies, feeding him, he fell for him too. Tom and Nazra had a talk. Tom is so practical, once he sets his mind to something, he gets things done.

Tom's face is turning purple, a shade deeper than his sunburnt red. 'Have you given Salimah a piece of your mind? It is not her place to make these kind of decisions anymore.'

'The head-shaving, it's this Malay ritual, they shave the head and donate the weight of the hair in gold to charity. It is a part of their culture. His culture too. We must respect that part of Boy.'

Tom groans. 'We need to get that kid a real name.'

Anna nods but says nothing. She can't imagine him with any other name.

Tom continues. 'We need to speed things up, so they can't do things like this again without discussing it with us. I've been doing some research and have registered us for this pre-adoption workshop. And I have met with a lawyer. Nazra will need to sign an affidavit stating she will give up the baby. I already talked her through the information the lawyer sent me, she seems happy to proceed. We'll just have to keep our fingers crossed she doesn't change her mind. After the affidavit is signed, things will officially get started. Obviously there will be a whole slew of red tape to get through afterwards, but it's the first step.'

He looks at the sleeping baby, and seeing the loving look in his eyes, Anna realises this is no longer only about her in a dark room needing that tiny body. This is real. This is happening. Yet she is still scared to talk about it with Salimah. Things are happening so fast. In Asia things take time. Tom looks at Anna tetchily. 'Well, what do you think? We need to be absolutely sure ...'

Anna nods and tries to find the right words. 'Of course I want this. But ...'

'But what? If you aren't sure, we should cancel the whole thing right now. We'll make our own baby soon.'

There is no romance in his voice and Anna recoils. She

cuddles Boy, who is sleeping in her lap, close. 'He is our baby. I want him.' She needs him. 'But why all that paperwork?'

Tom looks at her urgently. 'Anna, what is wrong with you? You used to be an intelligent woman. I can't even have a normal conversation with you anymore.' His eyes soften as he touches Anna's hand, that is on Boy's head. 'Are you still hormonal? Is it the climate? Where are you, where is your mind? In that notebook?'

So he has noticed that Oma's diary is back on her nightstand. The blood slowly leaves Anna's face and before the echo of footsteps can start approaching from behind Tom, she shakes her head vigorously to scare them off. 'This house, you know, it brings up memories. It's like a project, researching my family history. I need to exercise my brain.'

And when her son is grown up, she needs to be able tell him where he comes from. Tom looks satisfied with Anna's answer. 'True, and it is interesting for sure. Have you spoken to your father?'

'Yes, but he still doesn't like to get personal. He prefers to talk about Indonesian independence in general, how as a colonising power we screwed thing up. He finds it hard to talk about our own family's role.'

'It might be easier when you next see him in person? They plan to visit, right?'

'Yes, but it won't be until next year. Actually, what I really want is to visit Sumatra. To see the place with my own eyes.'

Tom nods. 'Sure we can do that, some time.'

'Not some time, I'd like to go now.'

'Now? We are in the middle of an adoption! I'm in the middle of a joint venture! Don't be ridiculous.' He pauses then says: 'You should research useful things. Go online, talk to the lawyer. Make clear arrangements with Salimah. It is not as if you have anything else to do, you are at home all day. You have help. He sleeps half the time.'

When Anna looks at the floor Tom's voice goes up a pitch.

'I, in fact, do have a lot to do. So it would really help if you do this. The joint venture with the Vietnamese isn't going well, it seems like the Chinese will outbid us. I am trying to do business in this bloody continent, but it's ... Never mind.'

Anna cannot not mind. What does he mean, not going well? She hasn't been asking him about work, his project, and veiled guilt creeps up; she knows she needs to do something with that, be interested, support him in the project that is so important to him, to his career. But she hasn't got the space in her mind to fake an interest. Then the veil comes off and a new fear erupts: if Tom screws up this project they will need to leave Asia. It is an emotion too big to process and the angst rolls up around itself and curls up in her stomach to nest there. She looks up at Tom.

Tom is looking at his phone, but when he sees her stare at it too he stuffs it in his pocket and says. 'I need to go to Vietnam tomorrow. Please, read up on adoption. Talk to Salimah and Nazra. Make sure that they are one hundred percent sure, I don't want to be disappointed. Not again.'

His face now loses all its determination and instead Tom just looks hurt. The Tom that can't talk about his pain crumbles and Anna realises this is hard for him too. He really wanted the baby they lost. Losing this one will be as hard for him as for her. She feels her love for Tom deeper than she has in a long while. The three of them. They will be a family.

But when she wants to say something, to renew their

connection, the moment is gone, and overworked, rational Tom is back. 'So, can I trust you to sort out the practical stuff? There will be house visits and such. Actually, the thing is, you will need to be the main person adopting. I can't. I'm British.'

Anna finally finds her voice deep in her throat. 'What do you mean, you're British?'

'The British are banned from adopting in Singapore. Not sure why, but it says so on the website. You have a Dutch passport, so it is better you are the main applicant.'

'That is so weird. Aren't there close historical ties between the two countries? It makes no sense.'

'These things rarely do. Maybe the ties aren't close enough.' Then, slowly grinning, 'Maybe the ties were rather too close.'

The phone is back in his hands before Anna has had time to mull things over. 'I'll message you the link to the adoption website. Read it!'

It sounds like a command and Anna begins to cry silently. Tom is absorbed in a work email when she hands the baby to Tom. He puts Boy up against his shoulder without pulling his eyes away from the screen, until the baby's calming scent works his magic on him too. Tom smiles over Boy's head, and kisses him gently on his stubble. He sticks the phone in his pocket and cradles the boy to his chest. 'You are right, he is a person, not a pile of paperwork. But still, without the paperwork we can't keep him.'

Anna rubs the wet corners of her eyes and smiles back. 'I know. I'm on it!'

24

One of the things Salimah likes about cleaning is that her hands are occupied but her mind is free. She mops Anna's wooden floor and her thoughts wander off to her grandson, fast asleep in the master bedroom. Ahmad still sleeps there at night. Salimah feels awkward enough taking Ahmad away from Anna in the daytime, even for an hour or so. She seems to have taken him on fully – as if he were her own. She knows they need to talk about this; she and Nazra, she and Anna. But how can she talk to Anna and Tom about the baby without settling things with Nazra first? The girl is rarely here, and when she is, she sleeps or shuns her mother. She looks nervous, haggard.

It seems Tom and Nazra have worked out some kind of arrangement that Anna and he will help out, and that he is fine with that. It surprises Salimah, Tom doesn't seem the type; it is Anna who does impulsive things like that.

Father keeps urging her to bring the baby over so he can spend time with him. Pak Long even suggested to take the boy to the masjid for prayers. Isn't he too small for that? And how could she explain the baby there anyway?

Shoving the sofa aside to mop under it, Salimah continues to reflect. Nazra is too young to make these kinds of decisions anyway. What was she herself doing at that age? Focused on her studies, mostly. The first years at her new secondary school were hard, there was always the dilemma of being different. The only way to compete with the brainy Chinese girls was to be smarter than them. Getting the same grades was not enough. Gone were the taunts, the gossip, the chilling looks in corridors that tainted the last months of an otherwise happy time at primary school. Because nobody at that exclusive secondary school even knew what a Boyanese was, to them a Malay was a Malay. And those girls were too well-bred to say these things to her face. Their style was to simply ignore.

Salimah sighs and tries to conjure up cheerful thoughts. Kampong games. Playing masak masak by cooking up logs and leaves, five stones with her agile-handed friends, climbing trees, catching dragonflies by the stream. Life was carefree, fun, easy; everyone was different but it did not matter, not yet. Why did that change all of a sudden? What is the significance of a silly playhouse in a tree? She doesn't want to stir things up, but how can she decide on the future without understanding the past?

She mops and broods, messy thoughts, until she forces herself to stop. What nonsense, to think that the events of so long ago have anything to do with this baby boy. She pulls her mind back from the past, and towards the future. If Nazra can't be relied on, Salimah needs to come to a decision without her. A small seed inside her starts to germinate, one planted by her mother all those years ago, hidden in the dark until Anna brought it to light. The thought has been mulling inside her for the last few weeks, concealed by tiredness and stress. Salimah would like to become a teacher. But how can she do that if she has to raise another baby? On her own, without Nazra to rely on.

Salimah puts the mop away. She is hungry. If she cooks a big batch of fried rice now, she can have some for lunch and take the remainder home to dinner for Father and Pak Long. Tom is away, and she is not sure where or what Nazra eats. Anna eats as little as a bird. She is still in bed with the baby and Salimah does not dare disturb her to change the bedsheets or bring her food. Anna is not likely to want fried rice but might want some toast – she should go and ask her. Salimah makes a cup of tea and gently knocks on Anna's door. She is lying in bed, Ahmad in the crook of her arm. He is asleep, she halfway there. Anna looks at Salimah with heavy-lidded eyes. Salimah sets the tea on the nightstand.

'Are you not feeling well?' she asks.

Anna looks up. 'Too tired. I couldn't sleep last night. He kept me awake, he is so hungry all the time. I am not sure I have enough milk for him.'

Confused, Salimah thinks of the two full tubs of formula in the kitchen.

'Do you want me to take him tonight, so you can rest?'

Anna shakes her head. 'No, I like having him here, especially with Tom gone. He pacifies her.'

'Pacifies who?'

'The white woman. He hates the footsteps in the corridor, but he makes the woman that lives in the banyan tree happy.'

Salimah feels her throat constricting. Doubts that have been gnawing at her for the last few months intensify, and with a final grunt, the wall she built around herself all those years ago comes tumbling down. There is no future without a past. The treehouse is back, and she hears the whispers clearly, *they do black magic.*

'Anna, please explain what you are talking about.'

Anna's pale face looks vacant but she does speak. 'I could not get him back to sleep. He is calmer when he is moving, so I went round and round the rooms – it was raining so I stayed inside. He finally fell asleep in my arms, but then, stupidly, I walked into the corridor where the footsteps are and they woke him up again.'

'What footsteps?'

Salimah thinks she knows what Anna means. She can sense them, but distantly.

'They aren't hers. The footsteps come down the corridor opposite, by the spare rooms,' explains Anna. 'They don't have a voice but still they shout. They like to order me about. I don't go there with him but I was so tired I forgot and he started crying straightaway, even before I heard them. So, I took him outside, despite the drizzle. She was there, floating above the pool. Thankfully she smelt sweet today. Frangipani.'

Salimah shudders.

'Sometimes she smells terrible, like rotting flesh. Those times she is angry, I think, looking for someone. If she is like that, sniffing the baby's neck makes the stench go away. She loves the baby. That's what Nazra said too, that she wants the baby.'

When Salimah doesn't respond, Anna continues, much calmer now, 'She is scared of the footsteps. They scared her out of the house, onto the roof.'

Salimah only hears one sentence reverberating in her head. *Nazra said she wants the baby.* Anna keeps talking and Salimah needs to listen so can figure this out.

'Boy fell asleep again and I took him back in and put him in his crib. He slept for several hours after that but I could not, the footsteps left their corridor and went to this ceiling.' She points to the white beams above them. 'They must have taken off their boots, they don't stomp here, just scamper, but they were at it until morning light.'

Salimah brushes Anna's sweaty hair from her warm forehead.

'They are gone now. Look at how soundly the baby is sleeping, why don't you get a little more sleep yourself?'

Anna is so tired she doesn't even argue.

Salimah walks back to the kitchen whilst a feeling of terror engulfs her. *She wants the baby.* A smell of sticky sweetness fills the air around her as she visualises it: floating white rags, long dirty hair, hands like claws. Can Father have been right, a pontianak, here? A chill settles in her bones when she realises what that means; this creature could be seeking revenge. Revenge on the man guilty of her death. Or his offspring.

Salimah's hands tremble when she messages Nazra to meet her at home for a family dinner. To Salimah's relief, she answers straight away – she will come. Salimah will fry chicken, a childhood favourite, to go with the fried rice. And on the way she will stop by a hardware store to buy some metal nails. The biggest she can find.

25

When a screaming Boy wakes Anna up she realises with a shock that it is early afternoon already. Boy is sleeping next to her on the bed, in Tom's spot, wedged in by pillows. Did he sleep all morning without a feed? Then she notices an empty bottle on the bedside table. Tom must have fed him before he left, and let her sleep. She feels disoriented. Was Salimah here in her room earlier or was that just a dream?

Boy's loud screams make it clear how real he is. She changes him, and dresses him in a clean outfit, then walks to the kitchen to prepare a fresh bottle. As the milk heats, she looks in the fridge, but sees nothing she can imagine eating right now.

Her phone pings, and as she looks at the long list of unread messages on her WhatsApp, she realises there is playgroup this afternoon. If she hurries she can still make it. She ought to get out of the house. The WhatsApp group with the mummies in the playgroup has eighty-six new messages. Anna scrolls through them without taking them in, trying to remember who is hosting today. She struggles to put faces to the names in the list. When she looks up the address, she sees it is close to Orchard Road. Maybe she can take Boy shopping after? He grows so fast.

She manoeuvres the baby into a more comfortable position, so he can drink whilst she scrolls her messages. If he drinks fast like this, Anna might be able to squeeze in a quick shower before she leaves.

There is an old message from Tom, still unopened. She clicks on the link he shared and stares at the website of the MSF, the Ministry for Social and Family Development. The tone is business-like, as if adopting a child is simply a matter of signatures and briefings. Anna can't bring herself to read it, and opens her Facebook page instead. She is on it several times a day, mostly on the Expat Wives page, but hasn't posted in weeks. When Boy is done drinking, she burps him, then takes a selfie with his round, milk filled cheeks next to hers, and posts it before she can change her mind. *Loving the new 'do, with my cool Boy.* She puts the phone on the side table. First, she needs that shower.

At playgroup Anna feels in her element. The other women are used to her and Boy and there is no more awkwardness. Anna says little today, but soaks up everything the others say. Only occasionally does she ask a question, seek some advice. Like where to buy Boy clothes that can withstand both Singapore heat and the icy battering aircon that confronts them on the inside of any building. Layering, they all agree, light cotton fabrics.

So now Anna finds herself in Takashimaya fingering Petit Bateau rompers that remind her of the ones she wore when she was little – but surely her mother never paid these extortionate prices? She hesitates – should she go down the road to H&M instead? A loud wail rises up from the stroller. With a shock Anna realises she only brought one bottle of formula – and she gave him that already at playgroup. Anna wiggles the pram trying to soothe Boy, then gives in and picks him up. It has only been an hour since his last feed. Is he having one of these growth spurts where babies need extra feeds? Anna goes round and round the baby department, trying to rock Boy back to sleep. She feels the judging looks from other shoppers. It will take her at least half an hour to get home. Even if she bought some formula in the basement supermarket, how could she clean and sanitise the dirty bottle in her bag?

Desperate, Anna squeezes the baby firmer and firmer until she spots a sign on the wall, with an image of a mother with a baby on her lap. A nursing room! She slips into one of the little cubicles that has space for her pram, and sinks into a beige armchair. Her body takes over as her minds shuts off and she lifts her top and Boy latches on. He drinks for a minute only, one side first, then the other, before he falls asleep again. Anna looks at his dark head against her creamy white breast, traces his bare little arm with a finger, wishing some of the perfect brown could rub off on her.

It is cold in the room. Anna falls against the back of the chair and wonders if it would be ok for her to take a nap here.

Anna startles awake. How long has past since she dozed off? She puts her son in the pram, pays for the overpriced rompers and drives home. At home, Salimah waits with a clean bottle and takes Boy from Anna's weary arms.

Anna has another shower, a cold one, then walks to the kitchen where Salimah is washing up and chatting in Malay to Boy, behind her in a bouncer chair.

'Hi,' Anna says shyly and Salimah turns with a smile. 'He is so happy, look at him smiling!'

Anna smiles too. 'He has had some busy days. First your hair cutting ceremony, and then playgroup. He is getting so grown up.'

'I know, it all goes so fast. It is a shame Nazra is missing this important part of his life.'

The comment confuses Anna. But she tries to stay polite. 'How is Nazra? I haven't seen her much lately?'

Salimah turns around and hands Boy the plastic toy he threw on the floor.

'I don't know. I'm worried about her. Has she said anything to you?'

Anna blushes. She has been avoiding Nazra. 'No, Tom is the one who has been talking to her, arranging things, didn't she tell you?'

'She talks to him, not me,' Salimah huffs.

'Tom is good at that sort of thing. I suppose we are all too emotional. Especially Nazra and me, too hormonal.'

Anna laughs shrilly and Salimah smiles, but only with her mouth. She looks nervous, Anna thinks, not herself at all.

Anna searches for the right words to assuage Salimah. 'Tom and Nazra have worked it all out. He says this is what Nazra wants.' She pauses. 'But it will be me doing it. I'm a little tired right now, but I will sort it all out, I promise.'

Salimah picks up a tea towel and starts drying the plates she just rinsed. Her back faces Anna and it takes a while for her to respond. 'Of course, you do all the hard work. Thank you for being there for Nazra.'

'No problem,' Anna says. 'She needs all the support she can get. What she is doing is the hardest thing.'

The last thing Anna wants to think about is what Nazra is going through right now, but she can hardly admit this to Salimah.

Salimah puts down the tea towel. 'You need to rest. Why don't I take the baby home with me for dinner. My father wants to see him again.'

Anna hesitates. She could use the break. Tom has a dinner with clients, he won't be home until late tonight, he told her not to wait up. They will surely be back before him. How can she say no, when they are Boy's family too, and Salimah looks at her so desperately. 'Sure.'

Anna wants to say more, wants to ask Salimah whether she thinks Nazra is doing the right thing. 'You have a brave daughter,' she says instead.

26

After she marinates the drumsticks in turmeric, pepper and some egg, Salimah rolls them in cornstarch. The hot oil in the wok sizzles and the sound is comforting. When she tosses in the chicken, the oil crackles and the smell draws Nazra to the kitchen, the baby in her arms. 'Keep him away,' Salimah warns, 'the hot fat spatters.'

Nazra turns her back to Salimah and the oil, and starts to hum to Ahmad softly. *Mana kucing, mana kucing*. The song melts Salimah's worries away, she hasn't heard it in such a long time. But when Salimah starts to sing along, *di dapur, di dapur*? Nazra breaks off. Salimah is still singing, *curi makan ikan* when Ahmad lets out a wail and Nazra quickly picks up again at the *miao*. Salimah sighs. Even when things seem sort of okay, everything has to be difficult. Well, now is as good a time as ever. 'Sayang, have you thought about what are we going to do? With him.'

Nazra cradles him until he is silent. 'Why? He seems happy enough.'

'You know what I mean. He spends most of his time with Anna. We can't go on like this.'

When Nazra does not reply, Salimah continues. 'I spoke to Anna. She seems happy to care for him, but we can't impose on her for too long. She said you have spoken to Tom. What did he say?'

She turns around, the slotted metal spoon pointed upward. Nazra stares at the baby with eyes that don't seem to be able to focus on anything.

'Nazra, talk to me. Do you want this baby or not?'

Nazra closes her eyes and Salimah feels like slapping her round the ears with the ladle, but it is hot and Nazra is still holding the baby, her nose against his. She stares at her instead until Nazra whimpers. 'Maybe.'

'Then you need to step up and take care of him!'

Nazra crumbles and tears appear in her eyes. She hands the baby to Salimah and walks out of the kitchen. 'I don't know! Leave me alone!'

Dinner is tense and uncomfortable. Nazra says nothing. Father sits beaming at his grandson. Pak Long tells Nazra off for not breastfeeding Ahmad. 'Qur'an prescribes this, it is what is best for the baby.'

When everyone ignores him he tries something else. 'Isn't it time for you to move back home? You have imposed on these Mat Salleh's long enough. Your place with him is here. I pray for him but he needs to be surrounded by his people. These people, these Christians, how can they take care of his needs?'

Salimah feels increasingly uncomfortable. She blurts out: 'They aren't Christian.'

That does not go down well either. 'What are they? Free thinkers? I insist you bring the boy home.'

For the first time, Nazra speaks up. 'That is not your decision to make. Stay out of it.'

Pak Long looks at Salimah. 'Will you let the girl talk to me like that?'

Salimah turns to Nazra. 'Please mind your manners.'

The girl looks furious. 'Isn't it best for everyone if I give him to them to adopt? It's the best for him.'

'Nazra!' Why did the stupid girl not speak out when they were alone? Angry and frustrated, she adds: 'He is yours, and if you want to make decisions about him, you need to take responsibility first. Be around so we can talk about this.'

Nazra stands up and her hands shake. 'I can't. I tried to be good. But she ... She scared me. And now I know I can never make a good mother.'

It takes a while before Salimah realises who Nazra is talking about. 'I know you are scared, sayang, but can't we fix this together?'

Nazra shakes her head, and before barging out of the house shouts. 'You know nothing!'

Salimah wants to shout after her – *and why is that* – but the girl is gone already.

When Salimah returns to the house that night it is already dark and the sultry smell of frangipani singes the garden air. Anna is lying on the sofa in front of a blaring tv, her face red and moist, sound asleep. Salimah switches off the tv and walks to the back of the house, the baby on her hip. Nazra isn't there. Salimah puts the sleeping baby in the corner of the mattress, and finds a hammer in the storeroom. She walks outside, takes the nails from her pocket and hammers them into the many trunks of the banyan tree.

27

Anna lies in bed, surrounded by darkness. Once again, a pounding sound echoes directly above her, like the scurrying of giant rats. She wonders, can rats really grow that large in this country? She rolls over in bed and notices the sheets are damp and feel icy against her burning skin. She turns over again and groans, why is it so hot in here? Is the air-conditioner even on? Suddenly, a sharp pain shoots through her left breast. As she turns onto her front, the pain intensifies, now striking her stomach like a bolt of lightning. Anna curls up into a foetal position, clutching her belly in agony.

An hour later she wakes up with a shock. The sound above her has abated and there is silence in the room. Too much silence. It takes a few minutes in semi-sleep for a feeling to seep in that things are not as they should be. The silence is scarier than the earlier rumble. There ought to be sound and she suddenly realises why: Boy has not cried all night. Panic takes over. Is he still breathing? Anna gets up but before she can rush over to the crib she tumbles to the floor and bangs her elbow painfully on the side of the bed. She sits up and lets the blood rush back into her legs before she tries again and stealthily, foot by foot, walks to the cot, clutching her heart.

The cot is empty. Anna's belly clenches again and as she lays her hands on it, it feels full of something. Noise fills the room again and it is Anna who is making it. She has only two settings lately: silent or screaming. She runs outside and shrieks into the open air and the bright night. There is a full moon hovering over the garden, bathing the clump of banana trees in silvery light. When the screaming stops, stillness envelopes her and she realises that not only is it quiet – no barking dog, no howling baby – but also the air is fresh and clean. There isn't a whiff of frangipani in the air, let alone a smell of rotting flesh and Anna calms down. She sits on the step of the decking and buries her face in her hands and wet tears roll over her heated cheeks until she sinks back and she barely feels her neck hit the wood.

She wakes up with Salimah standing over her, the moon painting a halo around her face. 'Anna, are you okay?'

Anna bolts upright and immediately remembers. 'The baby!'

Salimah sits down on her haunches next to Anna, and strokes some wet strands of hair from her eyes. 'He is in my room. Don't you remember, we discussed it when I helped you into bed? You are not well, you have a fever. Come inside, I'll give you some more paracetamol.'

He, Anna thinks, wasn't the baby a girl?

Salimah forces Anna into the shower whilst she changes the bed sheets and lays out fresh pyjamas. After swallowing the two white pills Salimah puts into her hand, Anna falls into a dreamless sleep.

Tom comes home to an Anna curled up into a ball around the pain. 'Anna, can you hear me, what is wrong?'

When Anna just groans he grabs her by the arm and pulls her to her feet. Her fresh pyjamas are now damp and cling to her legs, revealing red stains around her crotch. 'How long have you been like this? Come on, we need to get you to a hospital.'

It is the middle of the night, and in A&E they put Anna to bed with IV antibiotics and fluids. In the morning, she is seen by the gynaecologist who sticks a speculum up her to assess her empty insides, which turn out to not be empty after all. 'Look,' he points with a gloved finger at the monitor. 'It is about the size of a dollar coin. I am surprised you did not get sick earlier, how long has it been since your miscarriage, months?'

Anna says nothing but nods and the doctor continues. 'And you have experienced more bleeding recently?'

Tom talks to the doctor, holding Anna's hand, and the words fly over her.

'Sometimes after a delivery, some debris gets left behind. This looks like some properly attached placenta, with blood flow to it. Eventually it gets expelled, usually. But this has become infected. Normally I'd treat it with antibiotics and perhaps wait a little until it sorts itself out. This one appears obstinate. We'll have to organise a scrape.'

'A scrape?'

'It's a surgical procedure where we ... well, we don't actually scrape, it's more like a vacuum cleaner. We clean out the uterus.'

Instinctively Anna's hands go to her stomach to protect it. 'You can't do that! You can't just suck up my child!'

The doctor and Tom exchange looks.

Tom is the one that speaks first.

'That is not a child, darling, it's just a lump of leftover cells. Infected cells that are making you sick. They need to come out to make you better.'

Anna hugs her hands over her belly and the doctor addresses Tom as if she isn't even there. 'We'll do some blood tests too, see what her hormone levels are. Check with reception to book yourself in, we need to do this as soon as possible. But first we'll wait until the antibiotics calm things down in there.'

After the procedure Anna feels empty. Not only her body but also her brain feels scraped clean. She had to go under a full anaesthetic and when the liquid crept up cold into her arm she wondered for a moment whether she would ever wake up again. The thought of not waking up brought nothing but peace. But here she is again, groggy and hollow. They asked her to stay overnight and it wasn't until the middle of the night that Anna remembered Boy and instantly felt guilty for not thinking of him earlier, for not asking Tom about him when he was here holding her hand. As if the vacuum cleaner sucked him out of her life too. She feels ashamed for even thinking this. She brings her hands to her breasts and realises they feel cool like they haven't in a long time – less swollen, less red. She massages the nipples until a drop of white pearls around the tip. Anna picks it up on the tip of her finger and brings it to her lips. The sweet taste fills her hollowness inside.

When Tom arrives in the morning to pick her up, Anna is asleep. She half wakes but keeps her eyes shut when he talks to the obstetrician who just came in clutching an iPad that Anna notices through slits in her eyes. Why does the doctor talk to Tom, not her? And why does she not mind?

'We should do another blood test before she goes home, her hormones were extremely elevated, which explains her …' The doctor pauses a second and looks straight at Tom. 'Her mental state.'

In a louder voice he continues: 'Things should settle quickly now. And the antibiotics should take care of the rest, she'll be back to normal in no time.'

Anna opens her eyes and stares the doctor right in the face. She doesn't even know what normal is any more.

A few days later Anna is out of bed and feels good physically. Well, not good, but not bad either. Which in British English means really good, something that took some time to wrap her head around. Anna means *not bad* in the Dutch way: she does not feel terrible anymore. She sits on the sofa, hesitating whether to open her laptop. Worried what she will find when she opens her social media. Wondering whether she should check the job searching sites.

The laptop balances on her empty belly. Now she really isn't pregnant anymore. But somehow, in the last few months, she seems to have become a mother.

Anna had felt confused when Tom brought Boy's crib back to their bedroom. Anna's memories of the past weeks are hazy – what exactly has been agreed? Ashamed of her ignorance, she doesn't dare ask. She picks up the baby and walks around the room with him on her arm. It feels right holding him, as if her body knows what her brain does not.

Looking out of the window they observe the large palm tree outside. 'Look, see the birdies?' The top of the palm is at the same height as the window, with huge green fronds spread in a circle, in the middle of which large orange seeds grow, on which a couple of doves are feasting. A squirrel jumps from the roof to one of the leaves, which sways under the animal's weight as it runs up to the centre, grabs a seed and crawls back. Anna points the squirrel out to Boy and wonders if he can see it yet. She turns him around to face her, coos and smiles – and fills with happiness when he smiles back a toothless smile. Being his mother is not bad. Not bad at all.

At breakfast, after a night of little sleep, but only because Boy keeps waking up, she asks Tom about the adoption process and he tells her there has been a delay. Nazra had shown up for the lawyer's appointment and signed what she needed to, but Salimah wasn't with her. Since Nazra is a minor Salimah too has to sign. 'Can you ask her, please. You speak to her more often than I do. We need to get Salimah to sign all the paperwork.'

Anna nods and Tom continues. 'Ideally the father needs to sign too. And his parents if he is a minor. But since Nazra is not giving his name, we need to apply to the Court to skip that step and list the father as unknown. And then we keep our fingers crossed that he does not suddenly show up and make a claim.'

They go through the procedure once more together and Tom gets impatient. 'I have told you this so many times? How can't you remember?'

Anna feels like she is hearing it for the first time, and smiles meekly. But Tom drones on, explaining what they need: the endorsement of the Dutch Embassy, showing they will acknowledge this adoption and give the child a passport; and a Home Study Report to assess their suitability as parents. That last requirement makes Anna even more nervous.

Tom shoves a pile of papers Anna's way. 'So, I can leave this to you? It's straightforward paperwork, the most urgent is to get Salimah to sign the affidavit.'

Anna takes a deep breath. 'Why did Salimah take the baby when I was away?'

Tom blushes. 'I was in the hospital most of the time, what else could I do? She is his biological grandmother, and she does technically work for us, right?'

The words pierce Anna in her still slightly sore stomach. She looks at Tom's flushed cheeks and sees all the things he isn't saying. He was afraid, for her, that day he found her in bed bleeding. He still is. He can't lose her like she can't lose him. And that is what has been happening here in Singapore, they are slowly drifting apart. Anna doesn't want that to happen, especially not now they are going to be a family. She loves Tom. This, his emphasis on the paperwork, this is his way of saying he loves her and Boy and wants to keep both of them safe. She holds out her hand and places it on his, and he rubs it absentmindedly. Anna squeezes Tom's thumb. 'I'm tired, I think I'll go back to bed, lie down.'

Tom nods. 'Me too. I'll join you, let's take advantage of the fact the baby is finally asleep.'

On the bed they roll together and as Anna feels his body against hers, she starts to feel like solid ground is slowly appearing beneath her body again.

Later, when Tom has gone out for a run, Anna realises she hasn't seen Nazra since before she became ill. Does the girl still live at their place? She hopes she is alright, but at the same time, Anna wants her gone. Not only Nazra, but Salimah too. As long as they are here, things will be awkward and when they move out, Anna, Tom and Boy can be a family. Anna needs to find a job, and a proper helper who can do the childcare whilst she works. She will have the normal, productive life she planned to have here. Salimah too should move on, find a job that suits her skill set better. Above all, Anna needs to talk to Salimah. She has no idea how she feels.

She marches to the back of the house where Salimah is

hanging laundry but when Anna sees her, her courage fails her. 'How is Nazra, I haven't seen her in a while?'

Salimah looks up, her face deep with worry. 'Neither have I. I haven't seen her in a week. I have no idea where she is, she hasn't been at school either. She ran away again that night you got ill.'

The fact that the girl is missing unsettles Anna. She can't ask someone who isn't even here to move out. Nor can she bother Salimah with her plans to move on. 'But Tom saw her a few days ago? He said she looked okay.'

Salimah drops the sheet she is holding back into the basket and exclaims, 'Tom saw Nazra? Where? How?'

Anna stutters. 'At the lawyer. He mentioned you weren't there.'

'Me? No, I wasn't. What lawyer? Why?'

Anna stutters more. 'To sign the affidavit. He said he had expected you to be there too.'

Salimah's eyes become as big as saucers. 'He did not tell me, I know nothing. Why would I need to sign an affidavit?'

Anna straightens and says firmly. 'For the adoption. To give permission, since Nazra is a minor.'

Salimah mutters something Anna can't understand, then picks up the basket of wet laundry at her feet. She walks down to the laundry area, plops down the basket, wet sheets unhung, and turns to Anna. 'I'm not signing anything.'

Anna's jaw drops. Is it possible that she and Salimah never discussed this before, not once during those cloudy months? But Tom has, hasn't he? Or Nazra? Surely Salimah has agreed?

As she walks away, Salimah screams at Anna. 'Stop trying to take over my life! You give me a job, take in my daughter, make us all dependent on you. And now you think you can be a better mother to my grandson too? Well, the girl is gone, so neither of us has her. And as for that job: I don't need it. I quit!'

28

Salimah walks to the bus, fast, and pulls her tudung tighter around her head. She is furious with Anna, but even more so with Nazra. How can she have signed those papers without telling her, her own mother? She wants to shout at Nazra like she did to Anna but she can't as she has no idea where the girl is. Whatever Nazra has decided, or thinks she has decided, Salimah needs to know.

Where can she be? A shiver runs down her spine when she thinks about the pontianak. Slamming those nails into the tree trunk should have exorcised it, right? Was she too late?

When the school calls to ask her why her daughter has not been coming in, the receptionist's voice is curt and shrill, as she says, slowly, condescendingly, that she knows things have been difficult lately. The school knows Nazra has been in the hospital, but she isn't sure the counsellor has formally reported the pregnancy. It all happened so fast. 'We do need a MC,' the receptionist says, and Salimah can hear the judgement in her voice. It takes a few seconds for Salimah to realise that her nodding cannot not be heard on the other end.

'Yes,' she says, 'I'll get the certificate.'

Salimah feels nauseous. How can she get a medical certificate with no daughter to show to a doctor?

Salimah has no idea where to even search anymore. For days she has been wandering around foodcourts, kopitiams, even bars that teenagers might frequent. She calls Jerina, the only schoolmate of Nazra's she has a phone number for. Nazra is no longer her friend, the girl says. 'She hangs out with another group, not from school.'

Jerina sounds disinterested and aloof. Friends from Nazra's previous school, haven't heard from Nazra either. Salimah feels she's running out of options. Should she call the police? Something deep down keeps stopping her whenever she picks up the phone. A Malay teenager goes missing, why would they even care?

Nazra has stayed away overnight before but she's never stopped going to school. Helplessness and panic grow and Salimah knows that besides Nazra she has Ahmad to worry about. The boy whose eyes look so much like those of his namesake, his great-grandfather. It is only a matter of time before Anna will call her and talk about the signing of papers again and Salimah needs to talk to someone about what to do. Someone who is not Anna. She can't think about Anna now. She needs to find Nazra. Ahmad, for now, is safe.

Singapore may be small, but it is still too big to locate one girl in, not by herself, and Salimah doesn't know whom to turn to for help. She has not kept in touch with colleagues from work – with their common link broken, contacting them feels strange. She has not spoken to her other friends, Aziza, Rhynna and Lee Ing for a while either. Why did her mother and her husband have to die and leave her like this? Why has she no brothers and sisters, and only a handful of cousins she hasn't seen in years? There is just Father and Pak Long, wiry old men who will outlast everyone, possibly even her. If only Father was still his reliable self. He loves Nazra like Salimah does. For herself.

When she gets home, Pak Long isn't there and Father seems to be having a good day – he is sitting in the living room reading a newspaper. He looks at her with clear eyes when Salimah, very carefully, repeats what Anna told her: that Nazra signed an affidavit to give Ahmad up for adoption to Anna and Tom. And that Salimah needs to decide whether she will do the same. She stops there, not mentioning that she walked out and quit her job. Not mentioning either that Nazra has gone missing. She isn't sure what that disappearance means for her decision.

Father just nods.

Tears well up in Salimah's eyes. How come this does not upset him? Has Nazra confided in her grandfather? Father starts babbling, but not about the baby … about the house. The last time the house was mentioned he had a fit as if Satan himself lived there, but now, when he talks, he makes it sound like paradise. He mentions Rafi, the gardener next door, and his Indian banana trees. 'Bad quality, those ones, so I planted decent Malay ones. Good for goreng pisang.'

The gardener in him is back as he describes how you have to cut the baby shoots loose from the mother plant to propagate them. Salimah stares at him and the shiver returns. How does this all tie together? What does he know? She has a lot of questions but asks none of them as that would make answers unavoidable. Father drones on. 'If you want the pokok pisang to grow more babies, don't treat it well. It makes more babies when distressed.'

Salimah becomes increasingly frustrated. She doesn't want to talk about banana trees. She needs a serious conversation about her daughter and grandson. But Father looks happier than he has in a long time, and Salimah listens on.

It was his garden, he says, different from all the parks he

worked in later, where bosses told him what to do. 'Those ang moh trusted me, so I could plant and trim and they knew it would be good.' Father would have a fit if he saw the current state of the garden. Gardeners come in weekly, a team of Bangladeshis, often different people each time. They cut the grass, blow the leaves, cut back branches with blunt knives. When Salimah asks them to plant something they shrug. They don't speak much English. 'Call boss,' they say.

On days that Anna is out, or cooped up in bed, they finish even faster and leave dead flowers and leaves attached. Yet Anna seems to enjoy the garden jungly like this. Salimah nods encouragingly to Father, glad to see his smile again. Then he says: 'The boy would be happy in a garden like that.'

Just in time to overhear that last sentence, Pak Long comes in. 'What do you mean?'

Salimah jumps. She doesn't want Pak Long involved, not before she makes up her own mind. But it is too late, he won't let go now. Carefully, she explains that Nazra is considering giving up Ahmad for adoption, to Anna and Tom. She doesn't mention affidavits and lawyers, not yet.

Pak Long purses his thin lips. 'She cannot do that.'

'Well, she can. It is her child, but since she is a minor I need to give my approval too. I would need to sign an affidavit stating I agree.'

'You will not sign that!' Pak Long exclaims.

Salimah said the exact same thing to Anna but coming from Pak Long it makes her angry.

'We need to consider it. Nazra is still young; she has school, exams, university. Should she give up her life?'

Pak Long shakes his head. 'She has you. You can look after

the child.'

'I need to work, someone needs to make money to feed all of us.'

'You think only of yourself. How can you give away your grandson to heathens?'

'I think only of myself? I spend my days cooking, cleaning and caring for others!' Including him, in fact. The words pierce Salimah's core and nestle there.

Pak Long continues: 'You need to accept who you are. You are a Malay and so is he. This is not what we do. Do you not remember the Dutch girl?'

Salimah is confused. 'Anna? What do you mean?'

'No, not her, the one that caused the riots when the courts took her away from her Malay mother.'

What on earth does she have to do with anything, Salimah thinks. 'You mean Maria Hertogh? But, Pak, that was 1950. This is the twenty-first century. Things are different now.'

'Are they?' Pak Long asks.

'Yes, they are. We have a choice now. If Ahmad goes to them it is because we decide so. They cannot take him from us. The courts would not allow that. It is our country now.'

Pak Long's eyes become dark slits under a frown.

'You have a duty,' Pak Long states, 'to your religion. He needs to be with a Muslim family.'

The words hit Salimah in her sore spot. How can she argue with Pak Long about religion? No one speaks for a while until Father does. 'If the boy lives at the big house, I will build him a treehouse. A better one. A safe one.'

Pak Long looks at him in horror but Salimah says, 'Sure, it will be nice, and we can visit him there together.'

'No, no, tak boleh,' Father says. 'Cannot visit. It is their garden.'

'Of course I can.'

She said the words unthinking, then clasps her hands in front of her mouth. She quit her job. She can't go there. Not anymore, not after what she said. Thinking of Anna hurts. Betrayed, that is how she feels. She looks up to see both men shake their heads. Father speaks. 'Once the boy is theirs he will no longer be ours.'

Salimah lets that truth sink in as Pak Long draws a deep breath. 'I will ask around at the mosque, I am sure there are people willing to adopt a healthy boy like him.' He looks at Salimah with disapproval. 'If you can't take him.'

Salimah wants to respond but can't think of anything. Ahmad is happy with Anna and Tom, she has seen him nestled in her arms, seen her burp him on her shoulder and rock him to sleep. She has seen how Tom looks at the baby, and how he bestowed his first ever smile on him. She pictures the expensive items they've bought for him. There is also Nazra's apparent decision to give the boy to Anna and Tom, should she not respect that?

Drained, Salimah walks into her bedroom and shuts the door. She needs to be alone, to think. How can she make any decision when the girl has disappeared? Which she acknowledges is her own fault, being a bad parent. Tak boleh tahan, Salimah despairs. She can't take it anymore.

It is not that she doesn't want to keep the baby, raise it properly, she just can't see how. Even if she gave up the idea of becoming a teacher, she'd still have to take another job – someone has to pay the bills. The boy would start school and need supplies.

School. Thinking of how Nazra might never finish hers, Salimah starts to cry. How come she didn't notice before that things were going so wrong, how unhappy the girl was? How could she not see the danger of letting her stay at that place. The house has taken both her daughter and her grandson from her.

She reclines on her bed and stares at the fan blades turning. Her thoughts fly back to the kampong and to her own mother whose advice she so badly needs. How had Mak done it, work whilst raising a child? When she went out to clean she simply left Salimah with Aunty next door. Or with Pak Long in the pondok, a community where women she barely knew cooked her food and she played with a muddle of kids.

Here, there is old Mrs Ng next door, whose house is much too clean and who can't stand noise. The people one door down she barely knows. Should she get a maid? An Indonesian, one that can cook halal. She could help with Father too if that becomes too much for Pak Long. In her mind Salimah wanders around her apartment, that she once took pride in being so large with its three bedrooms. Pak Long, Father, herself, Nazra and the baby. The maid would have to sleep on the kitchen floor, it's impossible, even if she could afford it. Salimah sighs deeply.

A figure in white, slowly streaking with red, appears in her mind. It disappears when Pak Long's voice echoes in her brain 'You have a duty.'

Salimah slides off the bed and does the only thing she can think of: she prays.

29

Tom becomes increasingly impatient and grumpy. 'Just get the woman to sign. Yes, the girl is not here but we don't need her, she has signed already. It's the mother who needs to sign. Has she changed her mind?'

'Grandmother,' Anna points out. She looks sideways to the playpen where Boy is sleeping. She doesn't know what to say to Tom, she feels like she has woken up from a dream with a brain that has suddenly been switched on again, with some very strange things happening during its shutdown. How come Salimah knew nothing about this adoption? A blush creeps across Anna's cheeks, not just her face but all the way to her toes, when she thinks of what Salimah slung at her. All she wanted was to get to know her, be her friend. To help. Was that such a bad thing? She hasn't spoken to Salimah since and isn't sure how to explain that to Tom. He doesn't know that she's quit. She has been working hard to keep on top of laundry and the house presentable.

She looks at Tom standing over the baby, a soft look in his eyes. Why does he want this adoption? He seems to genuinely care about the baby, plays with him when he is home, does night feeds and nappy changes. Has he forgotten their own child, already, that little alien girl?

Everything she says to Tom these days seems to fall badly, and not like she intends it to. She has tried to point out to Tom that Salimah has more things on her mind than the affidavit – that Nazra is missing. But she isn't sure how to phrase that diplomatically. And Tom too has other things on his mind.

Tom turns his gaze from the baby. 'I am so fed up with this. What is wrong with Asia? Why can't people don't just do what they say? Make agreements, follow them up. Say what you really feel, not yes to your face and something different behind your back. I'd like to once work with someone I feel I can trust to stick to their side of the deal.'

Salimah never said yes, Anna thinks, but she is pretty sure Tom is no longer talking about her.

'Let's hope that when I speak to the Vietnamese again, we can finally get this joint venture to work. I'll probably be back next week having found they already settled with the Chinese.'

He points at the adoption paperwork sitting on top of the new antique Chinese sideboard. 'Do you think you could have it signed when I get back?'

He hurriedly kisses her on the lips as he looks at his bleeping phone. 'Taxi is here. Call me if you are not ok, please? I'll be straight back. I mean it!'

Anna is sure he means it, but also that she won't make that call. She has been feeling so much better these last few weeks. Earlier today she walked into that corridor, needing to know, staring at the hairs on her arms, waiting for them to stand up. Which they did eventually, but by then she wasn't sure what made them. Having read her grandmother's diary, finding out the history of the house, how Japanese soldiers imprisoned people here, has made her realise who those footsteps belonged to. And now she knows, they are less scary. They belong in the past. Only their echoes remain.

It is the white woman she can't stop thinking about. She can only see her now when she closes her eyes but her long hair, a yellow so pale it is almost white, her claw-like hands, and her bloodshot eyes, are etched on Anna's retina forever. Did she piece her together from some crappy eighties horror movie?

Anna has been back to yoga, and to baby group with Boy. She has even been looking at employment websites. On the outside, it looks like her life is shaping up. But she still feels like she is trapped inside a glass jar. She can see through, and people can see her, but everything is muted, as if she is missing half her senses. She takes the adoption papers from the sideboard and stuffs them inside, sliding her finger over the rough wood. The front of the sideboard is painted in little figures, a mountain, bright red flowers. 'Chinese antique, very old,' the salesman had insisted.

'Definitely fake,' Tom laughed.

When Anna turned red and became defensive, he had hugged her. 'But beautiful, I'm glad you are taking an interest in the house again.'

Anna has also bought a pretty wooden crib for Boy, the one she has been eying since she first found out she was pregnant and didn't want to buy then, so as not to jinx things. Things got jinxed anyhow. She still hesitated, but Tom said they should get it, to celebrate Boy.

Anna doesn't know what to say to Salimah. For what Salimah accused her off, apologies aren't enough. She picks up the phone, but when she brings Salimah's name up on the screen, she can't make the call. She wants to shout at herself, but at Salimah too. Shout really loud. Why didn't Salimah speak out earlier? Or, Anna worries, did she? She can't trust her memory anymore.

She looks at Boy and knows she needs to make things right,

for him. She also knows Salimah won't make any decision before speaking to Nazra. She has sent the girl dozens of text messages, but there is no reply. She even tried calling the police but they said that since the girl is sixteen, and left by her own free will, it isn't a priority to find her. Anna hung up before they started asking questions she couldn't answer.

Anna cooks, cleans the house, does the laundry. Every day her brain becomes more clear, and her love for Boy grows as she bathes him and feeds him, even when he sprays her with a beam of urine, right in her face. She is becoming his mother. Salimah hasn't called, hasn't once come to see him, which makes Anna hope she will sign. That she just needs time.

When Anna has a doctor's appointment, she leaves Boy with Marivic from next door. The doctor tells Anna her hormones are back in check. Only when he mentions nothing is stopping her getting pregnant again, Anna quivers. Back home, she looks in on Boy, sound asleep in his new cot. Next week she will interview one of Marivic's friends who is looking for a new employer; getting a fulltime helper makes sense now.

When Anna speaks to Tom on the phone he sounds distant, and not only because he is in Vietnam. She tells him about the doctor's visit and asks about his work.

Tom goes silent. 'I don't know Anna, sometimes I think it was a mistake coming to Asia. We don't belong here.'

The conversation soon dries up.

After the phone call Anna sits down on her bed and stares at Oma's painting. The two volcanoes convey strength and resilience, which she needs right now. She lies down, feeling drowsy and defeated. *We don't belong here* echoes though her glass jar, resonating off the slippery walls that offer no escape. Anna never really felt as if she belonged in the Netherlands. England was easier, as a foreigner, belonging wasn't expected, and marrying Tom gave her an excuse to stay. But would she ever be allowed to belong in Asia? And if not, could Boy ever belong with them?

Anna picks up Oma's photo album from her nightstand. The plantation, waterfall, the whitewashed house ... she stops when she sees the photo of Oma on the lap of her babu. Pulling out her phone Anna scrolls until she finds what she is looking for. Boy on her lap. Colours reversed. What does it mean?

She knows Tom is having a hard time at work, that his frustration is real. Things work differently here and he can't help the way he is – impatient. His all-boys school in the north of England is ten thousand miles from these heated shores where relationships count more than logic, where you need to invest time to build those. She thought she would be better at it, but seeing how she screwed up her relationship with Salimah, Anna worries Tom is right. Was it a mistake to come here?

Early the next morning, Anna spreads out the photos and the camp diary on her bed, then takes the painting off the wall. There is another reason she hasn't called Salimah. The white shape flashes through her head and she hears the footsteps echo in the distance. She isn't ready and she knows the answers lie here in Asia, but not in Singapore. Her body starts to tingle all over with excitement and she messages Tom. 'We both need a break! I'm planning a holiday to Sumatra. When can you take time off?'

Tom doesn't reply, it seems he hasn't even read the message.

Anna drops an email to her father, who is still asleep, telling him about her plans. She really needs to know the location of the family plantation. Anna also messages Bea. 'Do you want to drop by for a coffee? I need your Sumatra tips!'

Unlike Tom, Bea responds straight away. 'I have to be in your neighbourhood later, I'll drop by.'

When Bea arrives, Anna shows her all the papers on the bed, as well as the painting. It feels good breaking the silence of all those years. *People from the Dutch East Indies don't talk,* her father always said. *It happened before my time, I know nothing.* Which isn't true, Anna found out when she was older; he did spent the first eight years of his life in Indië, or Indonesia as it would be already have been called then.

As she shows Bea the old photographs, the footsteps retreat from of her mind and the room around her steadies. The footsteps go back into their own corridor where they will stay. And then something becomes suddenly clear: it is no longer the war that interests her, or how horrible those camps were. The war was merely a catalyst, pushing the inevitable ahead. What happened after, and what is happening now is what she needs to understand. *Asia for the Asians,* the Japanese had said, and she used to think that made more sense than colonisation, but then the Japanese proved to be more brutal than the Dutch ever were.

'What I need now is to wrap up my own story. I want to visit Sumatra, see it for myself. My family lived there for generations. Close to Medan and Lake Toba, but I'm not sure exactly where.'

Bea points to the painting. 'Those look like the mountains in Berastagi. It's just north of Lake Toba, you can easily combine them both in one trip.'

Anna's heart jumps. 'Oma stayed in a camp in Berastagi

during the war!'

She briefly sketches Oma's story, her years in the camp, and how they stayed on after the war until the Indonesian government nationalised all companies and kicked the remaining Dutch out. Bea nods, she is surprisingly knowledgeable herself. Still, Anna is relieved when they move back into lighter, standard expat-wife territory. Bea has exactly the kind of information she needs: a good itinerary taking in enough tourist sites to convince Tom. He loves climbing mountains. Slowly her Sumatra jigsaw is coming together. Medan, Lake Toba, Berastagi. The only thing Anna still needs is the exact location of the plantation. If it even still exists. Anna checks her phone, but neither Tom nor her father have responded.

Bea traces the trip she made on a map of Sumatra on the screen. 'Berastagi is lovely, very cool, as it is high up in the mountains. There are still some old Dutch bungalows there, it used to be a popular mountain retreat for colonials in Medan. And still is a popular destination for town-dwelling Indonesians, it gets really crowded on the weekends. You can hike up mount Sibayak, if you go up early morning you can watch the sunset from the top, it's an amazing view across the highlands. And you have the best view of the other volcano, mount Sinabung.' Bea points at the painting, at the perfect cone.

Bea looks pensive. 'I don't think you can actually see the two mountains together like they are in your picture.'

Anna nods, and jots it all down as Bea continues. 'So, then there's Lake Toba. I know a lovely little garden resort on Samosir Island. You must stay there to explore the island. It has a great vibe, it's like Bali, but unspoilt mostly.'

Anna smiles. Bea's down-to earth attitude relaxes her.

Bea now points from the lake to the east coast. 'This area is hideous, don't go there. It's desolate, just endless palm oil plantations.'

Anna nods absentmindedly.

Bea continues. 'So you have no clue where your grandmother lived? What did they do, were they planters?'

'Yes,' says Anna, 'they had a plantation. Rubber, I assume.'

'That reminds me,' says Bea, 'the Karo highlands near Berastagi are lovely too. It's like a huge vegetable garden, all smallholder farms. Such a different landscape from the monotonous palm oil plantations elsewhere.'

Anna makes more notes, then puts her pencil down. 'You have been here how long now, more than ten years?'

'Fifteen,' Bea confirms.

'Do you feel this is your country now?'

Bea laughs. 'Yes, this is home for me. Yet when people ask me where I am from and I say Singapore, I get strange looks. They ask where I am really from. But Singaporeans, they ask, ah, are you PR?'

What's that?' Anna wonders.

'A permanent resident. It's a long term visa, not tied to a job like an EP, you know, an employment pass. When I say I am not PR, they look doubtful. We never applied for it. The thing is, if we do, my son would have to do military service. It is my choice to live here, not his. I don't think its morally right to serve in an army of a country where you don't have citizenship. So we are still on an EP. If my husband loses his job or dies, we have a few weeks to leave the country.'

'Weeks!' Anna exclaims.

'Yes, didn't you know? Did you think we were better off than those construction workers and helpers? We are still foreigners.'

'But if you did get approved for PR, would they accept you as a Singaporean?'

Is a 'chop', a stamp, a piece of paper all that is needed to belong?

Bea shrugs. 'I suppose it shows you are committed, ready to contribute. And to give up your son if need be.'

With a shock Anna realises she too has a son now. A Singaporean son.

When Tom finally calls it is evening already. Bea has left, Boy is asleep and Anna listlessly trawls though Netflix. The excitement of the afternoon is muted by her annoyance with Tom's delayed response. He isn't excited at all. 'Why can't we just go to Bali?'

When Anna explains she wants to explore her family's history, that parenting Boy has made her question her roots, Tom sighs. 'It will be very remote, does it makes sense dragging a baby there? And anyway, as long as we don't have the adoption settled, we can't take Boy out of the country. He doesn't have a passport and he isn't legally ours.'

As the truth of that last comment sinks in, Anna realises she has to let go of her trip – for now. They talk about inconsequential things, but Anna is too sleepy and bids Tom goodnight.

When she lies in bed, Anna considers her options. She can't give up now she is so close. Can she ask Salimah to take Boy? Or Marivic? Neither are really viable options and Anna's focus drifts to the now familiar bouncing and scratching above her. Tom has heard it too, so she knows she's not crazy, not anymore. Rats, he says. Surely it is too loud for that? She tosses and turns, restlessly, annoyed she can't take full advantage of Boy's sleeptime; he'll be up for a night feed soon.

Anna turns on the light and looks for her book on the nightstand, hoping to read herself to sleep. There is nothing there but Oma's photo album. Anna flips the pages and stops again at the photo of big pink baby Oma on the lap of her babu. Her light grey complexion a stark contrast to the dark skin of the woman. She slams it shut, turns off the light, and as she slowly drops off, the footsteps come back, *Asia for the Asians* they pound, whilst the thing above her scratches *you don't belong here*.

30

Salimah's gloved hands are plunged down her toilet, scrubbing as if her life depends on it. She is desperate to scour away the contents of the letter that blackens her handbag. The letter that has caused Salimah's whole world to collapse. The envelope, which arrived with yesterday's mail, looked like any other government missive so Salimah had simply tossed it into a heap of mail in the kitchen, too tired and frustrated to deal with it, and had gone to bed early. But this morning, as she opened the letter and read the first few lines, the hard truth slammed into her like a freight train. Nazra.

Emotions surface one by one. A sliver of relief, for at least she knows where the girl is now. That she is alive. Then anger wins over, anger with the government especially. How is it possible she did not hear this earlier, that nobody called her? Nazra is in prison, in remand, awaiting trial as she is charged with possession and consumption of illegal substances.

Prison. The word echoes in her mind as Salimah violently scrubs the toilet. There is a number on the letter that she can call for information, and to make an appointment for a visit. Salimah hasn't called, hasn't told Father or Pak Long; she just shoved the letter back into the envelope, hid it in her bag and took out her yellow gloves. Cleaning clears her head. She sinks onto the toilet seat as she feels any grip she still has on her life slipping away. She removes her gloves and buries her face in her hands and sits there for what feels like hours. Then she gets up, puts on her tudung, grabs her bag off the chair and walks to the bus.

When Salimah walks into the house, the front door open as usual, Anna is sitting on the sofa, reading a book. 'I know where Nazra is.'

Anna jumps up and wraps her arms around a crying Salimah. For a moment she indulges in the warmth of the embrace, then breaks away and looks Anna in the eyes. 'She is in prison.'

Anna looks back with wide, shocked eyes, and pulls Salimah down onto the sofa. She sits down across from her, as if uncertain about getting too close. 'What happened? Do you want to talk about it?' Anna says hesitantly.

Salimah feels a strong urge to confide in Anna, something she hasn't done in months, and everything gushes out. 'She has been in remand for two weeks already. That is why her phone was turned off, I suppose. She is charged with consumption and possession of drugs.'

'Only possession, that's not that bad, right? It is not as if she was caught selling the stuff.'

Salimah shakes her head. 'This is Singapore, even possession is an offence.'

It takes Anna a minute to collect herself. 'So what happens next?'

'I'm not sure, I just saw the letter this morning. There is a number to call, and I can arrange a visit, it says. I have no idea how this works.'

'She must have been influenced by some bad friends, she might even be innocent. You need to go see her.'

'Well, if they found the stuff on her, it would be hard to prove innocence.' Salimah wails. 'I should have kept a better eye on her, I suspected she was hanging out with the wrong friends, but I had no idea it was that bad. What kind of mother am I?'

'I'm to blame too, I suspected it from the look in her eyes. I should have told you.'

Another cry rises up, from Anna's bedroom this time, and Anna gets up.

Salimah calls after her, 'So one of those, those drug guys, I suppose is his father?'

And that is why Nazra refused to name him?

When Anna comes back in holding the baby, she says. 'I think so, yes. She did say he was a bad guy. Fun to hang out with, but not one to marry.'

Salimah looks at Anna feeding Ahmad a bottle, it seems so natural, and she sighs. Isn't this the best for everyone? 'Anna,' Salimah says softly. 'I want to sign the affidavit.'

Anna does not respond as Salimah expected her to. She mumbles something about a trip to Medan, about how she needs Salimah's help, but that she can't impose on her right now, of course. Salimah gets annoyed with Anna all over again. Her daughter is in prison, she offers this woman her grandson, and she talks about a holiday? 'Medan, what do you mean?'

'I want to find my family roots, the old plantation.'

Salimah nods, puzzled why it has to be mentioned right now. Anna moves the baby around on her lap, so he can drink more comfortably. 'But let's not talk about me. You are in shock. Why don't you go home, think things over?'

Going home and facing those two old men is the last thing Salimah wants to do. 'No, I won't. I want to sign those papers first. I can handle only one thing at a time. One lawyer at a time.'

'Do we need to get one? A criminal lawyer, I mean, for her?'

The word criminal hurts when Anna says it, her daughter – a criminal. She shakes her head, she doesn't want Anna's help right now, not with that. She wants her to take the baby so she has one less thing to worry about. She needs to start acting decisively, as she hasn't done for a while. The old Salimah, corporate, efficient, the one who gets things done, needs to come back and fix this.

Anna fumbles with the baby, lets him burp, then hands him to Salimah. Salimah cradles him, expecting Anna to go fetch the papers but to her surprise, Anna sits down again.

'I don't know where the papers are. Tom is away. I don't know where he put them. I'll ask him where they are later.'

Salimah frowns. 'No. You know where they are.'

Anna blushes. 'They are in the Chinese sideboard,' she says softly.

Salimah gets up, hands the baby back to Anna and takes the documents from the dresser. They are crumpled, and Salimah smooths them on her lap, her heart beating loudly when she sees her daughter's handwriting on the dotted lines. She turns back to Anna who sits there sheepishly.

'Are you really sure?' Anna says.

Something inside Salimah breaks. 'What do you mean? You said you wanted this! I am sure, are you?'

When Anna doesn't answer, she almost yells, 'You cannot turn back now! I need you to do this!' She grabs a pen, and immediately signs all the lines that have a little yellow sticky note attached. 'Can you get me the number of the lawyer? I assume he needs to notarise this?' She stares at the form. 'Ah, his number is on here. I'll give him a call.'

From now on, Salimah is going to be in control of her life.

She will give her daughter her full support. So when this is all over they can both go back to school – and Salimah will not let Nazra out of her sight ever again, not even for a minute. She stuffs the papers in her bag, then changes her mind and pulls them out again. She waves them in the air at Anna. 'You know, my uncle says, that if I want to give him up for adoption, he needs to go to a Muslim family. But I can see he is happy with you. I don't want to upset his little life again.'

Anna looks pale and smiles at Salimah hesitantly, which makes Salimah worry whether she has done the right thing. She doesn't understand, shouldn't Anna be ecstatic? Salimah shakes off the thought as she puts the papers back in the cabinet. Let Tom deal with Anna, and with those papers. She has her daughter to take care of. First, she'll inform Father and Pak Long. Then she will call the prison officer.

When Salimah gets home she sits both old men down with cups of coffee, before she can change her mind, then freezes. Tell them what first? The men look at her questioningly and Pak Long looks like he is going to talk and she needs to beat him to it. She clears her throat and spits it out. 'I have signed the affidavit for the adoption. He will go to Anna and Tom.'

To shut Pak Long up, she lays the letter on the table between them. 'Nazra is in prison, she is charged with possession and consumption of drugs.'

Father stares at her and even Pak Long is temporarily stunned. Father then grins and pokes his brother. 'Hah. Abang, like you.'

Pak Long grunts at Father as if to silence him and Salimah stares back defiantly, more at Pak Long than Father, briefly wondering what Father means, but mostly preparing for a sermon on what a terrible mother she is to have let this happen. Father is probably just thinking about banana trees. But when Pak Long speaks his voice is gentle. 'You weren't even born, but those riots in 1950 left 18 dead and 173 injured. Did they die for nothing?'

Salimah sighs and sinks back. Why is he mentioning the Maria Hertogh riots yet again? It all happened during colonial times, when the Brits were still in charge. Of course they ruled that the girl return to her parents in Europe. That infuriated Muslims like Pak Long who thought the girl, raised a Muslim, should stay with her Malay godmother. The girl also agreed to that, she knew nothing else than the woman who raised her. But she was older, thirteen already; Ahmad is still a baby, although he too has grown attached to his foster parents. What is Pak Long trying to say?

She doesn't answer and Pak Long seems lost in the past as he continues. 'It was a morning in December. The verdict only took five minutes. Word spread fast. When I arrived there were hundreds of us, soon thousands, carrying green banners, shouting. We pulled over cars, pulling out white people. They had no business taking our Muslim children. Allah provides for all of his.'

Salimah knows where this is going. 'Did you ever expect the Brits to rule differently? Those Dutch were her biological parents. But the Brits left and handed over control after that, well, eventually. We are independent now. If we give Ahmad to these people it is because we choose to do so, not because someone makes us.'

'Are we truly independent?' Pak Long asks. 'Not as long as the Chinese are in charge. Our religious rights still aren't respected. In Malaysia, you think they would allow a Muslim baby to be adopted by foreigners?'

Salimah grunts. Why does everything have to be political for him? When Salimah doesn't answer – what can she say? – he continues. 'Anyway, we need to ask Allah for guidance and protection, for it is he who has been protecting us always. The boy, we did the cukur rambut, he too is protected by Allah. It is Him we must follow.'

'Yes,' Salimah says, 'but Allah provides sustenance to all of humankind, whether they are believers or non-believers. How do we know what Allah means for this boy? I have prayed for him but still I am lost.' Hot tears fall from her eyes. 'What you just said, Pak Long, is true. We are all in God's hands. But He also asks us to think for ourselves, right, and to do our best? I think this is what is best for the boy. And for Nazra.'

Father mutters softly but it is Pak Long who speaks out. 'I know you feel you cannot care for the boy. I will find him a good family.' Salimah shakes her head but Pak Long ignores her. 'You think you are a modern woman, a Singaporean first, then a Malay. You abandoned our traditions and customs. It's those English schools that teach that, you and the girl. That is why she lost her way.' He fiddles with the hairs on his chin, and as if it is all settled, continues: 'So, the girl. What to do?'

Salimah gets up, in a flash of determination. 'I'm not asking for your help, Pak, I just needed to tell you. Now you know. I will deal with this.'

Looking at Pak Long, she feels combative and adds. 'Anyway, what did Bapa mean when he said "just like you" earlier? Did you ever do drugs?'

Pak Long clenches his teeth. 'No lah never.' He gets up and walks past Father who still sits like a statue and stops in front of Salimah. 'Nak, no one but Allah knows everything, what will happen, how people will die, how they will live.'

Salimah sits back down. 'I know. But I need Him to guide me.'

'He can only guide people who listen.'

Salimah wrings her hands. 'I try, but there is so much noise.'

She feels like she is drowning in her own small self, underneath God the almighty, the all-powerful who is there but out of reach. She can't hear him inside her.

Pak Long lays his hands on Salimah's head. 'You call this officer, go see the girl. I will talk to some people I know. We will get through this. Alhamdulillah.'

Salimah takes her phone and goes into her bedroom, the door closes behind her. She pulls the letter from its envelope and dials the number.

31

Anna walks outside and sniffs. What idiot would have a barbecue for breakfast? Quickly she steps back inside and closes the windows to keep out the foul-smelling air. Salimah told her that in the old days everything was open, there were no glass windows, the whole living room basically a veranda that was open to the outside. There was a slanted slit at the bottom of the walls which allowed for air circulation. Everything to encourage a breeze. Since they don't have airconditioning here, Anna has been considering opening everything up again and removing the plexiglass from the white lattice above the windows. Let the house breathe. But now, she's glad she hasn't.

She looks around, unsure what she will do today. There is a lot of laundry to do, but she doesn't want to do that. What she really wants is to climb back into bed and hide under the covers. When Salimah signed the affidavit it was exactly what Anna wanted. She wants Boy more than she ever wanted anything in her life. So why is there a *but* looming inside her still?

Tom is still abroad and the papers sit safely in the cabinet. She hasn't told him about them, nor about Nazra's arrest. Poor Nazra. She'll have to call Salimah later today to ask how she is doing, whether she has even managed to see her yet. She looks at Boy, still asleep, and grabs her laptop. Facebook might cheer her up. As she opens the computer her heart leaps. Her father's reply is finally there.

He starts with some chitchat and Anna quickly scans the rant on colonialism that follows, nothing she's not heard before. She reads on greedily. "*To answer your question about Hemelrijk, the family plantation Oma grew up on? It wasn't rubber, Oma's family were tobacco planters, Deli tobacco was famous once.*"

Anna looks up from her email. She can still taste this morning's smoke from outside in her throat. Tobacco? How come she always thought it was rubber?

"*But my grandfather, Oma's father, was a man with a vision. He was one of the first to change over to palm oil. The crop of the future, he said.*"

Anna swallows, forces herself to finish the last paragraph of her father's message.

"*But after the war, Opa did work for a big rubber corporation, maybe that is what you were thinking of? I grew up between rubber trees. Sumatra was a wild place then, full of tigers, but also pemudas, young freedom-fighters, terrorists some people called them. Opa sent me away for my own safety.*

I think what you and Tom do is great, focus on modern Asia. Be there, be equals, and support their progress. Your mother and I will come and visit soon! I'm not sure if I dare go back to Sumatra yet, you go first. I went to a Dutch primary in Siantar, which wasn't too far from the plantation your Opa worked in, you should be able to find it. It's south of Medan. As for the planation Hemelrijk, it had ceased to exist by then, it got eaten up by one of the big corporations. I visited the area once with my parents, in the early 50s. The family home had been shot to pieces in the war. There was nothing there anymore, even then. I remember a muddy river? It wasn't far from the coast. If I remember more,

I will let you know. Do you have Oma's old photos? I can't find them.

Keep us posted, darling, and take care. Your papa."

Anna sinks down, trying to make sense of the whirlpool in her gut, and the toxic smoke in her nostrils is not helping. She has a sudden urge to drive to Changi airport, get on a plane and hug her father tight. There is so much more to ask him, but those questions aren't for an email, or even over the phone. Anna thinks of the forms sitting in the cabinet. Next time she sees Papa, he will have an Asian grandson.

Then Anna's phone beeps. It's Vicky. *'How are you hun? Catch up? Join me at Botanics?'*

Anna snaps the laptop shut and gets up. She definitely needs to get out and escape her thoughts. She texts back: *'Things quite smoky here. How about coffee at Tanglin?'*

When they have settled over a cappuccino in the cool freshness of the shopping mall, and have exchanged pleasantries, the conversation turns – of course – to the haze covering the city. 'These Indonesians, why do they keep burning their forests?' Vicky laments.

Anna feels stupid and ignorant, she hasn't paid attention to any news recently, buried as she has been in the past. She has no clue about these things. 'Is that what is causing this smoke, forest fires?'

Vicky nods. 'They burn down forests to clear it for palm oil plantations. Or clear old palm trees, I'm not sure. All I know is that it stinks.'

Anna's throat constricts though the air is fresh inside. Too fresh. 'Palm oil?' she mutters. 'How long will it last?'

'I don't know, a few years back it lasted for weeks and it was horrid, much worse than this.'

It takes a while for Anna to answer. 'So these palm oil fires, where are they? In Indonesia, you say?'

'Yeah, Borneo, Sumatra. I hope it will blow over soon as I can't stand another period like before. It's not only that they cut and burn rainforests, they drain the swamps, set the dry matter on fire and those just smoulder forever. Last time it was terrible. For weeks we couldn't go outside. The smoke was everywhere, in your nose, your throat, it gave you headaches. I try to avoid using palm oil because of this. But it really is in everything you buy.'

Anna tastes the smoke again even though the mall air is crisp. She takes a big swig of lukewarm coffee and swallows it down. Her father's words come back to her bluntly. *The crop of the future.* So much for her great-grandfather being a visionary. The foul smoke layers on top of other feelings that have amassed in her stomach and when she looks at the baby on her lap they amplify. His future. Boy sweeps a spoon from the table to the floor. When Anna bends to pick it up she hits her head. While she rubs it, Vicky changes the subject and is now talking about a trip to Thailand she is planning a few weeks from now. They chat about beach resorts, air travel with babies and some more, and Anna shares her plans for the trip to Medan.

'A trip down memory lane? But wait, if it smells this bad here, isn't it going to be way worse there?'

Anna's mood sinks further. Vicky points at Boy, who is sitting at Anna's lap, groping a napkin now. 'And how about him? How is the adoption going anyway?'

Anna explains how Salimah has signed the documents, and that a Home Study Report to assess their suitability is on the way.

'You don't seem excited,' Vicky says. 'That is great news, right?'

Anna nods. She is excited. She inhales a big gulp of tinny mall air and sees Salimah again, just before she signed the affidavit, with that forlorn look in her eyes. 'I know. It is great. But sometimes I wonder, what gives me the right to take him away from his own culture?'

Vicky shrugs. 'So many people adopt from other countries. And you would be giving the boy opportunities he would never have otherwise. Education, money. I mean, isn't he better off this way?'

Anna feels defensive. His grandmother is an educated woman, with a university degree. There are plenty of good schools and opportunities for him here. 'It's also about religion, some family members think he should go to a Muslim family.'

She picks up Boy and holds him high, his wide smile bolstering her mood. When Boy pulls her hair she turns him back onto her lap and hands him his dummy, which he sucks blissfully unaware of the turbulence in his young life. 'We aren't religious at all. I don't like religion, it only seems to divide people.'

Vicky looks at Anna with half a grin and doesn't speak for a few seconds. 'You know I'm a Christian, right?'

Awkwardly, Anna replies, 'I'm sorry, I didn't realise. The Dutch are mostly secular.'

Tom is originally Anglican, but never talks about religion.

'It's okay,' Vicky laughs. 'I'm not hung up about it. It is just that I feel there has to be more between heaven and earth, things you can't see or touch, it would be too depressing if not.'

'But there is plenty more, isn't there? Love, for instance.

Commitment. Responsibility. Art. Faith in humankind.'

'Isn't it all the same? You call it love, I call it God.'

'I suppose, but calling it love just feels more inclusive to me. If there were a god, he should be there for everyone.'

When Vicky nods and smiles; Anna is glad she isn't insulted. She ought to have this talk with Salimah too, but the idea of talking to a Muslim about religion scares Anna. She pulls Boy to sit up straight on her lap. 'It is not just religion, it is the whole colonial history of my family.'

'Why on earth would you bring that up? That happened ages ago. You need to think about what is best for the baby.'

Boy hits her on the arm with the spoon, and Anna straightens her back. Vicky is right. That is exactly the thing: adopting Boy is what Anna wants. But is it best for him? 'I wish Tom was around more. He is always travelling, I worry we are growing apart.'

Vicky takes her own baby from her pram and fiddles with her clothes, until the baby latches on and sucks loudly. She looks pensive, then whispers. 'You know how many expat marriages go to pieces? All those girls throwing themselves at our men at business meetings. You need to keep an eye on him.'

'No, Tom isn't into women like that, he always complains how embarrassed he feels when that happens.'

'Well, that is what we all think, have you heard about ...' Vicky starts a juicy gossip about a woman from playgroup, who's husband left her for their Filipina helper.

Anna allows herself to get lost in the gossip, and after they do some shopping and she is driving home, she realises it helps to say things out loud. But it is even better with the right person.

32

It is as if Salimah is watching her daughter on tv. Nazra is probably in the same building but seems excruciatingly distant on the screen. She can't touch her, can't smell her – she can hear her but she sounds strange. The whole thing is surreal; as long as Nazra is in remand, there can be no face to face visits, the officer says. Only later, after conviction, Salimah can see her in person – but still with a wall of glass in between. 'You are looking at two years, most likely,' the officer says. Two whole years where Salimah won't be able to touch her child. Not that she touches her that often anymore, but seeing her so small on the screen makes her want to do it more than ever. She wishes Nazra was a baby again, a baby she can cradle and keep safe.

Salimah looks at Nazra on the screen. She has lost weight.

'Do they feed you well?' she asks.

The girl just shrugs. Their conversation is stiff and difficult, with Nazra not saying much and Salimah asking questions but not the ones she ought to. Only, almost at the end, she looks straight in the camera. 'Why Nazra, why is this happening to us? You have a good family, a good life. You do well in school, nice friends.'

'Nice friends? At that school? They barely talk to me! But yes I made nice friends, other ones, that accept me the way I am. They don't expect me to be something I can't be.'

Salimah turns pale. 'So these friends, are they the ones that gave you the drugs? Why did you take them?'

Nazra doesn't answer for some time. Then she says. 'It started for fun. At a party. Why not?'

Salimah wants to scream out all the reasons why not but hisses them out through her teeth. 'Because everyone will see you as this haram girl, not someone they can take home to meet the family. Think of your reputation and how people will judge you.'

'Judge me?' Nazra answers. 'Like you do, you mean?'

Suddenly it isn't like Nazra is in another room but right in front of her, stabbing her.

'You always need to compare me to others. So-and-so made a good marriage and is such a helpful wife and has a perfect job too, and lots of babies. So-and-so has better grades than me, so-and-so has gotten into Yale-NUS. Well, maybe so-and-so didn't have to babysit her grandfather at the weekend. You want me to be the perfect student, be the perfect Muslim girl. I'm not superwoman. I'm not like you. It is too much.'

Before Salimah can come up with a reply, the officer signals that their time is up. Salimah promises Nazra that she is still her little girl, that she will look after her no matter what.

Nazra smiles carefully, as if she doesn't believe it, and that wrings Salimah's heart. Just before the officer kills the connection, Nazra asks in the tiniest of voices, 'How is Ahmad?'

Just hearing her say his name makes Salimah break down, but not until the camera is turned off.

The following day, Pak Long takes her to the mosque to meet a woman, Cik Nor, from a community action group that supports Muslim inmates. She explains the process Nazra will be going through and how they can help. Here, Salimah finds her tongue again and asks away. How does visiting work, will she be fed properly, and what about her record, will it stay forever? Won't she make all the wrong friends in prison? Friends that are on drugs. And, more pragmatic, shouldn't she get Nazra a lawyer?

'Don't waste your money,' Nor answers, 'most of these drug cases are done without a lawyer. If they found the product on her, and she failed the urine tests, there is little a lawyer can do. At her age she might get sentenced to training and rehabilitation, but she'd still be locked up.'

She explains that they can help after Nazra is convicted, that there are programmes. Nazra could even study in prison for her A-Levels, but only if she gets a longer sentence – unlikely for a first-time offender. 'What we need to focus on is how you will support her when she gets out. Most drug addicts relapse, go in and out of prison. She needs to have something to come back to, that will motivate her to stay clean.'

Salimah thinks of a crying Ahmad.

'You said she attended school until her arrest? That is good. Many young drug users run away and end up living on the streets. It seems like she hasn't been lost that far.'

Further than you know, Salimah thinks, but Pak Long says it: 'There is the baby, of course.'

It doesn't seem news to Nor. 'Actually, babies can have a good effect on young mothers, it means having something to take care of other than oneself. It gives them a sense of responsibility. Some even deliver in prison, keep their babies with them; they are born there and stay until they are about a year old, sometimes longer.'

Salimah shudders. No way she is sending her innocent grandson to prison. Anyway, she signed the boy away. He is not theirs any more.

Cik Nor is friendly and candid. When Salimah gets up, Nor puts her hand over hers. 'Don't despair. You will need to work though this, but rezeki does not come by itself. Usaha first.'

Afterwards Salimah sits in the corridor feeling lighter, while she waits for Pak Long – he always takes forever here, knows everyone. She realises that at no point Cik Nor had judged Nazra, or Salimah. She accepted. She looked forward. She was positive and supportive.

Salimah looks up to see a purple veiled shape coming towards her. It's Aziza. Salimah has been avoiding her friends, but Aziza makes to sit down next to her. Is she here to gloat?

'Kak, what am I hearing, why are you hiding? Why did you not tell us?'

Salimah looks into Aziza eyes, open and plain, and suddenly the whole story comes out. She has missed her friend. Aziza mutters, shaking her head. 'What a stupid girl. These kids, they are our curse, right? Who will marry her now? What sensible man will love her?'

Salimah gets up and bursts out. 'I will love her! And one day there will be a man brave enough to love her too. She is strong and beautiful, my girl.'

Aziza looks at Salimah with shocked eyes. Salimah sinks down. 'But, yes, she is also very stupid.'

Thankfully, Aziza laughs. 'She is.'

Aziza strokes Salimah's arm. 'We are still your friends, do you think our kids aren't stupid?'

Then she lowers her tone and whispers conspiratorially. 'Did you know my Hamid failed his exams?'

Salimah smiles sadly, and Aziza continues. 'But Salimah,

how can we help you if we never see you? You never come to the mosque anymore.'

'I have failed my daughter, Aziza, what help would be any good?'

Aziza smiles. 'We can cook, we can listen, we can get you things for the little one. We can be there.'

Salimah shakes her head. 'The little one has enough things. He is not staying with me. Nazra plans to give him up for adoption.'

She can't bear to say it as if it's a fait accompli. Even though she signed already.

'Aduh, Kak, you need to take him, a baby is rezeki from Allah.'

The word rezeki echoes in Salimah's mind. It is the same one Cik Nor used. Sustenance from God. But usaha first; she needs to work for it.

When Pak Long returns, Aziza takes her leave, and Salimah feels soft inside. Pak Long sits his old body down. 'Give me a few minutes, Nak. My bones are tired.'

Salimah rehashes what Aziza said, about her kids, and about how she could help. Aziza never said these thing before. Why do women pretend not to support each other? Is she herself like that too? The thorn of Nazra's earlier words, *you always judge me,* settles more solidly, painfully, into her side. Hesitantly, another understanding creeps up. Nazra might seem different from Salimah when she was young, but she is facing similar problems as she herself did at that age. How did she not notice how unhappy the girl was, has she become so cynical she thinks it is normal? Nazra does not accept what Salimah did all that time ago, she has higher expectations of life. Sure, she should have allowed her more fun. But such a bodoh girl, if her idea of fun is doing drugs and chasing ghosts. Now that ghost got her revenge.

Salimah looks at Pak Long. Did he start all this, long ago? He looks very innocent, and smug, sitting there. It is true, today he helped her. 'Thank you for introducing me to Cik Nor.'

He smiles his crooked teeth bare. 'We take care of each other here.'

Salimah wonders, did she judge Pak Long too harshly? Or not hard enough? She should have shielded Nazra from his judgement. She, who suffered it herself, should have seen how it hurt the girl. The old man smiles his lop-sided grin, and Salimah isn't sure whether to love or hate him. 'There is more, there is a family looking to adopt a son. I will introduce you.'

Salimah shakes her head.

When she reaches home, having picked up groceries on the way, Mrs Ng is in the corridor watering Father's plants. Salimah cringes. Salimah got rid of the dead plants, but left some that still had the tiniest of green on the edges. She has been meaning to water them, but she is as bad a gardener as a mother, obviously. 'I'm so sorry, Mrs Ng, I keep forgetting to water them. I've been so busy lately.'

Mrs Ng puts down the watering can. 'How is your little grandson? He is so cute.' She walks over and smiles. 'I haven't seen him in a while. And I heard about his mother, poor child.'

Salimah doesn't know if the poor child is Nazra or Ahmad. She stares at the concrete barrier on the side of the corridor, wishing she could jump over. Of course people know, there is no avoiding that, but thankfully most are polite enough not to mention the unspeakable. She nods, silently.

'Do you need help?' Mrs Ng asks, nodding at Salimah's grocery bag. She has adopted Anna's habit of bringing reusable ones, even though they try to push plastic on you in most supermarkets. 'I can help. My life, well, I'm alone a lot these days.'

Salimah is stunned. 'I thought you, ehm ...' She regrets starting that sentence, how can she end it without being offensive? 'I thought you were enjoying the quiet life now your grandchildren moved out?'

'I love babies. Yes, these children, when they got older, so noisy. But I don't hear yours much, he must be a good baby?'

Salimah doesn't want to admit Ahmad lives elsewhere, so just nods. 'He is.'

'I can babysit, you know?'

'Babysit him?'

Somehow tears start dripping from Salimah's eyes and she stands there, not even trying to wipe them.

'Why don't you come inside for a minute and sit down?' Salimah has never heard Mrs Ng speak kindly like this, and follows her into the apartment. Mrs Ng pours iced water for Salimah, nodding for her to sit down on a red flowery sofa. 'You know, my daughter when she was young, all sorts of problems too. Not so bad like jail lor, but still. Then she marries this guy I can see mile away good for nothing. And who ends up with her and the kids after he leaves her? Me. But I love those kids, especially when they were small, not yet misbehaving. Now in school already. You want to talk?'

'No,' Salimah starts, but then it does come out. How hard it is taking care of those two old men with a daughter in prison, and also needing to provide an income. How she worries whether Nazra can find her way back when she gets out. How she signed away the baby. All these things she hasn't been able to tell her friends she now tells the nasty next-door neighbour. Mrs Ng snorts. 'I can check on your father, he is a good man. I miss his plants and his talk in the corridor. I don't mind.'

She looks quite different now, embarrassed only. 'My daughter and the kids, they were noisy and annoying but now so quiet here lah.'

It is the first time Salimah is inside this apartment, even though they have lived next to each other for years. She looks around. In the corner is an ancestral altar with photos. Salimah recognises Mrs Ng's late husband, and two old people who must be her parents. On a low side table are photos of the children. Mrs Ng follows her gaze. 'They don't visit much. Being retired is nice, but sometimes quite lonely. Did you know I was a teacher once?' Salimah didn't.

'Lecturer, at university. Can't deal with the young ones.'

They chat a little longer, and Salimah leaves feeling much lighter. As she crosses the corridor she thinks about how her life has changed in just a few months. Not long ago she had a proper job, a not yet senile father, and a daughter in school. Now, she has a Chinese neighbour who is just as vulnerable as she is but who is offering support. As the late afternoon sun plays through the pillars she looks down to the ground and the empty storm drain she can just make out below. Storm drains may appear peculiar, empty concrete channels that seemingly hold no function. When heavy rain pours, their crucial role emerges, as they prove to be the safety net that keeps everyone's feet dry. They brim with swirling currents of murky water, swiftly channelling it away. And once the storm subsides, the relentless sun dries up the drains, returning them to their unassuming state.

33

Anna strokes Boy's head as she suckles him to sleep. She mostly bottle-feeds him, but in the privacy of her bedroom she finds offering her breast the easiest way to put him to sleep. Seeing his dark stubble next to her bare skin makes her feel sentimental. She can see Nazra in the jut of his chin, the fold of his ear. And it no longer bothers her when she does.

Even here she can taste the haze – the windows of this old house don't close properly. It hurts her throat. The smog clouds her brain too, her mood has been spiralling down with every breath of toxic air she inhales. She looks up the problems palm oil creates online and reads how her former employer is the largest buyer of palm oil worldwide, using it in soaps, margarine, foodstuffs. Palm oil is the biggest cause of deforestation in Indonesia, Anna's head aches from both the bad air and the terrible facts. Local people lose their land and livelihoods as small farms get swallowed up. Indigenous peoples lose the forests they need for survival. And all the profits go into the deep pockets of foreign owners in liaison with corrupt government officials. *A visionary?* Indeed. The mindset of people like her great-great-grandfather is still prevalent in this part of the world.

Anna forces herself to snap out of the thought spiral. Tom will be back tomorrow and she needs to show him Salimah's signature on the paperwork. Looking at Boy lying there, his bare skin next to hers, his milky scent, makes her so happy. There is nothing she'd rather do than raise him, see him turn into a boy, then a man. Then why has she not yet told Tom about Salimah signing?

Anna sighs. Because he is not here. She and Tom need some time alone to talk about their relationship, their future. This child. She pictures the resort Bea recommended on the shore of Lake Toba, with cottages in a flowering garden. It would be the perfect place. But it will be a while before they can travel there with Boy. It might be too late. Boy bites her nipple and Anna jolts up. Too late for what?

Carefully she manoeuvres the baby off her breast. She needs to start focusing on the positives. This amazing child is going to be hers. His smiles, his intelligent eyes, his gorgeous curls that are growing back. Maybe he is the key to a future where all can be well, where all can be equal? Carefully, Anna allows herself to dream. She needs to call the embassy, ask what the process is to get him a Dutch passport. And what should they do about his name? Formally the boy is called Ahmad, but Anna doesn't like it. Can they legally change it? Would Salimah mind if they did? They can hardly keep calling him Boy. All the questions make Anna's panic surface again, and so does her doubt. What happened in those weeks before Nazra disappeared? Was it her meddling that pushed the girl to start using again?

The silence in the house is oppressive, and Anna almost wishes she could see that ghost again. It is easier to have someone else to blame for your bad choices. Boy stirs and lets out a gentle whimper. Please, don't wake up, Anna thinks. She pushes her nipple back in Boy's mouth. The maternal feeling that it gives Anna relaxes her and then it dawns on her – she wants Boy. But keeping him means losing Salimah forever.

34

After her visit to the mosque Salimah sits on the bus and as she passes the Bukit Timah canal she experiences a strong urge to see baby Ahmad, so she alights and walks to the house. The front door is open, and out of habit she walks straight up, without thinking. Only when she stands in the living room she stops in her tracks. She doesn't work here anymore. This is not appropriate. But she can't make herself leave.

Salimah looks around, calls out softly, but there is no response. Anna's bedroom door is closed, she is probably asleep. Would it be okay if she waited here? On the sofa she eyes a heap of clean laundry, all baby clothes. She fingers the soft cotton of the tiny onesies, and suddenly she finds her fingers folding them and piling them up. The pile is unbalanced, it falls over. The boy has so many clothes.

Rezeki, she thinks.

As she folds she thinks of Ahmad, of him sleeping in the beautiful new crib, of him with her father in the garden, of him taking his first steps on the lawn. A tear forms in the corner of her eye and softly rolls down her cheek. She pulls the tiny shorts she is holding away just in time. When she has a basket full, Salimah gets up, walks over to Anna's room to put everything away in the chest of drawers next to the crib, and, without thinking, opens the door.

Her feet stick to the floor. Anna is lying on the bed. Her chest is bare, and Ahmad clinches to it, his head moving in a gentle rhythm. Anna startles, pulls down her top and hoists the boy over her shoulder. He is asleep. Anna looks at Salimah with embarrassed eyes. And a whiff of fear.

'I am so sorry,' Salimah stutters, 'I know, this is completely inappropriate. I came to see you, and as I waited, I ...' She points to the baby clothes in her basket. 'It's a habit I guess. I could not stop myself, and then. I just forgot.'

Anna too, stutters. 'No, no. I am the one. I mean, this is inappropriate. Me feeding him.'

She readjusts the sleeping baby before she continues. 'But it calms him. Both of us in fact.'

There is another pause where Salimah doesn't speak. She thinks of Pak Long, angry at Nazra for not breastfeeding the boy. Then, of Nazra, so small on the screen.

'I wanted to call you, but then ...'

Anna looks so helpless, like a little puppy, that Salimah can't help to burst out laughing. It is infectious, for now Anna starts too. 'Shush, you'll wake him up,' she whispers with a snort.

Anna sits up and settles back against the wall.

Salimah tries to align her thoughts. 'I saw Nazra yesterday.'

Anna nods. 'How is she? I think about her a lot, you know. When I look at him, drinking like that.' She pauses for a moment. 'You must think I am crazy.'

Salimah grins despite herself. 'No. It's fine. Actually, you are mahram to him now. That means family. It's encouraged you know, in Islam, to breastfeed an adopted child. By breastfeeding you establish the mahram relationship, which means he can see you without hijab.'

Anna pulls down her top further, self-consciously.

Salimah sits down on the edge of the bed. 'Can we talk?' Anna looks at Salimah questioningly as she continues. 'Did you tell Tom about the papers, that I signed?'

'No, I didn't.'

'Why not?'

Anna drops a kiss on the head of Ahmad before she answers, quietly. 'I am not sure.'

'Neither am I.'

For a few moments neither of them speaks. And when they do, they both do at the same time.

Salimah: 'A baby brings rezeki.'

Anna: 'It's complicated.'

They laugh again, and the new bout of laughter clears the air further.

'You first,' says Anna. 'What did you say?'

Salimah smiles. 'Babies are a gift from God and a door to more rezeki. It is hard to explain what rezeki is in English, it means sustenance, divine lot. It is everything that God gives us that we need.'

Anna looks pensive and doesn't answer.

'I made a promise to you. But I needed to tell you how I feel.'

Slowly, Anna speaks. 'I think it is good that we talk finally, how is it possible we just stopped talking when things got hard? If we hadn't, we'd not been in this mess.'

'You were ill. I don't think your brain was right. And you are also you, just a little too enthusiastic, too keen to be helpful. You don't always think first.'

Blushes appear on Anna's white cheeks. 'I didn't mean to take over your life.'

'It is my fault too, I let you do it. I am the opposite of you. Too indecisive. I was distracted, worried about Nazra, my father, my uncle.'

And her denial let that pontianak wreak havoc for far too long, Salimah thinks, but doesn't say it out loud. She wants to talk about the living right now.

'What do you want now?' Anna asks. 'Can you tell me how I can help?

Those needy eyes look serious and Salimah laughs despite herself. 'If only I knew.'

Anna wriggles the baby and stretches her body. 'I just want what is best for the boy.'

'Yes,' exclaims Salimah, 'but what is best for him? My uncle, Pak Long, thinks he needs to be raised in Islam, but you know, Allah provides sustenance to all of humankind, whether they are believers or non-believers.'

After a short break she adds. 'He is my grandson.'

'And that means he belongs with you,' says Anna, rocking the baby gently in her arms. 'I'm not like him, I can't give him what he needs'

'No,' says Salimah, 'that is nonsense. You are his mahram now too. Family.'

After a short pause she continues, 'I think the boy will be fine with you, that is not it. It's Nazra. He is her son, her way to rezeki. She will need him when she leaves prison.'

'And,' Salimah adds, 'maybe I need him too.'

She looks at Anna and the baby and suddenly a feeling of panic rises up inside her. She laughs again, hysterically. She has no idea where all of that came from, she was not planning to say that at all. She raises her hands in agony: 'What am I saying? I can't look after him, I couldn't even look after my own daughter!'

Anna leans over and puts the baby in Salimah's arms. 'You know what the best thing is? When you smell his neck. Seriously, try it, it makes all bad thoughts go away.'

Salimah puts her nose in his skin, just below the dark hair that is turning soft again now it's longer. He smells like sweet milk, innocence, and very, very familiar. 'Nazra smelled just like that. But how would I to do it? My father suffers from dementia, my uncle is too old to work. I need to support everyone, I need to be there for Nazra.'

She stops and thinks of Aziza and Mrs Ng. Who else is out there? 'I had to raise Nazra on my own, her father died when she was only two.'

And see how that worked out. Times haven't changed, no matter how hard Salimah has worked to prove herself as a Malay woman. There are just as many prejudices today, and they are even harder to stomach for a modern girl like Nazra.

'How long will Nazra be in jail, you think?' Anna asks.

'The officer said two years is likely. But she might be able to complete her A-levels inside. It is something.' It is something Salimah has been holding on to all night.

Anna gets up and takes the old photo album from her nightstand 'Can I show you something?'

She turns the album around and points at the photo of an Indonesian woman with a white baby on its lap. 'This is my grandmother, and that lady was Ayu, her babu. Oma always talked about her. Babu Ayu was like a second mother to her. She tried to find her after the war but she never found out what happened to her, or even whether she had survived.'

Salimah looks at the photo. Where is Anna going with this?

Afraid to ask, she stares at the photo. 'Rambut sama hitam, hati lain-lain.'

Anna looks up, 'Sorry, what did you say?'

Salimah hadn't realised she said that out loud. 'It's a Malay saying, it translates into, well, that everyone has the same black hair, but everyone's heart is different. It means, I guess, that people have different opinions. But looking at that photo, or you and Ahmad just now, I think the saying should be the other way round. We all have different hair colours, but our hearts, they are the same.'

'That sounds lovely, but it isn't reality,' says Anna. 'Most people act as if hair and skin colour do matter. It makes me worry whether he can be happy with us.'

Salimah doesn't know how to respond and Anna continues. 'Would he be alright growing up outside his own culture?'

Salimah gently strokes the hair of the sleeping baby. 'This isn't about that. Not even about you and me.'

'You are right. It is about Nazra and Ahmad.'

It is the first time Salimah hears Anna say his name. 'I just want to help, really help this time. Be like Babu Ayu to him.'

Salimah laughs again, but this time silently. 'You, my nanny? I can't afford you.'

'No, I am talking nonsense about babus, I have been reading too much colonial literature, it's gone to my head. What I mean is, I can help you take care of him. I love him, but I hope to have my own children one day and there is no need to take yours. I will, but only if that is what you want. If that is what Nazra wants.'

Salimah smells Ahmad's neck again and this time everything seems possible. She gets up, and puts him in his crib. 'I'm not sure Nazra isn't in the right position to make this kind of decision right now. I need to step up, be her mother. After all, she is only a child herself.'

'So how do we do that? Do I take him home? I need some time to sort things out for Nazra, and ...'

She looks at Anna helplessly but Anna nods firmly, suddenly in charge.

'Take all the time you need. I've got him. I need to talk to Tom first, he is home tomorrow and I have no idea how I am going to explain this to him.'

'He is a man,' Salimah says and they both laugh.

'What about your uncle?' Anna asks.

Salimah beams. 'I think he will be very happy.'

Suddenly, a loud noise erupts above them. Anna instinctively covers her ears with her hands, her face turning pale as she trembles in fear. 'Not again! This usually only happens at night. This whole house is haunted, I can't take it anymore. Make it go away!'

Salimah stares at the ceiling, 'You have heard this before?'

'Usually at night, never during the day. What is it? Goblins?'

Salimah laughs. 'That's not a goblin. It's a musang.'

Anna stares back blankly. 'I need to move, I cannot stand living here anymore. The footsteps of the Japanese soldiers in the corridor, the white woman in the garden. And now a musang in the roof. It is too much. I am going to get Tom to rent me a nice little condo. With marble and glass and none of these, these ... ghosts.'

The noise above them intensifies and Salimah laughs again.

'It's not funny!' Anna exclaims.

Salimah points at the ceiling where the noise has diminished to a light scratching. 'A musang is a, how do you call it in English, a civet cat. Musang berbulu ayam – literally "a civet cat with chicken feathers", like your wolf in sheep's clothing. They are sneaky animals but completely harmless. It's probably fighting with the rats up there. We had them in the kampong. You know, the longer I stay in this house, the more it reminds me of my old village. I always thought this house was so different from ours, but it's not. Staying here with you, I found my village again.'

Salimah picks up the basket and starts putting away the laundry, feeling calmer than she has in months. They will find a way. It takes a kampong to raise a child. So she will have to build one.

35

Salimah has taken Ahmad to the wet market so Anna can talk to Tom in private. When she hears the taxi pull up, Anna waves at him from the window. Tom looks up, grinning. He stumbles up the stairs with his luggage and swoops her up in his arms. 'Hello beautiful, I have missed you!' He kisses her on the lips, spreading warmth.

'You are in a good mood, your trip went well?' Anna has no idea how he will react when she tells him about Ahmad. He might go ballistic. She tries to distract him by asking about work.

'We sealed the deal!' Tom exclaims. 'We are going out tonight to celebrate, you too, everyone is coming. This is what we have been working on for months. Champagne tonight!'

He slows down and looks around. 'We'll need to get a babysitter. Where is Boy? Is he asleep? I want a cuddle. What did I miss? Is his hair growing back yet?'

Anna pulls Tom down on the sofa. 'Salimah took him to the market. We need to talk.'

Tom looks at Anna. 'What is wrong? Did she refuse to sign?'

'Actually,' Anna begins, 'she did sign.'

'Excellent,' Tom interrupts, 'even more reason for champagne!'

'Wait, not so fast. Nazra was arrested a few days ago.'

'Oh my god, what happened?'

Anna is happy for the respite, and explains the drugs charges, and how Nazra is expected to spend a few years behind bars. Tom nods. 'That is terrible for the girl, for Salimah. But it means we are doing the right thing, doesn't it? She is in no position to care for him. I'm glad Salimah agrees, and finally signed.'

Anna takes a deep breath. 'Actually. No. Salimah did sign the affidavit, but she was in shock.'

Anna feels more sad than she had anticipated, but knows this is right. She is afraid Tom might not feel the same and her voice wavers. 'We can't take him if Salimah has doubts. Nazra needs him.'

Tom gasps, baffled. 'Anna, you are ranting. Nazra is in prison, so how can she look after him? Have you even spoken to her? This is what she wants, she told me so herself. We can't give him up. Do you still have the papers, because legally ...'

Anna interrupts. 'I have no idea what it means legally, but does it matter? Salimah thinks Nazra is in no position to make this decision now. She thinks she will regret it later.'

Tom turns red. 'They can't just flip-flop like that. And what, next week they change their mind again? We need to be firm Anna. We need to fight this in court.'

Tom's words sound harsh but his face shows he could start to cry any minute. Frustrated, Anna searches for words. 'He is their blood-relation, we can't force a child away from his biological family. How would we explain that to him when he's grown up? The biggest loser would be him, regardless of who wins.'

Tom buries his face in his hands. Is he really crying? Anna expected him to be angry, but not this. She sits next to him and hugs him tight. 'I know it hurts.' She has spent the last few nights crying too. 'I love him. I love him so much. But we need to think about him. And that means letting him go.'

Tom sighs, rubs his eyes on his sleeves. 'Okay. Fair enough.'

Anna has never seen him like this, so emotional, so vulnerable, but he quickly composes himself. 'Do I get to see him again, at least to say goodbye?'

Anna looks at Tom and throws her arms around him again, squeezing him so hard he gasps. She explains what she agreed with Salimah, how Ahmad will keep living with them for a while, until Salimah knows what is going to happen with Nazra. Salimah will come every day and they will share responsibilities, taking turns to care for him. In time he will move back to Salimah's place, but when, or how, they haven't decided yet. 'Think of it as fostering. It happens all the time, right, foster parents taking care of a child temporarily whilst the parents can't?'

When she explains it this way, the whole setup starts to make sense. They will be his foster parents. Tom frowns at her. 'You are a crazy woman, you know?'

Anna bites her lip. Tom grins. 'But I do love you.'

Salimah takes Ahmad home that night, so Anna and Tom can go out. Anna stares at herself in the mirror, at her huge breasts that bulge out of her bra. Her stomach, that never carried a grown baby but look flabby nonetheless. She has no idea what to wear. The wives of Tom's co-workers all look so manicured. Her tall body and sensible Dutch wardrobe feel awkward. She pulls out a new dress she bought at Tanglin. When she bought it, she imagined herself at a fancy beach resort, it is too airy for a night out, but it will have to do. She can't remember when was the last time she applied mascara. She feels like a new woman. Or perhaps, like her old self?

In the taxi she shivers and Tom puts his arm around her,

warming her up, and when they arrive at the bar it is evident many of his co-workers have been there for while; the mood is cheerful and loud. Someone pushes a shot glass in Anna's hand. Without thinking, she gulps it down. It goes straight to her head. She hasn't drunk alcohol in ages. Julia, Tom's boss, comes over with a bottle of prosecco and pulls Anna away. 'Come join the ladies.'

Anna sips the cool liquid with relish. Conversation ripples easily on the flow of bubbles and Anna relaxes. Everyone is happy after this week's success. Nobody talks about feeds, nappy rash or weaning. After an hour or so, Tom taps her on the shoulder. 'Come on, we're going dancing!'

They taxi to a nightclub where the music leaves no room for thoughts as Anna sways with the sound. The once so familiar smells – stale beer, smoke effect, sweat – invigorate her and she closes her eyes and envisions herself back in London. How come she hasn't been here before? Has she become that old, buried in dusty books and times long past? She needs to enjoy life more, now she still can. She has been given a second chance to explore Asia unencumbered. Looking around as laser beams bounce over the sea of people, she sees hair in all colours of the rainbow. Black, brown, blonde and blue and pink as well. What was it that Salimah said, about how everyone had the same black hair but different opinions? Well, not here, in this club, in this town, on this tiny island in South-East Asia.

Anna can't remember much more of the night when she wakes up in a puddle of sweat – they forgot to turn on either the fan or the airconditioning and the window is closed.

Very hungover, she sips her coffee, while Tom makes a big mess in the kitchen frying bacon and eggs. He definitely knows how to deal with hangovers. Ouch. She is happy Boy, no, Ahmad, isn't here this morning. How do parents have babies and a social life? Her stomach churns thinking about his smelly nappies.

The greasy food settles Anna's acid belly, and she looks at Tom, trying to remember their drunk conversation last night. The music was so loud that she isn't sure she remembers correctly. Did she really tirade about her Dutch family's colonial past to her British husband – in a Singapore nightclub? She has become just like her family, tight-lipped and then annoyed when people don't understand them. She remembers shouting in her husband's ear: *I need to go to Sumatra and face the ghosts of my past. If not, they will keep haunting me forever.* He agreed. When drunk.

'You really want to come to Medan with me, and Lake Toba, as soon as Salimah can arrange to take Ahmad for a week?'

'Absolutely,' Tom says, his mouth full of eggs. He swallows, takes a slug of coffee. 'I should be able to take some time off now we managed to secure the joint venture. I want to climb those mountains of yours.'

'My mountains? Oh, you mean Oma's volcanoes?'

'Yes. I'd love to see those. But what about that haze, the fires you were talking about the other day?'

Anna grins. 'It turns out there was a fire at a landfill in Johor, where they burn garbage – probably ours. Nothing to do with palm oil. Or Sumatra.'

'So you are off the hook?'

'Me, why?' says Anna with feigned attitude.

'Your family didn't start those fires after all.'

'Well,' says Anna, getting up to clear the empty plates. 'Not this time. But whether we are off the hook, we'll have to go see about that.'

36

Salimah looks at the baby, who is lying on the rug contentedly. Then, she looks back at her screen, clicks the button and waits for the confirmation. Application sent. She has registered for a course at the Ministry of Education; they are looking for mid-career professionals to train as teachers. She needed to do this before she tells Father and Pak Long. So they can't change her mind again. She hasn't told Nazra yet, she has no means to get in touch with her until the next visitation. It doesn't matter. She will do this anyway.

Ahmad has started to commando crawl and is moving around the rug. Salimah sits down cross-legged, and sets out cups on the low coffee table. Soon they won't be safe there anymore, she thinks, looking at Ahmad rolling and grabbing.

She looks at the men on the sofa. 'Pak Long, Bapa, I have some news. Good news.'

Pak Long looks up, but Father fiddles with the hem of his shorts. He picks up Ahmad and pulls him onto his lap. 'Ahmad won't be adopted, I will be his guardian. Anna will help take care of him while I study. I'm going to be a teacher.'

Pak Long nods approvingly.

Father is quiet.

'Bapa, did you hear me? I'm talking about your grandson! You'll be able to play with him as often as you like. But he will be staying in the big house some time still. You can visit him there. Maybe one day you can build him a treehouse?'

And abruptly Father is no longer quiet.

'He can't go to that house! It is dangerous there!'

He gets up, squeezing the baby tight. Ahmad starts to cry. Father shakes him violently until Salimah jumps up and grabs his arm. 'Bapa, let the boy go! You are hurting him.'

Slowly she wrestles the baby from Father's arms and rocks him to sleep. 'He has been in that house all his life already. What is going on, the other day you said he was fine to stay there?'

I exorcised her already, I hammered those nails into the banyan tree.

Father starts talking, again about trees, and how things aren't safe. How they will kill people. He mumbles about it all being his fault. That he cut off some of the aerial roots of the banyan, and how that destabilised the tree. That he never meant to use black magic but maybe he did, by accident? 'Or maybe someone set me up,' he says, glaring at Pak Long.

Ahmad has fallen asleep on Salimah's lap and she looks at Pak Long. 'Do you have any idea what he is talking about?'

Pak Long sighs. 'I think I do.'

And after a pause. 'Remember how he lost his job at that house?'

Salimah remembers. 'Did they fire him after something happened in the treehouse? Is that it?'

'They never fired him. The girl and the father moved away.'

She didn't know that. 'The father? What about the ma'am, the mother?'

Suddenly Salimah sees her. A figure with long blonde hair, in a white dress with dark red cherries and embroidered lapels. Can it be?

Pak Long continues, 'They found her body in the garden, not long after it happened. It was never clear why she had been on the roof of the house. Whether it could have been an accident.'

Salimah feels dizzy. 'After what happened? I don't understand.'

Father, in a sudden flare of lucidity, says, 'Ma'am lost her baby when she fell out of the treehouse. After that, she was never the same. She went crazy. And it was my fault.'

Pak Long exclaims: 'It wasn't your fault. These people never blamed you. Nor me. It was just those fools in the kampong that pointed fingers.'

'And maybe they were right,' says Father. 'These people lived in this big house, like rich white people always have, always will, who is to say I did not want to hurt them? I hammered the planks together, they were rotten. I should have seen. Anyway, because I remember it one way, it doesn't mean that is the way it was. Maybe I did do it. My memory, you know, it isn't good.'

Father looks up at Pak Long as if he is a little child and Salimah can't help but feel protective.

'Whose memory is?' says Pak Long, 'Do you think mine is always clear?'

Salimah thinks about this for a second. 'People remember what they want to remember. Just like they believe what they want to believe. We will probably never find the truth, if there is such a thing. But I know how proud you were of that treehouse.'

Then something else slithers its way into Salimah's mind: Father was so adamant she never went near the place. *Because it was dangerous?* Immediately, she dismisses the thought. Her father is the nicest, kindest man, he only ever spoke of his employers with pride. They were good people, gave generous ang pau – as a child she would get a red envelope from them even though neither of them was Chinese, and the amount wasn't auspicious.

Salimah shudders. How can she be sure the pontianak is gone? Anna says she can't see her anymore, just sense her, in the background. In the past, thinks Salimah, she is in the past now, where she belongs. She's had her chance at revenge. And Salimah will make sure those games she played will not have the intended effect. Salimah is in charge now.

Cradling the baby she looks at the two old men in front of her. 'Isn't it time we let the past rest? The future is here,' she says, nodding at the boy in her arms. 'We have lived on this small island for hundreds of years with so many races and all our lives are intertwined. We can only go forward together. We will give him a good Malay upbringing and, who knows, maybe Tom will build him a new treehouse.'

At the word 'treehouse', Father suddenly convulses and he screams at Pak Long: 'Why do they say I do black magic? It was you, you who put the blood on the wood, not me!'

Salimah looks up, startled, terrified. 'What blood?'

Pak Long's face knots up and he glares at Father. 'Nothing, what you talking about, Adik? I just cut my hand is all. Cut myself sawing the wood, dripped blood on the wood. And then people said I cursed the wood, made that woman fall. Because I'm Boyanese. Because we Boyanese are always accused of black magic.'

Pak Long turns away from Salimah, avoiding looking into her eyes, but then he turns sharply towards his brother and she sees a flicker in his eyes that scares her. Suddenly it all becomes clear; the judgement of the kampong people, the prejudice, fingers pointing at the Boyanese. How can this world work if even we

Malays can't find peace amongst ourselves?

As if she said that last sentence out loud, Pak Long replies. 'It is Islam that binds us Malays together.'

Everything tumbles trough Salimah's mind. Her old friends, the baby, the pontianak, the question of the blood, her father's scrambled brains. And now Pak Long brings up religion? Anna once said that religion divided people. Can both be true?

Father stands up and shouts at his brother. 'You always were a batu api! How did I trust a trouble maker like you?'

A long rant in Boyanese follows, and Salimah sighs and sits until Father sinks back down, deflated. She looks at Pak Long, angry now as well as scared. 'What does he mean?'

The look on Pak Long's face is hard to fathom. Defiant? Guilty? It makes Salimah wonder; does she really know this man she has known all her life?'

Resignation sweeps over his face as Pak Long says. 'I told you about the riots for the Nadra girl in 1950?'

Again? 'Yes, you told me, you were part of the riots when they gave the Muslim girl to the Christian parents, who put her in a convent. I told you, it is not the same now. Why talk about it again?'

'It's not that riot I want to talk about. I was just a boy then. It's the other ones.'

Salimah sits up. 'How many riots have you been in?'

Is he blushing? Pak Long likes to complain about Chinese dominance, but he worked for a Chinese family all his life. She always thought him a man of words rather than action. She pictures the young him, with raised fist, shouting merdeka, freedom.

Pak Long ignores the question but says, 'It was in 1964. It

was the birthday of the Prophet Muhammad, peace be upon him. Singapore was not independent then, but the British were gone and we were part of Malaysia.'

Salimah nods, she knows her history. 'You mean the race riots, Malays against Chinese.'

'Yes,' says Pak Long. 'We were angry, Lee Kuan Yew and his PAP government were not listening to us Malays, to our needs. They could become violent against us, kill us even.'

'So you and your friends, you just became violent yourselves?'

Pak Long's eyes now turn even darker. 'No! They started it, they very havoc, throwing rocks and bottles at us. We were praying, it was a procession. There was singing, children, it was festive. But we also needed to show ourselves as Malay, we needed to take back what was rightfully ours.'

'And where did that get you? Split up from Malaysia and a minority in your own country.'

Father cuts in, more clear today than he has been for some time. 'Got him locked up. Your daughter isn't the first in this family.'

So that is what father had meant the other day, when Pak Long had tried to brush it away. Her straight-faced, preachy uncle – in jail! It is hard to believe and Salimah can't help but smirk. 'How long? I can't believe I have an uncle with a criminal record. Did you hurt an officer, or other people? Or was it just vandalism?'

Pak Long turns crimson, she has never seen him like this. 'It wasn't like that, I wasn't a criminal.'

Salimah suddenly feels defensive. 'Neither is Nazra. Yes, she was damaging herself, but is that criminal?'

'In this country, it is,' says Pak Long. 'She knew the drug

laws.'

Yes, thinks Salimah, but she is only sixteen. 'Nazra never hurt another person.'

'I only did it to protect my people!' Pak Long retorts. 'How else could we get someone to listen to us?' He regains some of his colour and straightens his back before continuing. 'I changed, I no longer support violence. True Islam is peace. But you, who never lived through that period, you cannot understand how we were back then, during those turbulent times. Every race was suspicious of the other. We needed to protect ourselves as Malays.'

Salimah is glad she doesn't understand, but maybe remembrance is more needed than she realises. But there is more she can't grasp. 'Why are you telling me this now, what does all of that have to do with what happened in that treehouse?'

'They knew I disliked the mat salleh, the white people, as much as the Chinese,' says Pak Long. 'They called me a trouble maker, and this is why they accused me. Yes I hated them, but killing a woman like that? A baby?'

Pak Long seems to brace himself for more but Salimah has suddenly had enough. More than enough. She needs a break, to get out of this house and put her thoughts in order. She lets out a long sigh and picks up Ahmad. 'We are out of milk. I'm going to go down to the shops.'

37

There are rows and rows of palm trees on both sides of the road. Progress is slow, the roads are narrow and full of holes. They have to slow the car to a walking pace whenever they get stuck behind a truck. There are trucks everywhere, filled with red clusters of palm seeds, piled high like red pineapples. Some carry pebbles, and the narrow vehicles sway from their heavy load.

Hendra, their Sumatran guide, who sits in front next to a friendly driver who speaks no English, points at the lorry crawling along in front of them. 'They take stones from the river, to fix the roads.'

'Don't they fall over,' Tom asks, 'they seem very unstable?'

Hendra laughs. 'Yes, sometimes. They overload them. This is the problem, the heavy trucks, they break the roads. The roads aren't strong enough. They plant more and more trees but they don't make more roads.'

Anna has been quiet for the last hour, staring out the window. Usually she loves being on the road, the feeling of wind in her hair, new views around every corner, observing people from the comfort of her seat, and being able to pull over whenever something worthwhile presents itself. But this has to be the most boring road trip ever. Palm trees in straight lines in all directions. There are no other plants or wildlife, save the occasional herd of scrawny cattle. There a few people to be seen either, apart from those on the roads. The landscape is a far cry from the bright green padi fields with waving rice stalks that Indonesia is famous for. When they pass a big factory with a palm tree logo planted outside in bright orange flowers, she asks Hendra, 'Who owns these factories and plantations?'

Hendra turns around to face them. 'Last time, it was a company from Germany. Now it is a Chinese company.'

Anna thinks back to the village they stopped at for lunch. There had been a Chinese temple, many of the signs were in Chinese. 'Ah yes, I saw a number of Chinese things in the village we passed earlier. So the Chinese community here runs these plantations now?'

Hendra laughs. 'No, a Chinese company from China. But yes, we have Chinese people here too.'

'How come there are so many Chinese here?' Tom asks.

'They were brought over to work at the plantations, a long time ago. We Batak, we didn't like plantation work. So the Dutch brought in Chinese and Javanese. They said we were lazy.' He breaks into a sly grin. 'Lazy because we refused to work for them.'

Anna hopes the purple rushing to her already red cheeks isn't visible in the heat. She hesitates; should she tell Hendra why they are here, why she wants to stop in Siantar?

'Are you from around here?' she asks Hendra.

'Yes, close to Medan.'

'Anna's family was originally from around here too,' Tom says.

Anna turns her head and looks at him sharply.

'What?' he says. 'You wanted to do this.'

He continues towards Hendra, 'Anna is tracing her roots.'

Hendra nods but doesn't say more. When Tom asks him how

he feels about the Dutch colonial period, he smiles evasively. 'It's a long time ago.'

So Anna asks him about now, today, about palm oil. It must be something all tourists ask, Hendra has his answers ready. 'We lose more and more forest to the palm oil. Bad for the animals and people who live there. Also the people, they lose their land to farm. They bring a lot of foreigners to work at the plantations. And their trucks, they ruin the roads. The palm oil, it goes to Europe, China. America. Our land is rich but the people are poor.'

The car swerves to avoid a pothole, making Anna nauseous. 'And the fires?' she asks.

'Yes, this year, not so bad, the dry season was short. A few years back we had a lot of fires, the air always smoke.' Hendra is amazed when Tom tells him that they can smell those fires all the way in Singapore. 'Maybe better, that way they also notice our problems.'

Anna snaps, 'They should, as they cause it. They – we – not only own the plantations but also buy the products it is used for.'

Hendra turns back to face the front and they sit in silence.

Anna stares at the trees and thinks of Ahmad. She misses him. She messaged Salimah this morning from the hotel, who replied all was well. Sideways, she glances at Tom, who is looking at his phone. She nudges him. 'No work!'

Grudgingly, he puts the phone in his pocket. 'Don't worry, I don't have any network here.'

Anna grins. 'Another upside of travelling to such a remote place. We are forced to wind down completely.'

She hopes there won't be network in the mountains either. She'd love an evening unspoilt by interruptions. So much has happened over the past few months, they need some quality time together.

Anna spots some wooden shacks up ahead by the side of the road. 'Can we pull over?'

At a small warung they buy fresh whole coconuts, floating in a bucket of ice. Glad to be able to stretch her legs, Anna walks into the palm trees. The ground underneath is dry and bare. There is nothing to see and she turns back to where Tom has sat down at a concrete table with round concrete stools perched next to it, shaded by a palm tree.

Lately, she finds herself lost for words around her husband. There is so much to talk about, but nothing she wants to say now, in this surreal place. She takes her phone from her bag, and scrolls though the snapshots of the old black and white photos she took before she left – the waterfall, the lake and other scenery.

'Hey, you said no phones!'

'I said no work. Look.' She holds up the screen to Tom. 'Some of these places should still exist.'

Her father messaged her more old photos, and she scrolls through those too. Papa as a toddler, in front of a whitewashed building, one of him in the mountains, perhaps near Berastagi? A boy in white shorts in front of a big palm tree. The images look so ancient she struggles to believe this is her father.

Hendra nods enthusiastically when he sees the waterfall. 'I'll take you there, after Berastagi, on the way to Lake Toba. Very nice place.'

They should arrive in the mountains, in Berastagi, in an hour or so. Distances here are measured in time, not kilometres. 'After Berastagi you can go see the Karo highlands. They are very different from here, much better to see,' Hendra says. 'No palms grow there, it's cold. Maybe when we arrive you want to go to the hot springs?'

Tom wipes his face with the top of his shirt. 'I'm more up for a cool pool.'

'When we get to the mountains it will be cold,' says Hendra. 'The springs are at the foot of the volcano, very good view.'

Hendra explains to Anna that on the way back from Lake Toba to Medan they will pass Siantar, if they leave early enough they can stop there for lunch and still catch their flight that evening. Anna needs to get her head round Sumatran roads and distances. The hundred and seventy kilometres between Medan and Parapat, on the shore of Lake Toba, takes over four hours by car.

When they arrive in Berastagi it rains, the mountain views Anna was looking forward to are shrouded in mist. Anna shivers, her body struggling to remember that she was boiling hot less than an hour ago. In the lobby, as they wait for their keys, she looks at Tom, who is frantically trying to get onto the hotel wifi. 'Shall we try those hot springs?'

'We just got here. Can't we relax a little first? I don't fancy going back in the car now.'

Hendra grins encouragingly, 'It's just out of town, maybe fifteen minutes.'

With a look from Anna, Tom gives in.

They drive down the same road they just came up, then turn onto a small track into the green. There are small vegetable plots on either side of the road, planted with lettuce, beans, carrots, even asparagus, and many vegetables Anna doesn't recognise. They have been driving for almost forty-five minutes when Tom starts to suggest they turn back. He whispers to Anna so Hendra doesn't hear, 'Why can't these people ever tell the truth? He must have known it wasn't fifteen minutes?'

Anna nudges Tom to be quiet as she gazes out the window.

When they reach the hot springs – a group of dark pools cast in concrete – the clouds in front of them magically part, revealing a towering, majestic mountain. Hendra points proudly, as if he set up the spectacle especially for them: 'Mount Sibayak!'

Anna stares at it and tries to see Oma's painting projected over it but they are too close to see it properly. Tomorrow they will get up before first light and climb it, through the dark, to experience the sunrise from the summit.

They change into swimwear and lower themselves into the hot sulphuric water. Anna snuggles up to Tom. Hendra and the driver have taken off their shirts and have picked another pool, the one furthest from them, where they sit splashing each other and laughing.

Dusk settles and up above tiny stars begin to sparkle. The effect, together with the shadowy outline of the mountain that is now barely visible, is mesmerising.

'I'm sorry,' Tom says softly in her ear, 'I haven't been there for you lately.'

'Shhh, let's not. Tonight, I want to enjoy.' She pauses. 'I wasn't there for you, either. Your work, I should have been more interested. Supported you or at least noticed your struggle.'

Tom puts his hand over hers. 'I know, but you needed me more, I mean …'

Anna sits up, the hot water dripping from her hair into little whirlpools in the water. They are the only visitors here tonight. Maybe they should talk, right here, right now. 'It is just, my head, it is so full. It drives me crazy.'

'Why don't you tell me? Let it all out?'

Anna hesitates. 'You are so rational. I'm afraid you won't understand.'

She waves her hand gently through the water, creating two sets of ripples that collide and merge in the middle to form a new, mesmerising pattern.

'Then start with what I can understand. Your family. Your grandmother. She was imprisoned here, in this very town. Do you want to go and find the location of the camp tomorrow, if it is still there?'

'No,' says Anna quietly. 'I think just being here, breathing the air, seeing the mountains – is enough for me. Just to get a taste of the place. Like, I always imaged she would have been so hot all the time. But it is cold here.'

Anna tells him more about her grandmother's ordeals, about the Japanese guards, the transport out of the last camp, the long wait after. About how reading the diary made Anna realise that the biggest drama – for Oma at least – didn't happen until after the Japanese were defeated.

She explains her father's story too – how he was sent to school overseas in the Netherlands when he was eight and never came back. 'He always refused to visit, but now he is as excited as I am about this trip. He sent me those photos, and asked me share with him ones I take here. But what depresses me when I drive around here, through all those palm trees, is …' Anna struggles to put her feelings into words. 'I thought things would have changed more. People here still get screwed over. A lot of money is being made but they see none of it, most leaves the country. I feel guilty, I suppose, for being a rich tourist. My country colonised and exploited Indonesia for centuries, bringing us wealth and them poverty. I have no idea what I can do about that.'

She bites a bit of loose fingernail. There is a pit in her stomach with a vortex of feelings being thrown around and sucked inside.

Tom gently rubs Anna's wrists. 'Yes, the world is still unjust, unequal and exploitative. Neither you nor I can change that.'

The stampeding boots in the hallway of her house resonate in Anna's brain. A catalyst, that's what they were, but there is so much more to the story. 'I tried looking at it as a historian, to see if I could make sense of it. Rationally. Both from books and information my father sent me. It's a lot. After they won the war for independence the Indonesians had a lot of internal turmoil. And initially the Dutch were still very involved, since they owned so many of the businesses. Until all the companies were nationalised and all the remaining Dutch, like my grandparents, were expelled in the late 1950s. Which ruined the economy.'

She is silent for a minute. 'That is the part my father struggles with, I think. His parents decided to stay on after the war, to help build the country up again. They meant well. Papa was too young to understand why they had to leave. As an adult he felt he could not blame the Indonesians for throwing them out, and I think that is why he refused to talk about it. When he was older he became fiercely anti-colonial.'

'I can see how conflicted he must have been,' says Tom.

Anna looks up to him. 'I can't step over all of that so easily. So when it came to the adoption, I wasn't sure we should take Ahmad. Is it right to take a kid away from his culture? He had a family. I must have sensed Salimah had doubts even though she never said it out loud.'

She stops talking and looks at Tom.

Tom takes some time trying to formulate an answer. 'Why would adopting a Malay child have anything to do with our colonial history? A lot of different people are responsible for this current mess, not just you and your family, not just the Dutch and the British. How about all the corrupt officials lining their pockets? Yes, we colonisers started a lot of that shit and we should feel guilty for it. We have a responsibility to bring it out into the open and talk about it and make sure that it stops happening. So, are you going to wallow in it or try to fix it?'

Anna thinks of Salimah, her anger when she accused her of taking over her life. If she wants to fix things, she need to make sure she is doing it right. But what is right? 'I don't know,' groans Anna, 'it's complicated.'

'You make everything complicated,' Tom says.

He gets up with a big splash, steam rising from his chest in the cool air. He sits on the edge of the concrete pool. 'This water is a bit too hot for me.'

Each pool is a different temperature, depending on how close they are to the spring. Tom and Anna sit in silence as they watch a motorcycle arrive with a couple and a little boy, perhaps around five years old. He strips down to his underwear and skips over to the other side, into one of the cooler lagoons.

Anna looks at the boy frolicking in the water and wonders whether Tom is thinking the same as she is.

'We never really talked about Boy properly. Ahmad, I mean. He sort of happened.'

Tom nods. 'True. We should not have taken adoption that lightly. I thought he would make you happy. I guess I was being selfish, it was an easy way for me to not have to worry about you; if you had him to keep you distracted. But I also fell for him myself. I wanted him too. I have emotions, you know.'

Anna laughs. 'You manage to hide them well sometimes.'

Tom splashes Anna with his feet. Then he looks serious again. 'We would have figured it all out if we had kept him, isn't that what parents do? I miss him.'

'Yes, me too. And that is what scares me. What if we eventually leave here? That will be so hard. And what if what we are doing is screwing that boy up?'

Tom laughs. 'As I said, you always make things too complicated. He is young. Plenty of kids have foster parents, nannies, caregivers. Many Singapore households employ helpers, to help raise their kids. And think about the poor helpers who leave their own children behind to raise other people's kids. We are helping a family take care of a kid. It's really not that big a deal.'

'I suppose you are right. But leaving him will be a big deal to me.'

'And to me.'

Anna imagines having to leave Asia – that too would be a big deal for her. But she can't see Tom staying here the rest of his life. 'Do you think we can we remain a part of his life, long term, realistically?'

'Why not? These days the world is so much smaller. There is the internet. Cheap flights. I'm sure we will manage something.'

Things have always seemed easier to Tom, and for now that mollifies Anna. Maybe he is right. Maybe she does make things too complicated.

They don't say anything for a while, until Tom suddenly asks, 'Why didn't you tell me all of this earlier? All that stuff about your family, how your father was born here and the Indonesian government forced them out against their will. I knew your grandparents lived here, but that was about it.'

'My father doesn't like to talk about it, it embarrasses him. I guess I inherited the guilt.'

Tom sinks back into the water and pulls Anna to him. 'Can we promise never to stop talking to each other again?'

Anna nods. 'I thought you hated Asia and I couldn't cope with that. I love it here.'

Tom sighs. 'I don't hate it. I just don't love it like you do. I do find it rather frustrating a lot of the time.'

Anna points at the completely dark sky above them, the mountain somewhere behind them that, although invisible now, is etched in her mind. 'Isn't this the most beautiful place you have ever seen? What is not to love?'

'Well, the lack of clean changing rooms,' Tom points out, 'and the fact that I need to go to a toilet balanced above a hole with no paper. And that that guy says it's a fifteen-minute drive but it takes almost an hour.'

He kisses her wet hair. 'It's rather romantic actually. Can't we go back?'

Anna turns to him and hugs, then kisses, him. 'Not yet. I'm enjoying this too much.'

'Me too,' Tom says, pulling his lips free for just a minute, 'it is magical here. And please remember, you are not alone. Just tell me what you need.'

'For now, I need you to enjoy tonight and look at the stars with me.'

They sink back and look up, together, to where they know the mountain is and talk longer than they have in months until their fingers resemble prunes and Anna sees Hendra and the driver pacing in front of the car impatiently.

38

'Bapa, come with me to the house? Together with your grandson?'

Tom and Anna are in Sumatra, and Salimah needs to go and water the plants. She also likes the idea of being in the house alone, getting a sense of the place without Anna present. She hopes that taking her father there, to the house and perhaps to the area their old house was in, will trigger his memory. There are so many undigested stories and emotions that rile her still. For better or worse, she just wants to shake him out of his elderly apathy. She needs to feel she isn't the only adult in this family. But he is adamant. 'No, sayang, I cannot. Cannot go there.'

Sighing, Salimah gives up. Part of her feels relieved. But still, she needs to talk to Father, find more resolution. For her grandson if nothing else. 'Go jalan jalan in the park, then? At the reservoir?'

Father agrees and they take a bus to McRitchie. They walk along the water's edge in silence, Salimah pushing a sleeping Ahmad in his expensive pushchair. She gazes at the mirror-like surface of the reservoir, which reflect the trees of the secondary forest lining the banks. A ripple forms some distance out and slowly a shape comes towards them. When it is close, Salimah sees a small head followed by a tail swishing rhythmically from side to side. 'Look Bapa, buaya!'

Father startles.

'Sorry, I'm joking. No crocodile, it's just a monitor lizard,' she shushes.

'Many like this in the garden, you know, in that house.'

Salimah nods. She has seen a number of monitor lizards there; a young one lives in a hole in the tree next to where she hangs the washing. It stares at her, but if she comes too close, it dives into the trunk. They are friendly but very shy.

'Do you miss it?' she asks. 'I mean not that house, but kampong life?'

'I miss your mother,' Father says.

Salimah squeezes his hand. Her mother was the glue that kept this family together, regardless of where they lived. Sometimes she feels her mother was lucky to be born in a different era, when things were more simple. People accepted their fate without asking difficult questions. Mak was a religious woman but never wore a tudung – few did in those days. Her Islam was so different from Pak Long's – much more accepting. What would Mak have thought about Salimah covering her hair? It isn't something she thought about deeply at the time, nor thinks about much now. It felt right to wear it. It still does.

When she first showed up in the tudung, people in the office had reacted politely, hiding their shock. But she could feel their looks piercing the fabric at the back of her skull. Some immediately treated her like a different person, as if she was no longer one of them. What they didn't realise was that she never had been.

Salimah knows that deep down Anna doesn't agree with her tudung either, but she never mentions it or treats her any differently – she accepts Salimah's choice. Salimah smiles, thinking of Anna. Anna can be annoying when she talks too much, tries to explain something that isn't hers to explain, asks impertinent personal questions or jumps to conclusions, but then Anna challenges her to be a better person, to think more. And most importantly, Salimah knows the baby is safe with Anna because she tries not to judge.

Thinking of the three of them together – Tom, Anna and Ahmad – makes her feel melancholy. They are such a pretty family. She knows Anna is looking for something in Sumatra – she isn't sure what, but she hopes she will find it. That it will give her the peace she badly needs. Anna will be a better person, make better choices when she has found peace.

Salimah sighs and turns to her father that stoically walks beside her. 'Remember how we used to sit in our old house, around the gaslight, that old lamp we had? The stories Mak told? Ghost stories, and fairy tales? Now we have tv. I something wonder what our lives would have looked like if we had stayed there, in the kampong.'

Father looks up, his eyes less cloudy. 'Your mother had to work so hard, no washing machines, no vacuum cleaner. And mud everywhere when it flooded.'

Salimah perks up at his sudden clarity. She has so much to ask, but since she will likely only have his attention briefly, she needs to be economical. Looking at sleeping Ahmad, she asks, 'Am I doing it right, Bapa? I try to follow Allah but sometimes I don't hear him.'

Father strokes the side of her tudung, like he stroked her hair when she was a little girl.

'You are beautiful, like her. Your mother had this lovely hair. God is for all, sayang, also for you. And for them.'

He points across the lake and Salimah assumes he means the house behind the trees. 'He will get the best of both worlds, won't he, our grandson?'

Great-grandson to him, Salimah thinks, but she doesn't correct him. 'But what about my daughter?'

Salimah has an appointment to see Nazra the following day. Now Nazra has been officially convicted, the visits are face to face with only glass separating them. Visits are still hard – painful confrontations where Salimah can't find the right words. There is an improvement though, she feels, for at least she is now trying to find the right words. Yet she can't combat that helpless feeling when it comes to Nazra. 'How can I make sure that she doesn't stray again when she comes out?'

She looks at Father pleadingly but he is starting to disappear, pointing at dead leaves near the water's edge; a sudden jet of wind propels them into the motionless water.

Salimah continues regardless. 'What about her reputation, her education? Nazra only thinks of fun.'

Father sits down at a bench. 'Maybe you should have had more fun when you were young. Then you would have understood her better.'

Salimah groans. He says that a few decades too late. They sit for a few minutes before they get up again, Father walking on at a crisp pace, cheerfully. It rubs off on Salimah; she too gets a spring in her step. She is enjoying this walk. She should listen to Anna, who told her to let it go. To let her go, as she no longer means harm. There are others out there more dangerous, like those crocodiles that preyed on her daughter.

The reason she brought her father here, to find out what really happened with the treehouse, now seems as fleeting as scattered dust on the wind-blown water. Everyone has their own truth, and as she watches her father walking peacefully ahead of her, she realises that she must let him be. He is a good man.

But when she sits facing Nazra the next day she does what she resolved not to, she tells her everything: the treehouse and its rotten wood; the lady that lost her baby and jumped or fell off the roof; the bullying she faced as a child after they accused her father of meddling with black magic; moving away and the new school where she struggled to fit in; and her resolution to become so successful nobody could ever talk down to her again. When she mentions the ghost that haunted Anna and the house, Nazra's eyes light up.

'This hantu, Mak, I saw her too. I followed her out one night.'

A sudden chill creeps up Salimah's back and her nose fills with the same dreadful stink. She swallows deeply and forces out words. 'What are you, gila? She could have killed you, or Ahmad!'

'Ya, I was, Mak, I was crazy then. And when I saw her, she made me feel so scared, I thought she was ging to take Ahmad, hurt him. I couldn't actually hear her voice but I could somehow feel what she was saying. She wanted me to go and give her the baby. I was so scared I left the baby with Anna and ran. I took drugs again.'

Salimah feels the blood rush to her cheeks. Now Nazra sits here, paying the price because her mother took so long to step up and protect her and her son. 'I'm so sorry, sayang, it is all my fault. I should have seen how you weren't coping. I should have realised it wasn't safe there.'

'No, I wanted to see her, that is why I agreed to stay with Anna in the first place. Somehow, I think this needed to happen. Things could have been worse, maybe I would have hurt the baby. In a weird way, I think she saved me.'

Nazra grins; she talks as if she is describing a movie. 'Pontianaks are badass. No one tells them not to go out after dark and 'ruin' their reputation. Instead, men are terrified of them.'

As Salimah looks on in silence, Nazra gets more worked up. 'I wish I could get back at men by clawing out their insides.'

When she sees Salimah's shocked expression, Nazra laughs. 'Sorry, just kidding. But seriously, I mean, did this ghost even disembowel anyone? Or is it just that, like all women, she can't escape a bad reputation?'

As Salimah shakes her head, Nazra continues. 'That's what so cool, just the illusion of them is enough for people to get all freaked out.' Then she breaks off. 'Wait, do you think she wants to hurt Atuk?'

'That's what I was worried about, and maybe to get to him through his great-grandson. She might have believed your grandfather was guilty, and wanted revenge. But Anna says she doesn't, not anymore. That she just wants to be remembered and understood.'

Nazra ponders a while, then slowly answers: 'Yes, that makes sense. She seemed lost to me. Lonely.'

Salimah nods. 'And as you said, maybe the illusion is enough, the fact that we know she is there and respect her.'

They both sit in silence a little while. Then Salimah says: 'But aren't you still scared of her?'

Nazra shakes her head. 'Not really. Humans are much worse, like the kids that bullied you and those that ignore us at school or work. All the demands society puts on girls. Do this, don't do that. Be so careful. So precious.'

Nazra curls her fingers in to create sharp claws and swings them at Salimah behind the glass. 'Ah, to be a pontianak!'

'Are you still on those drugs or what?' Salimah says, but lightheartedly. This fierce, creative Nazra impresses her. If only she can channel these thoughts into something useful, she could get somewhere in life.

'No, Mak, don't worry. I don't want to do that anymore. I have a lot of time in here to think about my mistakes.'

A glimmer of hope and pride fills Salimah as they talk, and they reach a level of understanding they haven't achieved in a long time. As Salimah leaves the prison, she feels a sense of contentment. Maybe, with time, things will begin to look up again and life can be good once more.

39

They have to get up in what feels like the middle of the night; the plan is to reach the top before the sun rises. As Anna and Tom hike up Mount Sibayak through the dark mist, wet branches slap their faces, and the smell of sulphur increases as they ascend. For Anna, it brings back memories of dark nights in her garden in Singapore, the smell of rotting flesh … suddenly she feels nauseous. She sits down on a rock.

'What's wrong,' Tom asks. 'Do you need a break?'

Anna hasn't told Tom about the ghost because she doesn't believe he would understand. She doesn't believe in such things herself, chalking it up to her hormones being out of control. However, the look in Salimah's eyes as she recounted her story told a different tale, and Anna shivers when she thinks about it. Salimah had told her about the pontianak, a vampire-like apparition from Malay folklore, the ghost of a woman who died while pregnant or giving birth. Salimah had explained how pontianaks prey on men, using their long claws to disembowel their victims. Anna had never seen Salimah so frightened. She kept talking about nails, urging Anna to carry some and hammer them into the back of the creature's neck if it ever returned. For once, Anna had to be the one to calm Salimah down. Now, as Anna sits on a rock on the side of a volcano in Sumatra, she inhales deeply through her mouth and spits out the foul taste of sulphur.

'Let's go or we'll miss the sunrise,' she says, eager to move on from such eerie thoughts. The floating woman seems to have disappeared, and Anna wonders if she ever saw her at all.

The mountain is still shrouded in darkness, but the air is gradually warming, and the sky is slowly brightening. Anna feels a growing sense of anticipation as they near the peak. As they climb higher, a few rays of light edge over the mountain ridges, and they arrive at the summit just in time to witness a magnificent sight. A yellow disc rises over the highlands, illuminating the lush green valley below in shades of orange. In the distance, the almost-perfect cone of Sinabung comes into view, a dark plume of smoke rising in a picture-perfect parabola towards the sky.

Tom nudges Anna. 'The second mountain, right, from your oma's painting?'

'Yes,' says Anna, 'Sinabung. It looks different though. It must be Oma's artistic interpretation, she made it more pointy.'

She has to admit, she can't really recognise either mountain from the picture but she knows it is them as they slide in place inside her like pieces of a jigsaw. This is her grandmother's country.

Hendra joins them, and gestures at the horizon. 'You see the smoke? Since 2004 the volcano is active again, for the first time in centuries.'

Anna nods. She read this already. The surrounding villages have been evacuated and tourists cannot visit. Hendra continues: 'A few years back, a massive eruption blew the top off.'

As Anna stares at the volcano, she inhales the frosty sulphuric air and thinks of Oma sketching the volcanoes. Her rocks, she called them, her anchors. And now the top of one of them is blown off. Anna feels like the other mountain, the one she is standing on, is crumbling to pieces and her feet are standing on thin air. Nothing is permanent.

Tom nor Anna speaks. They both stare at the mountain and the glorious views of the valley beneath them, where in the upcoming light they can see the shapes of small farms appear.

Anna remembers the photos she saw last night at the reception of the hotel. 'Imagine, such a green valley, all grey, everything covered in layers of ash? It's a disaster.'

'Yes, it looks horrid,' says Tom. 'But volcanic ash is fertile. Ash from eruptions in the past is probably the reason why this valley produces all those vegetables. It may take a while, but things will be fine.'

'True, but imagine living here. It's just too scary.'

'Yes. Your beloved Indonesia is sitting on some of the most active volcanoes in the world. It's on the ring of fire.'

Anna wraps her body around Tom's to absorb some of his heat as she lets the words sink in. 'I'd forgotten I'd married a geologist.'

Tom laughs. 'I had forgotten I'd married a historian. I guess we both got so carried away by our corporate jobs, that we forgot our real passions.'

Anna's passion had been for the past, but now she isn't so sure. Up here the air is cold and thin and the sharp chill of it clears her brain. 'Actually, I have been thinking I want a change. A different kind of job from what I did before. Less commercial. People here are still being exploited, only less openly, now by foreign companies and a rich elite. It is like colonialism didn't change but is less direct.' She looks at the plume coming from the mountain. 'Helping Salimah with Ahmad feels good, I'd love to make a career change. Maybe I can find a company that makes a positive, sustainable impact here in Asia?'

If Salimah can do it, follow her dream and become a teacher, so could Anna. 'I just haven't got a clue what or how.'

Tom smiles. 'Take your time. You'll figure it out.'

'I mean it! When I look at Boy, I'm reminded of the future, and seeing how we are screwing up the world depresses me.' She swivels around and looks Tom in the eyes. 'Don't you worry about the future of mankind?'

'Anna. We are in the most beautiful spot ever, can you just relax? This is so you, you see something and you get all worked up. Don't get me wrong, it's great that you want to do good. But maybe take it one step at the time and don't make problems bigger than they already are? Sit back, reflect, and enjoy where you are.'

As they begin their walk down in the bright morning light, they can finally see the path they took earlier. From yellowish rocks and pungent white steam billowing from crevices, to savanna flats dotted with small bushes and stones, giving way to rich greenery the further they descend. Anna remains silent, countless thoughts jostling for attention in her mind as she turns back for one last glimpse of the distant mountain.

40

It has been a long time since Anna and Salimah cooked together. Today they are making sambal kangkong and nasi goreng. When Anna says she can never get fried rice right, that hers ends up mushy, Salimah laughs. Today she's brought a Tupperware with cooked rice. Lesson number one: always use cold rice, ideally a day old. Hot rice is too moist.

Salimah shows Anna how to roast the belacan on a fork over a flame. The pungent smell of burnt rotten fish assaults their nostrils, and Salimah laughs when she sees Anna cringe. 'I know, it smells hideous at first. But it will give a lovely flavour to the sambal. You'll learn to appreciate it.'

Both of them know what the rotten smell reminds them of although neither says it out loud.

As they chop the chilli and garlic, they chat. 'You know, my uncle is so happy that Ahmad is staying in the family that he ordered an Aqiqah to celebrate.'

'A what?'

'Aqiqah is a Muslim tradition, the offering of a goat. Normally the parents do this, but he asked me if he could do it instead.'

'That sounds dangerous. Where will he slaughter it?'

Salimah laughs as she pictures Pak Long with a knife. 'No, he won't do it himself. Not in Singapore. A company in Indonesia does it, and the meat gets handed out amongst the poor.' As she explains how it works to Anna, she feels glad the boy is bought up in Islam proper. As he ought to be.

'Do you know of the Maria Hertogh case?' she asks Anna.

Anna looks confused. 'No?'

'She was Dutch, wasn't she, like you?'

'I never heard the name. Does she live here?'

Salimah is somewhat taken aback that Anna has never heard of Maria Hertogh, her story is so well known in Singapore. Ever since Pak Long bought up that case from long ago, Salimah can't stop thinking about it. Maybe the Malay name of the girl, Nadra, reminds her of Nazra? Or is it that Anna, like the girl's parents, is Dutch? 'In 1950, a young Dutch girl was the cause of one of the biggest riots we ever had in Singapore. Over twenty people died. My uncle was one of the rioters.'

Anna drops a chilli to the floor and as she bends to recover it, Salimah explains. 'The Dutch girl was separated from her biological mother during the war, in Java.'

She takes the chilli from Anna and rinses it again. 'Just before the Dutch mother was locked up by the Japanese with her other children, this girl was given to a friend of her Javanese grandmother – a woman from Malaysia called Aminah. The foster mother took her back to Malaysia where she was only found years after the war. They took her to Singapore and put her in a convent whilst the parents battled the foster mother in court.'

Anna looks at Salimah incredulously. 'So, why the riots?'

'Well, it's a long story, but the girl was raised a Muslim, so a Catholic convent didn't go down well with people like my uncle. After the court gave her back to her Dutch parents, well ... many white people got attacked.'

'But they were her biological parents. It makes sense she'd go back, doesn't it?'

'There were papers suggesting she gave the girl up for adoption, but the mother denied it in court afterwards. Giving up a child wasn't uncommon in those days; she had many kids, and there was a war on. It could have all been a misunderstanding, who knows?'

As expected, Anna has many questions.

'It had been eight years since she went to live with the foster mother, the girl had forgotten her Dutch language. She wanted to stay here. She had become a devout Muslim. Giving a Muslim girl to Christians, for someone like Pak Long, that was unforgivable.'

Anna, for once, stays silent. Then, she tries, 'But they never found out whether the mother had actually given her up for adoption? Whether she lied in court or not?'

'I guess we will never discover the truth. Quite possibly both parties have a different truth, and both could be equally true. But you seriously mean you have never heard of this case? It is so famous, every Singaporean can tell you this, even the Chinese. We haven't forgotten.'

Anna rubs her nose with her free hand. 'No, I haven't. I mean, it happened a long time ago.'

'It's not that long ago, my uncle was part of it.'

Anna looks apologetic, then adds, 'I'm sorry.'

After they blend the sambal belacan that they will stir-fry the water spinach in; Salimah shows Anna how to fry ikan bilis, tiny dried anchovies, to a crisp in hot oil. Anna picks at the tiny fish. 'These are so good. Like fish chips!' Salimah flicks Anna's hand away. 'We won't have any left!'

Salimah heats up the oil to fry the rice, and repeats: 'Fried rice is made with old, cooled rice. In a scalding hot wok.'

Remembering how she observed Anna at work in the kitchen when she first arrived, she adds: 'And please, do not just throw everything in together. If you fry too much at once, it will cool the wok down. Every ingredient has a different cooking time. And when you fry things separately, everything will retain its own flavour so it contributes to the whole the best it can.'

She stirs through the wok slowly, mixing all together and smiles at Anna. 'Just like people, the different ingredients all need the special treatment they deserve.'

41

They take their plates outside and sit down at the table underneath the attap. When Anna takes a bite from the kangkong, it brings tears to her eyes. 'Wow, that is spicy.'

It takes a minute for the flavours to develop in her mouth. 'You are right. The belacan gives an amazing depth of flavour to the sambal.'

'Do you want water?' Anna pours both of them a glass.

'My grandmother used belacan – trassi in Indonesia – in her cooking, but it never tasted this strong. She didn't roast it over fire, maybe that is the reason?'

When Salimah nods, Anna realises she has been making so many mistakes when cooking Asian food. Salimah would get a heart attack if she saw those plastic bags of ready-cut 'stir-fry vegetables' popular in Europe. She chuckles, imagining Salimah painstakingly picking apart and sorting the mix into separate piles, the onion to go in first, then one by one cabbage, beans, carrot, and the bean sprouts only at the very end.

Suddenly a cool wind wafts in, making the leaves of the banyan rustle. A stronger gust sweeps up a flurry of leaves which settle in the pool. Not long after, a flash lights up the sky, followed by an almighty crack. Anna looks at Salimah. 'That was close.' The air feels charged with electricity, and as she rubs the hairs on her arm, it crackles.

The next strike feels like it hits them right on the head and the large banyan shudders when thunder rolls over them. Around them it is suddenly as dark as night. A second later, rain hits the gazebo roof and imprisons them in a wall of water.

The wind has really picked up now and it howls through the banyan tree causing the aerial roots to whip through the air. The tropical downpour is deafening and Anna looks at Salimah nervously. A chill runs down Anna's spine as her thoughts return once more to the horror of the past months, the noises in the ceiling, the footsteps in the corridor, the stench of rotting flesh, the banyan with its alien roots and that women, that ghost, with whom she shares her home. Hysteria rises within her and then she remembers the child is alone in the house. 'Boy!' she screams. 'Ahmad!'

Salimah places a reassuring hand on Anna's arm as she follows Anna's gaze to the main house. 'He's fine. It's just a storm. Get used to it, there will be more this time of the year.'

Salimah stands up to turn on the light underneath the attap roof and immediately they are bathed in a warm glow. Anna calms down once more and, as they continue their meal, their little dry island in the sea of noise and water starts to feel cosy.

After Salimah goes home with Ahmad, Anna changes out of her dress, pulls on a bathing suit and lowers herself into the cool clear water of the pool. It is covered in a layer of leaves the storm blew off the tree. She gets out the little blue net and walks around in circles, scooping out the leaves one by one. Then, she grabs the lilo from the outbuildings and lies down on it. A proper lady of leisure, she thinks, with only a small pang of guilt. Hopefully not for long. The air is fresh and crisp after the earlier deluge, but the sun is heating it up again quickly.

Anna looks up at the banyan tree hovering over the pool. A flock of birds flies over, twittering loudly, and settles in its branches. For a few minutes, she manages to clear her mind and just be. A squirrel climbs onto the roof of the attap cover and sits there, looking around. Then it burrows under the palm fronds to bury its treasure, a red palm seed, before bouncing off quickly. A golden oriole perches on a branch of the palm tree, its black-masked face naughty and sleek. Anna feels happy and blessed.

She lets her hands trail in the water then covers her eyes to block the beating sun. Lying in the hot rays she gets hotter and hotter until thoughts steamroll their way back into Anna's mind and she can feel them running everywhere, even into the veins in her little toes. She splashes water in her face.

She needs to occupy her brain, to block these negative thoughts. Last week she visited the women's shelter with her neighbour Sonja, the one who does the counselling. If she wants, Anna can work there too, it would be a voluntary role, but it's part-time which means she can combine it with taking care of Ahmad. It is not the kind of job she wants to do long term, but it will give her time to think about a possible career change. Anna grins when she thinks back to how when she arrived, she felt the only way for her to prove her worth here was getting a high-profile corporate job.

She looked up the case Salimah told her about earlier, Maria Hertogh. The girl became miserable in the Netherlands, had a rotten life. Reading about her made Anna feel melancholy. Would she have been happy had she been allowed to stay here? The girl, with her white face, was clearly seen as one of theirs by the Malay. Does that mean a person can fit in anywhere they wish, can really belong? What would it take for Anna to be accepted like that?

In the back of her mind she sees the pontianak again, her blonde hair waving in a slight evening breeze, bound to this place forever in death. That woman too belongs here, whether she wants to or not. Was she really there? Anna shudders. Looking up at the house she feels the history of it weigh on her heavily. Then a sudden peculiar feeling comes over her as the taste of the belacan rises in her throat. Anna rolls off the lilo and swims a few strokes, then lets herself float on her back. The queasiness in her stomach makes her feel anguished and hopeful at the same time. She will worry about things later, today she lets the cool water, cold almost after the earlier downpour, support her as the hot sun batters her pale belly and chest. She didn't apply any sunscreen, soon she will turn red as a lobster. Unwilling to leave the soothing freshness of the water, Anna turns back onto her stomach and dives under. The future can start tomorrow.